Stranger on the Square

Stranger on the Square
Arthur and Cynthia Koestler

❖❖❖❖❖❖❖❖❖

Edited and with an Introduction
and Epilogue by
HAROLD HARRIS

Random House   New York

Copyright © 1984 by The Estate of Arthur Koestler and Cynthia Koestler
Introduction and Epilogue Copyright © 1984 by Harold Harris
All rights reserved under International and Pan-American Copyright
Conventions.
Published in the United States by Random House, Inc., New York.
Originally published in Great Britain by Hutchinson & Co. (Publishers) Ltd.,
London.

Library of Congress Cataloging in Publication Data
Koestler, Arthur, 1905–
Stranger on the square.
Includes index.
1. Koestler, Arthur, 1905–   –Biography.
2. Koestler, Cynthia, 1928–1983.   3. Authors, English–
20th century–Biography.   I. Koestler, Cynthia, 1928–1983.
II. Harris, Harold.   III. Title.
PR6021.04Z476 1984   828′.91209   [B]   84–42519
ISBN 0-394-53888-9

Manufactured in the United States of America
2 4 6 8 9 7 5 3
First Edition

Contents

List of Illustrations

Introduction

BY HAROLD HARRIS

This book is in essence a love story, but unlike any other love story I have read. Perhaps it would be more accurate to call it the story of an obsession.

It was in July 1949 that Cynthia Jefferies, a pretty but painfully shy and rather awkward girl from South Africa, answered an advertisement. A writer wanted a temporary secretary. The writer was Arthur Koestler. He lived at the time in a house near Fontainebleau with Mamaine Paget, one of the beautiful Paget twins, whom he was later to marry when the divorce from his first wife came through. Cynthia was living in Paris.

She got the job and worked at intervals as his secretary for the next six years, partly in France, partly in England, partly in the USA. During that time she herself was married and divorced. In 1955, she threw up her job in New York in response to a cable from Koestler, and returned to London as his full-time secretary. At what stage they became lovers readers of this book must decide for themselves, but there is no doubt that Cynthia loved Arthur almost from the moment of her first awkward interview with him in Paris.

From that reunion in 1955 their lives were shared. In 1965 they were married. On 3 March 1983, their bodies were found in the sitting room of their house in Montpelier Square which figures in the title of this book. Koestler was sitting in an armchair, a glass of brandy still in his hand. Cynthia was lying on a sofa, a glass of whisky on the table beside her. Each had taken a massive overdose of barbiturates.

Koestler was seventy-seven years old. For the past seven years he had suffered from Parkinson's disease, which had first been kept under control but had latterly taken its progressive toll. For the past four years he had suffered from leukaemia which, a pathologist testified at the inquest, was in its terminal stages. Cynthia was fifty-five and in perfect health.

To none of us who knew and loved them both did Arthur's suicide come as a surprise. He was a writer unequalled in his generation for the extraordinary breadth of his genius. Over the years his literary output had been witness to his many-sided imagination, to his intellectual power, and to his extraordinary literary prowess as a master of the English language – in his case, an acquired art. In addition, he was usually actively involved in some campaign and, as this book demonstrates, he led a very full social life. Even though he bore the handicaps imposed by his terminal illnesses with expected fortitude, with unexpected patience, and with his own unrivalled brand of wry humour, no one who knew him anticipated that he would quietly submit to the final removal of his physical and mental faculties. Indeed, on the last occasion on which I saw him (Thursday, 24 February 1983) I felt that he might have left it too late. He was unable to stand, his speech was disjointed, and he clearly found it difficult to concentrate on what was being said to him. I felt that he might not last the night and I begged Cynthia to send for me if she needed help. Next day she told me on the phone that Arthur seemed a good deal better and had told her that he had been hallucinating when I was there. But he was unable to speak on the telephone and Cynthia had to cancel their appointments for the weekend.

As has been widely reported, he was vice-president of the Voluntary Euthanasia Society, and the news of his death on 3 March was not unexpected. The finding of Cynthia's body at the same time, however, was not merely unexpected but came as a profound shock to all their friends. I do not think it had occurred to a single one of us that she intended to take her life at the same time as Arthur.

When did she make this decision? And why? These were the two questions we asked each other, blaming ourselves for not having foreseen it, for not having intervened in some way.

So far as the first question is concerned, we know that when Arthur wrote his farewell note 'to whom it may concern' in June 1982, there was no intention whatever that Cynthia would join him on his final journey. (He had written: 'What makes it nevertheless hard to take this final step is the reflection of the pain it is bound to inflict on my few surviving friends, and above all my wife Cynthia.') It is my belief that she had not considered doing so when I saw her on 24 February nor when I spoke to her on 25 February. All the evidence is that they took the fatal dose on 1 March, and I believe (although there is no proof) that Cynthia made her decision either on that morning or during the night of 28 February–1 March. We do know that it was on the morning of 1 March that she took her beloved dog, David (a twelve-year-old Lhasa Apso), to the vet and had him put down, giving as the reason that she could not look after him properly any more as she had to spend all her time caring for her sick husband. (She told their cleaner that she had given David to a friend. The 1st of March was a Tuesday, and the cleaner did not go to the house on Wednesdays.)

In a brief typewritten addition to Arthur's farewell note which I have quoted, Cynthia wrote: 'I should have liked to finish my account of working for Arthur – a story which began when our paths happened to cross in 1949. However, I cannot live without Arthur, despite certain inner resources.'

I believe that this realization was borne in upon her when she knew that the day had actually arrived when Arthur could no longer tolerate the burden of existence.

So much for the question of 'when?'. The answer to 'why?' took me longer to formulate in my own mind.

The manuscript of this book was among the papers found on Arthur's desk, and took me by surprise. Many of his friends, including myself, had been urging him for years to continue with his autobiography,* which ended in 1940. I do not remember exactly when, but I think it must have been towards

---

* *Arrow in the Blue* and *The Invisible Writing*.

the end of 1982 that he confided to me that, in fact, he was at last at work on a third volume. He swore me to secrecy, for he had a superstitious hatred of discussing work in progress. The manuscript that we found was, in fact, a kind of joint autobiography. Cynthia had clearly been writing about her own life with Arthur for a longer period, but had never mentioned this to me nor, as far as I am aware, to any other friends. The only other example of her writing that I knew was' the chapter entitled 'Twenty-five Writing Years' in the festschrift which I edited to celebrate Koestler's seventieth birthday.* Perhaps it was the favourable reception accorded to this piece that prompted her to enlarge it to a book in its own right.

At what stage did it occur to Arthur that the two books could be merged? It can only be conjecture, but I believe that he had completed chapter 1 of this book (taking him from 1940 to 1949) when he decided on joint authorship. The final sentence of chapter one does not appear in the handwritten manuscript, but has been inserted by hand in the typescript, thus neatly paving the way for what Cynthia had intended as chapter one of her own book.

What in fact we found as the basis of the present volume was 175 pages of Cynthia's typescript (a carbon copy of the original version has been preserved). Of these, the first eighty pages had been edited and, in some instances, cut by Arthur, with his own chapters alternating as they do now. Those eighty pages were thus increased to 122 pages, consisting of six chapters initialled alternately A.K. and C.K. (One further chapter by A.K. has been omitted from the main text of the book for reasons which are explained and inserted as an appendix.) Pages 81 to 111 of Cynthia's typescript seemed to have been partly edited by her, and the remainder hardly at all.

These bibliographical details have been given at perhaps tedious length in order to account for the present shape and content of the book. In the form in which it came to us, it

* *Astride the Two Cultures*, Hutchinson, London; Random House, New York; 1975.

was unpublishable. The question which I had to ask myself as editor, sadly unable to consult the authors, was 'How much revision am I entitled to make?' The obvious answer was as little as possible, and I have tried not to interfere with what they wished to say.

The first decision I made was to divide the book into its present two parts, and very little editing indeed has gone into Part One. Part Two presented more of a problem. It appeared that Cynthia had used as her sources the correspondence files which she kept so meticulously as his secretary;* his notebooks in which he sometimes made diary entries, comments on his mood, ideas for books, or just random jottings; and what she calls his 'Hermès diaries'. These were tiny French diaries, each of three months' duration, with an illustration on the cover of a horse-drawn phaeton and the name 'Hermès'. He used them almost exclusively for noting his engagements hour by hour, but occasionally entered a comment.

Evidently she wrote her script as she thumbed through these sources. The result is that, while the original version is chronologically exact, it lacks continuity. She might include a letter from Arthur on one page and the answer to it several pages later, and she switches from one subject to another and back again to the first with no thought of logical progression. I am sure that, if she had spared herself to finish her work, she would have altered this. I have, therefore, taken the liberty of rearranging some of the material in order to make for more consecutive reading. This in turn has entailed the inclusion from time to time of a few linking words, or the deletion of some superfluous ones, and for the sake of readability I have not indicated where this has been done. The carbon copy is available should any scholar ever think it worthwhile to compare the two versions.

I also divided Part Two into its present six chapters, and as the authors had given titles to the first two chapters of Part One, I added titles to the remaining chapters.

What I have not done is to eliminate any of the extremely

---

* To the end of her life, when signing letters as 'Secretary to Arthur Koestler', she used the signature of Cynthia Jefferies, her maiden name.

frank revelations she makes about her life with Arthur, his love affairs or passing fancies, his demanding nature, his temper, his depressive moods, his manic activity from time to time. All this she relates in a matter-of-fact way, hardly ever with any comment except a kind of rueful sympathy with him.

As I read through her pages, I felt that they confirmed the answer which I had already begun to form in my own mind to that question 'why?'. Why had this intelligent, healthy woman of fifty-five ended her life? Why had she written 'I cannot live without Arthur'? Other women (and men) have loved deeply and survived the death of the partner. In Cynthia's case, that cry, 'I cannot live without him', was, I felt, the literal truth.

He had never made any secret of the fact that he was difficult to live with. He made frequent references to the fact in his notebooks. He never tried to hide his demanding nature, the violence of his moods, his abrupt changes of direction, his obsessional chasing of women (which persisted long after the examples he himself mentioned in *Arrow in the Blue*). Behind all that was a man of intense intellect, a man who could show enormous kindness and generosity, a man of incomparable humour, and – most of the time – a companion of the utmost charm.

Cynthia was well aware of his faults which he did not try to conceal. Yet, in all the thirty-three years of their association, the only times that she was really unhappy were during the first six years when, occasionally, Arthur tried to break the links which bound them together. He did this, as he thought, for Cynthia's own good, because (at the time they met) he was exactly twice her age and because he knew that no partner of his could ever hope for a conventional ménage. She knew this too – but it made no difference.

There can be no doubt that Cynthia fell in love almost at their first meeting and she loved him for the rest of their lives. From 1955 to the end she shared his life. But even that was not enough. It is hardly an exaggeration to say that his life became hers, that she *lived* his life. And when the time came for him to leave it, her life too was at an end.

That is, I believe, the conclusion to which readers of this

book will be drawn, although Arthur and Cynthia lived for another twenty-seven years after it ends. Did Arthur return her devotion? He was not demonstrative in public, though he never called her anything but 'Angel' before his friends, even if he was accusing her of some supposed heinous crime. Both of them would have been acutely embarrassed if they could have read these lines, for both hated any suggestion of sentimentality. Of course he relied on her absolutely, but I do not believe it is being sentimental to say that yes, Arthur did also love Cynthia deeply. He was sparing of compliments, as she ruefully remarks. He knew she did not expect or wish for any reward for her years of devotion. But he also knew instinctively that the reward she would prize more than any other was contained in the concluding sentence of his farewell message 'to whom it may concern', written nine months before they died: 'It is to her that I owe the relative peace and happiness that I enjoyed in the last period of my life – and never before.'

Though hedged about with Koestlerian qualifications, that is the epitaph which Cynthia would have valued above all others.

Part One 1940-1951

by Arthur and Cynthia Koestler

I

Retrospect

by A.K.

I

A writer aged seventy-six has only two prospects before him: to be forgotten before he dies, or to die before he is forgotten.

Before I was fifty I published two volumes of autobiography, *Arrow in the Blue* and *The Invisible Writing*. They ended with my escape to England from Nazi-dominated Europe in 1940, at the age of thirty-five. These volumes were published in the early 1950s. In the thirty years that have passed since then, I have been urged by publishers and friends to continue where *The Invisible Writing* left off, but kept postponing it in favour of writing books on what seemed to me more worthwhile subjects. But if I were to temporize even longer, it might be too late.

However, before picking up the thread again, I must provide a brief chronology of my life up to 1940 for the benefit of readers who have not read *Arrow in the Blue* and *The Invisible Writing*, or read them so long ago that they have forgotten their contents – after all, thirty years are the standard measure by which we count generations.

CHRONOLOGY

1905
Born in Budapest, first and only child of Hungarian father and Austrian mother; brought up bilingually (Hungarian and German). Father prosperous industrialist but went

bankrupt in early twenties. Both parents non-practising Jews.

1919

Family moves to Vienna.

1922–26

Studies engineering at Vienna Polytechnical University. Joins Zionist duelling fraternity. Co-founder of Austrian branch of Vladimir Jabotinsky's radical movement (the so-called Revisionist Party) which later gave rise to Begin's Irgun.

1926–27

Abandons engineering studies, emigrates to Palestine. Works in a kibbutz; as a street vendor of lemonade in Haifa; as a draftsman to an Arab architect; as a freelance journalist, frequently on the verge of starvation. In 1927 obtains the post of Middle East correspondent of Ullstein, the biggest chain of continental newspapers, and seems set on the road to respectability.

1929

Transferred by Ullstein from Jerusalem to Paris.

1930

Transferred from Paris to headquarters in Berlin.

1930–32

Science editor of Ullstein's *Vossische Zeitung* and simultaneously foreign editor of their evening paper, *BZ am Mittag*.

1931

Attains the peak of his journalistic career: only press representative on board *Graf Zeppelin* on its polar expedition.

1931

Hitler *ante portas*. Joins German Communist Party as the only apparent alternative to Nazi rule. As a consequence sacked by Ullstein.

1932-33

Travels in Soviet Russia, Caucasus and Central Asia, sponsored by Agitprop Komintern,* to write a book on first Five-Year Plan.

1934

Book completed but rejected by Soviet censorship. Goes back to Paris, now the centre of anti-Nazi exiles.

1934-36

Paris. Active in anti-Fascist movement, writes propaganda pamphlets, edits various émigré magazines, starts writing *The Gladiators* – a historical novel on the abortive revolution of Roman slaves under Spartacus in the first century BC.

1935

Marries pretty German CP comrade, Dorothy Ascher.

1936

At the start of Spanish Civil War, visits General Franco's headquarters in Seville as special correspondent of the liberal London daily, *News Chronicle*, to collect evidence of German military aid to Franco. Denounced by a former Berlin colleague as a Communist, he makes his escape via Gibraltar. Writes propaganda booklet *L'Espagne Ensanglantée*, later incorporated into *Spanish Testament* (London, 1937).

1937

War correspondent of *News Chronicle* on loyalist side. Captured at the fall of Malaga by Franco's troops; imprisoned February–June under sentence of death; liberated by prisoner exchange arranged by International Red Cross. Writes *Dialogue with Death*.†

---

* Agitation and Propaganda Department of the Communist International.
† Originally incorporated into *Spanish Testament*, later republished as an independent book.

1938

Breaks with Communist Party under the impact of Soviet mass arrests and show trials. Finishes *The Gladiators*. Starts writing *Darkness at Noon*.

1939–40

At the outbreak of the Second World War, arrested by French police as a political suspect, interned in concentration camp at Le Vernet d'Arriège. Released early in 1940, completes *Darkness at Noon* a month before German invasion. Joins French Foreign Legion under the assumed identity of Albert Dubert, taxi driver from Berne, to get off the Gestapo wanted list. Escapes via Marseille, Oran, Casablanca, Lisbon to England.

This is where the existing volumes of the autobiography end. However, this skeletonized outline of the first thirty-five years of my life requires a few comments.

A chronological account follows of necessity a single line along the dimension of time – which does not reveal the complex, multidimensional pattern which provides the motivation and meaning. Thus the foregoing chronology must give the impression of a senseless zigzag course – a battered tennis ball bumping down a mountain stream, as the Zen saying has it, whereas – to change the metaphor – there are in fact several distinct leitmotifs underlying and entwined in this curriculum vitae which lend coherence to the seemingly disjointed sequence. Thus to embrace Zionism in Austria in the 1920s, the foul cradle of Hitler's movement, was a sensible thing to do – only the romantic aspiration to spend the rest of my life in a kibbutz was based on a naive misjudgement of my powers of endurance. Embracing Marxism and joining the Communist Party was certainly a tragic mistake but a mistake shared in the thirties by the intellectual vanguard in Europe and America – from Auden to Brecht, from Malraux to Silone, from Hemingway to Picasso. Nor was there incompatability, at that time, between devotion to the Promised Land – Palestine – and the Land of Promise – the Soviet Union. The Communist revolution was to solve all social problems on a global scale, but also reserve a niche for the 'Jewish National Home' in the new world order. It is now generally forgotten that in 1948 the USSR and the USA were the first two countries to recognize officially the State of Israel. 'Zionism' became a term of abuse in Soviet parlance only at a later stage.

In *Arrow in the Blue* and *The Invisible Writing*, as well as in *The God That Failed** I have described at length the complex psychological phenomena involved in the process of conversion to the Marxist–Leninist creed, and my personal experiences as a member of the Communist Party during the seven years 1931–38. In the present context I only wanted to reassure the reader that the bizarre figure of the foregoing chronology was more typical of his time, both in his beliefs and errors, than appears at a first glance.

Another curious aspect of this curriculum needs a word of explanation: the dual role I played for a while as science editor of a morning paper and foreign affairs editor of an evening paper. This strange combination came about by a chance event, but it reflected a basic lifelong dualism, a split mentality, one half of which was actively and passionately involved in political action, the other attracted by science and philosophy. I have spoken of this mental split in the earlier volumes of my autobiography and it will constantly crop up in the pages that follow.

The chance event I mentioned was the award of the 1929 Nobel Prize for physics to Louis de Broglie, for his revolutionary wave theory of matter. I called on him immediately after the news had come in from Stockholm; he was glad to be interviewed by a journalist who had a scientific education and we talked for three or four hours. The interview occupied a whole page in the *Vossische Zeitung* and convinced my Berlin bosses that I had a gift for popularizing difficult scientific theories. By pure chance the revered science editor of the *Vossische Zeitung*, Professor Joel, was reaching retirement age – hence the offer to succeed him, and the resulting happy schizophrenic state of holding forth on relativity and the coming age of space travel in the feature columns of the

* London and New York, 1950.

morning paper, and editorializing on Signor Mussolini's post-urings in the evening paper. It was too good to last. . . .

2

In the last years before the war, during the days of the great anti-Fascist crusade, I had made a heterogenous collection of British friends and spent an increasing part of each year in Britain – supervising the translation of *The Gladiators*,* writing *Spanish Testament*, lecturing for the Left Book Club, and learning to eat fried kidney for breakfast on night trains and in the houses of friends. I had also acquired an English girlfriend – Dorothy and I had parted amiably in 1937. The new girlfriend was Daphne Hardy, a young sculptress who had won a travelling scholarship to Paris; she appears as 'G' in *Scum of the Earth*. When war was declared, we intended to go at once to England, where I was to enlist as a volunteer in the British Army. I still had a Hungarian passport with a valid visa for England; but on the day after Britain declared war on Germany, all visas to the UK were cancelled, and new visas could only be granted to foreign nationals by special authoriza-tion from the Home Office. A month later I was still waiting for that special authorization when the French police dispat-ched me to the notorious detention camp for undesirable and politically suspect aliens at Le Vernet, in the foothills of the Pyrenees. A year later, after France had capitulated and I had made my tortuous escape via North Africa to neutral Lisbon, disguised as Legionnaire Albert Dubert, the game called wait-ing-for-a-visa, well known to tens of thousands of Europeans, started again. After two months of it, my patience ran out, and I boarded a passenger plane from Lisbon to England, without an entry permit.

This was the sort of thing which, by British standards, 'simply isn't done'. Particularly not when there is a war on, and the country is in the grips of a fifth-column scare. As a result, I spent the first six weeks in my new homeland locked

* Written in German like all his books up to and including *Darkness at Noon* – Editor.

24

up in Pentonville Prison, amidst a cosmopolitan crowd with
the somewhat paradoxical status, 'Alien refused permission to
land'.

The irony of it was that I owed my release from the Le
Vernet camp half a year earlier to the intervention of British
politicians with the French authorities – among them Ellen
Wilkinson, Under-Secretary of State at the Home Office.
Then why in God's name did the Home Office not authorize
the British Consulate in Paris, and later the Consulate in
Lisbon, to grant me a visa? I have never been able to discover
the reason. Did MI5 believe that I was still a Communist (one
must remember that at that time Stalin was allied to Hitler)?
Or did the Soviet agents who infested British Intelligence
like maggots in an overripe cheese take their revenge for my
defection? Forty years have passed and I no longer care, but
at the time I did.

It was in the visitors' room in Pentonville that Daphne and
I met again after our separation in France (she had managed
to embark on one of the last British boats from Biarritz, while
'Legionnaire Dubert' made his detour via Morocco). Until I
got to Lisbon neither of us had known whether the other was
still alive – but the visitors' room in Pentonville was not the
ideal place for a display of emotions.

It was also in Pentonville that I received the page proofs of
Darkness at Noon, and heard for the first time the English title
of the book – based on a quotation from Milton – which
Daphne had suggested, and which I liked.* There was irony
in reading, in solitary confinement, the proofs of a novel about
a man in solitary confinement, and I considered myself very
lucky indeed that I was in Pentonville and not in the Lubianka.

I was released from Pentonville a few days before Christmas
1940 and moved in with Daphne, who had a small house in
South Kensington and a job at the Ministry of Information.
The day after I was released I went to the Recruiting Office
in Duke's Road, Euston, and enlisted in the Army, but was
told that it would take several weeks before I would actually

---

* As related in *The Invisible Writing*, it was Daphne who translated the book from
the German original.

be called up. This gave me time to breathe – and to write *Scum of the Earth*, the account of my experiences during the collapse of France. In 1968, I wrote a new preface to it for the collected Danube Edition of my books:

Scum of the Earth was the first book that I wrote in English. It was written in January–March 1941, immediately after I had escaped from occupied France to England. My friends were either in the hands of the Gestapo, or had committed suicide, or were trapped, without hope, on the lost continent. The agony of the French collapse was reverberating through my mind as a scream of terror echoes in one's ear. Within the previous four years I had been imprisoned in three different countries: in Spain during the civil war; as an undesirable alien in France; finally, having escaped to England with false papers at the height of the Fifth Column scare, I was locked up, pending investigation, in Pentonville prison. The book was written in the blacked-out London of the night-blitz, in the short breathing space between my release from Pentonville and enlistment in the Pioneer Corps. . . .

Re-reading the book after all these years, I find these pressures reflected in its apocalyptic mood, its spontaneity and lack of polish. Some pages now appear insufferably maudlin; others are studded with clichés which at the time, however, seemed original discoveries to the innocent explorer of a new language; above all, the text betrays the fact that there had been no time for correcting proofs.

Nevertheless, the book was well received and – to my utter surprise – reissued in a Left Book Club edition, in spite of its savage attacks on the Stalin–Hitler pact and the French Communist Party. As for *Darkness at Noon*, it became a Book of the Month Club choice in America, while in England the editor of the *New Statesman*, Kingsley Martin, though a notorious fellow-traveller, called it 'one of the few books written in this epoch which will survive it'. No doubt the success of the novel was gratifying, but even more important for me was the political influence it had on the leftist intelligentsia in the USA and, after the war, in France.

Thus I found myself abruptly transformed from a member of the grey, piteous crowd of refugees – the scum of the earth – into a best-selling author. This is a dangerous experience for any writer, but before it could turn my head I was also transformed into Private No. 13805661 in 251 Company Pioneer Corps, which was not given to lionizing intellectuals. (The Pioneer Corps was at that time the only branch of the Army in which non-allied aliens could enlist.) My late friend John Strachey described the impression I made at our first meeting:*

In the spring of 1941, I was serving as the Adjutant, or maid-of-all work, of No. 87 Fighter Squadron of the Royal Air Force, at that time stationed near Bath. One day a pilot opened the door of the Mess and said, with disinterest, 'Someone to see the Adjutant.' There entered the rumpled, battle-dressed figure of Private Koestler of the Pioneer Corps, surely one of the oddest men ever to dig a British latrine.

Yet it was a priceless experience. Years later I described some touching episodes in a lecture to the British Academy† from which I quote:

My company – the 251 Company Aliens Pioneer Corps – was engaged on a fairly vital defence job to protect the petrol reservoirs in the vicinity of Bristol. (We were digging craters which, during air-raids, were filled with inflammable liquid and set ablaze to convince the raiders that they had accomplished their mission and could safely go home.) We were glad to do a useful job, but as you would expect from aliens, we became over-enthusiastic, so we asked our Commanding Officer (who was British) to do away with the ritual tea breaks – which, what with downing tools, marching to the distant cook hut and back morning and afternoon, cost nearly two hours of our working time, in addition to the lunch break. The CO expressed his appreciation of our laudable zeal and explained that we had to have our tea breaks whether we liked it or not because the British Pioneer Companies and the local unions of our civilian workmates would raise hell if we didn't. The time was about nine months after Dunkirk.

No less characteristic seemed to me another episode, which I quoted in the same lecture:

---

* *The Strangled Cry*, London, 1962, pp. 11f.
† First published on behalf of the British Academy by the Oxford University Press in 1973 under the title 'The Lion and the Ostrich'; reprinted in *Kaleidoscope*, Hutchinson, 1981.

I had to spend a few days in a military hospital somewhere in Gloucestershire, and asked for permission to use my typewriter. The sister in charge of the ward, a kind, middle-aged spinster, who had never before come across a British soldier with an accent like mine, listened to my request, thought for a while, then said: 'All right, you can have your typewriter, but on one condition: you must give me your word of honour that you won't do any Fifth Column work on it.'

The lecture went on to draw some conclusions which, I think, are still valid today:

But other experiences left us rather bewildered. While 'digging for victory', we came into intimate contact with working-class life, and found it fundamentally different from its Continental equivalent. In the NAAFI canteens, in the pub and later at the snooker table in a London ambulance station, I was taught to accept the stubborn persistence of the hoary cliché that people in general were divided into Them and Us. But that 'Us' had nothing to do with class consciousness in the Marxist sense, as it existed in the Socialist and Communist Parties of Europe. Marxist dialectics was as much double-dutch to the British working class as it was to the rest of the nation; instead of the fierce class hatred which had scorched the Continent with revolutions and civil wars, there was an almost smug acceptance of living in a divided world, as licensed premises are divided into saloon bar and public bar. On the Continent, the symbolic gesture of militancy was the clenched fist; here it was closer to a shrug, a deliberate turning of one's back on middle-class standards of value, codes of behaviour, vocabulary and accent. Off duty our British working mates were lively characters, full of fun and games; on the working site they moved like figures in a slow-motion film, or deep-sea divers on the ocean bed. They seemed to be conforming to a sacred doctrine, a set of unwritten maxims of life: go slow and take it easy or you are letting your mates down and we shall all be on the dole. It's a mug's game, anyway, and you are in it for life unless you hit the pools. In the Libyan desert, or as rear gunners in a bomber, they would have done a magnificent job; for in those circumstances the gulf would have been temporarily bridged by shared danger and hardship – and by the awareness of playing a man's game instead of a mug's game. The same lovable bloke who risked his life on D-Day to keep the country free would not lift a finger at Dagenham to put the country back on its feet.

It may seem to you that I am flogging a dead horse, but to

pronounce it dead does not make it so – or else this particular dead horse still has a kick.

Although my career in the Pioneer Corps was short-lived, it taught me more about the 'toiling masses' of this country than any amount of reading could have done.

After a few months of digging, I was made an Army lecturer, travelling up and down the country and trying to convince somnolescent audiences of the existence of Dachau and Buchenwald. After another few months, in March 1942, the Ministry of Information got me invalided out of the Pioneer Corps and employed me as a scriptwriter for propaganda films. I also wrote some radio plays, devised texts for leaflets to be dropped by the RAF on Germany, and did some night stints as an air-raid warden and auxiliary ambulance driver. I was bombed out once – by a V1, or doodlebug, as those murderous flying bombs were affectionately called – but got away without injury. In retrospect it seems to me that the three war years 1942–44 which I spent in blitzed London were among the most uneventful (I almost said peaceful) periods of my life. This paradox is not the product of a perverse mind: lots of people have almost nostalgic memories of the Blitz. It is also a well-known fact that while it lasted, less hospital beds were occupied by mental patients than before or after. 'Business as usual' turned out to be a potent therapeutic slogan.

3

In my spare time, I wrote a novel, *Arrival and Departure*,★ and a number of essays, which were collected in *The Yogi and the Commissar*.†

Arrival and Departure was the third volume of a trilogy of which the central theme is the conflict between morality and expediency – whether, or to what extent, a noble end justifies ignoble means. It is a hoary problem which obsessed me

★ London and New York, 1943; Danube Edition, 1966.
† London and New York, 1945; Danube Edition, 1965.

during the years spent as a member of the Communist Party. The first volume of the trilogy, *The Gladiators*,★ was a historical novel about the revolution of Roman slaves in 73-71 BC led by the Thracian gladiator, Spartacus, who for two years held half of Italy under his sway. The main reason the revolt was defeated was apparently Spartacus's lack of determination – his refusal to apply the 'law of detours' which demands that the leader on the road to Utopia should be 'pitiless for the sake of pity'. He refuses to execute dissidents and troublemakers, and to rule by terror – and through this refusal he dooms the revolution to defeat. In *Darkness at Noon* the old Bolshevik Rubashov goes the opposite way and follows the 'law of detours' to the bitter end – only to discover that 'logic alone was a defective compass which led one such a winding, twisted course that the ultimate goal disappeared in the mist'. Thus two novels complement each other, and both end in a cul-de-sac.

In *Arrival and Departure* the conflict between morality and expediency is restated in psychiatric terms. Peter Slavek starts out as a brave young revolutionary in a country under a Nazi-type dictatorship, without much insight into the unconscious motives of his own actions. When war breaks out he escapes to 'Neutralia' (Portugal), and is now faced with the choice to follow his fiancée to the still neutral USA or to volunteer for the Allied Forces. He has withstood torture and imprisonment in the past, but now, faced with an insoluble dilemma, he suffers a mental and physical breakdown – a so-called hysterical paralysis affecting one leg (which I had seen displayed by a fellow-prisoner in Seville gaol). He is treated by Sonia, a Freudian psychotherapist who makes him relive some traumatic experiences of his early childhood, and realizes that his crusading zeal was derived from unconscious guilt. Thus, on the analyst's couch, he is persuaded to say farewell to arms, and to opt for the choice which reason and expediency dictate.

In the type of psychotherapy practised by Sonia there was no provision made for ethical absolutes; its aim is to make the patient

★ London and New York, 1939; Danube Edition, 1965.

accept reality; and if the reality is Nazi-occupied Europe, it cannot be helped. Yet in the end her method does not work; Peter changes his mind – or rather some untouchable core inside him, a core apparently 'beyond the reach of cause and effect', changes his mind for him.*

He realizes that ethical imperatives, intuitive insights, artistic values cannot be explained (or explained away) by 'reducing them to conditioned reflexes, childhood traumas, frustrated sex and ultimately to electro-chemical processes'. This view of the irreducibility of values from higher to lower levels in the existential hierarchy ran counter to the prevailing reductionist currents of the time – Marxism, Freudianism, Behaviourism, Logical Positivism and Materialism in general. A novel is not a philosophical treatise, and thus the intended message of Peter Slavek's story could only be hinted at in an implicit, oblique way. But I have endeavoured to clarify it in later works, the first of which was *The Yogi and the Commissar*.

At the end of the novel, Peter Slavek is parachuted into his native country to join the resistance movement and his future remains uncertain. But fate gave it a bitterly ironical twist – as described in the postscript to the Danube Edition:

Peter Slavek was modelled on a young Hungarian friend of mine, the poet Endre Havas, whom I knew during the war in London. Though at one time he too had been disillusioned by the Communist Party, he rejoined it in the days of the Battle of Stalingrad, and went back to Hungary. In 1949, during the great purge which followed the trial of the former Minister for Foreign Affairs, Laszlo Rajk, Havas was arrested, together with virtually all Party intellectuals who had spent the years of the war in the West. He was accused of being a spy, but persisted in his refusal to sign the usual confession. Several of his fellow prisoners who were released during the revolution of 1956, and escaped to England, reported his end. Havas had gone insane under protracted physical torture. He would crawl on all-fours shouting 'Help, help. Long live Stalin.' He died in the prison infirmary in 1952 or 53. After the thaw he was posthumously rehabilitated as one of the victims of the 'Stalin personality cult', and

---

* *Arrival and Departure*, postscript to the Danube Edition, p. 190.

a biographical note, accompanied by his photograph, appeared in the official *Encyclopaedia of Hungarian Literature*.

The Yogi and the Commissar was a collection of essays, ·whose title became a kind of catchword which even found its way into the *Penguin Dictionary of Quotations*. The first and last of the essays, as already mentioned, contained a critique of Reductionist philosophy and some tentative suggestions for an alternative approach, which I shall discuss in later contexts. The hard core of the collection, which accounts for the impassioned controversies which it raised, were three consecutive essays: the first, 'Anatomy of a Myth', analysed the mentality of the fellow-traveller as a myth addict; the second, 'Soviet Myth and Reality', gave a detailed account, mainly based on Soviet sources and statistics, of the true nature of that regime; the third, 'The End of an Illusion', predicted the enslavement of Central and Eastern Europe. In the euphoric mood after D-Day and the Battle of Stalingrad, such Cassandra-cries did not find willing ears. And yet 'it required no prophetic gifts, only a sober assessment of the facts, to draw the obvious conclusions'.*

For light relief, the collection also contained some literary essays, among them one called 'The French 'Flu',† which started:

The people who administer literature in this country – editors, critics, essayists: the managerial class on Parnassus – have lately been affected by a new outbreak of that recurrent epidemic, the French 'Flu. Its symptoms are that the patient, ordinarily a balanced, cautious, sceptical man, is lured into unconditional surrender of his critical faculties when a line of French poetry or prose falls under his eyes. Just as in the case of hay-fever one whiff is sufficient to release the attack, thus a single word like *'bouillabaisse'*, *'crève-coeur'*, *'patrie'*, or *'minette'* is enough to produce the most violent spasms: his eyes water, his heart contracts in bitter-sweet convulsions, his ductless glands swamp the blood-stream with adolescent raptures. If an English poet dares to

* Preface to the Danube Edition.
† First published in *Tribune*, November 1943.

use words like 'my fatherland', 'my soul', 'my heart', etc., he is done for; if·a French one dispenses musical platitudes about *la Patrie, la France, mon coeur,* and *mon âme,* the patient begins to quiver with admiration.

Three works have come during the last year out of captive France, all three celebrated as literary revelations: Gide's *Imaginary Interviews,* Aragon's volume of poems *Le Crève-Coeur,* and Vercors' *Le Silence de la Mer.* . . .

The essay criticizes the three books as bogus; they have indeed been deservedly forgotten, nor would the essay be worth quoting except to establish priority, as it were, for the term 'French 'Flu' which is still current among literati.

4

Daphne and I never got married, mainly because I was still legally married to Dorothy (who survived the German occupation under a false identity in France), but to all intents and purposes we considered ourselves, and were considered by our friends, as a married couple. This intense relationship lasted for six years – from 1938, when we first met in Paris, till 1944, when it broke up, owing to the persistent and well-nigh pathological streak of promiscuity during my youth and early middle age, which I have confessed to in *Arrow in the Blue.* As a mitigating circumstance I may mention that Daphne and I are still close friends, nearly forty years after the breakup of our ménage.

Daphne's successor was Mamaine Paget, one of the brilliant Paget twins – stars, or rather twin stars, among the debutantes of the 1930s. They were identical not only genetically, but in appearance, and to such an extent that even close friends often found it difficult to tell whether they were facing Celia or Mamaine. They also had the same passion for poetry and the classics; for playing the piano, bird-watching and photography. Both spoke near perfect German and French.

One evening John Strachey invited Mamaine and me for dinner at the Etoile, then mostly frequented by writers and publishers. Strachey, in his capacity as Minister for Food in those hungry, rationed days, was much caricatured in the papers, so his presence had not passed unnoticed. Nor had Mamaine's – for some tables away from ours her alter ego, Celia, identically dressed, was dining with the philosopher Freddie Ayer. Strachey, who arrived a few minutes after us, and whose chair was facing in the opposite direction, had not noticed them. After ordering our food, Strachey excused himself and disappeared to the gents. At that moment I had a bright idea: I asked Mamaine to change places with Celia. The manoeuvre was executed quickly and expeditiously, watched by the fascinated diners. When Strachey returned from the loo he resumed his chair and continued talking to Celia, without noticing the substitution. He only realized that he was no longer talking to Mamaine when Celia and I burst out laughing, with other guests unashamedly joining in the merriment.

5

One essay in *The Yogi and the Commissar* (originally printed in the *New York Times**) was called 'On Disbelieving Atrocities'. It reminded the reader that those who throughout the 1930s had tried to warn the West of Hitler's intentions had been dismissed as hysterics or persecution maniacs.

At present we have the mania of trying to tell you about the killing of the total Jewish population of Europe. So far three million have died. It is the greatest mass-killing in recorded history; and it goes on daily, hourly, as regularly as the ticking of your watch. . . . But in the course of some recent public opinion survey nine out of ten average American citizens, when asked whether they believed that the Nazis commit atrocities, answered that it was all propaganda lies, and that they didn't believe a word of it. . . . And meanwhile the watch goes on ticking.

A few weeks after writing this, I learned that my mother's aged sister and her family were among the six million who

* January 1944.

perished in extermination camps. Six million is an abstraction; my Aunt Rose and cousin Margit, gassed like rats, were the reality behind the abstraction. Could anything be done to save at least some of those who had so far survived? There has been a spate of books and documents in recent years* which shows that quite a lot could have been done to save substantial numbers in the Nazi-satellite countries – Hungary, Bulgaria, Rumania, Yugoslavia – if the Allies had been willing to provide a haven for them, in Palestine or wherever else. But Allied statesmen turned down or shelved all such schemes. To them, the holocaust was indeed an abstraction – they had no Aunt Roses to mourn.

I had revisited Palestine, as special correspondent of the *News Chronicle,* in 1937, four years after Hitler's ascent to power. My friends of the old days had changed:

In the streets of Haifa and Tel Aviv, in the settlements of Samaria and Galilee, they went about their business with the calm, slow motions imposed by the heat, but underneath they were all fanatics and maniacs. Every single one of them had a brother, parent, cousin or bride in the part of Europe ruled by the assassins. It was no longer a question whether Zionism was a good or bad idea. They knew that the gas-chambers were coming. They were past arguing. When provoked, they bared their teeth. . . . I had become gradually convinced that partition of the country into an Arab and a Jewish state, as proposed by the Royal Commission of 1937 under Lord Peel, was, though not an ideal solution, yet the only possible solution. In 1937 partition could have been carried out with relatively little trouble and less bloodshed. The representative Jewish bodies were prepared to accept it. The moderate Arab leaders would have yielded to diplomatic pressure. The most influential among them, King Abdullah of Transjordan (whom I revisited in Aman during a lull in the riots), gave me an interview which, in somewhat veiled terms, amounted to an acceptance of partition. The Government of Neville Chamberlain, however, refused to implement the Royal Commission's plan, and for the next ten years British policy in Palestine was plunged into a dark night of indecision, error and prejudice.†

* Morse, Lacqueur, Gilbert, Bower, etc.
† *The Invisible Writing*, ch. 35.

In 1944, I was more convinced than ever that the Royal Commission's proposal was on the right lines. But I also believed that the Government could only be persuaded to implement the proposal by a show of strength of the Jews of Palestine. However, the Jewish Agency which officially represented them, was opposed in principle to the use of forcible means, and so was Chaim Weizmann, the president of the Zionist Organization (and later President of the State of Israel). On the other hand, Begin's Irgun and the so-called Stern Gang engaged in acts of terrorism (and rejected partition). As I had once been active in Jabotinsky's Revisionist Party,* I had some sympathy with its offspring, the Irgun – though not with their recent methods. But I also felt the urge to see for myself what was going on, to try to form a balanced opinion. Dr Weizmann, whom I saw fairly frequently at that time, approved of the idea – though he did not entirely trust me because of my Revisionist past. 'Talk to those mad friends of yours,' he told me, 'and try to convince them that partition is our only chance.' Thus encouraged, and armed with an accreditation from *The Times* as their special correspondent, I embarked, just before Christmas 1944, on SS *Exeter,* which was part of a convoy from Liverpool to Alexandria. In the Mediterranean, the ship behind us was sunk by a German submarine, but we arrived safely at our destination.

I stayed in Palestine from the beginning of January to 15 August 1945 – I remember the date on which I left because it was the day the first atom bomb exploded over Hiroshima. Most of these seven and a half months I spent collecting material for, and writing *Thieves in the Night.* Soon after my arrival I established contact with Irgun and the Stern group, both of which were underground; there was a reward of £500 each on the heads of their respective leaders, Begin and David Friedman-Yellin, both of whom I met in secret, under the noses, as it were, of the police. This did not involve any great risk on my part, as *The Times* accreditation lent me an odour of respectability. But the meeting with Begin had an added

* See *Arrow in the Blue* and *The Invisible Writing,* ch. 35.

spice: the head of the Jerusalem CID, whom I had repeatedly met socially, came for drinks at my flat, just before the man from the Irgun picked me up. For Begin and his outlaws the risk was, of course, incomparably greater, but they had devised an ingenious system for maintaining contact with the outside world. Essentially it consisted of my changing cars and travel companions no less than five times until I was safely relayed from my Jerusalem flat to a house in a slummy suburb in Tel Aviv, having no idea where I was. Two unsmiling toughs led me up some steps into a large, pitch-dark room, where I was told to sit down. Some distance away across the room, I sensed the presence of another human being – which was Menachem Begin. I asked whether I might light a cigarette, whereupon one of the toughs said I might not, but he would light it for me – which he did, shielding the light of the match as one used to during air raids in the blacked-out streets of London. The reason for this precaution I learned later: it was rumoured that Begin had disguised his features with a beard or plastic surgery. In his memoirs Begin says ironically that I wanted to strike a match to have a glimpse of him out of journalistic curiosity – whereas I was much happier not to know where I was, nor his appearance, in case I should, after all, run into trouble with the police.

We talked for about an hour. I tried to convince him that, once the war was over, British policy towards Palestine would change, and that the only hope was partition, with Israel becoming a Dominion of the British Commonwealth. Begin answered in substance that he did not believe British policy would change even if Labour came to power (which proved to be a woefully correct prediction); but that even if I were right, his task was to fight the Palestine administration, which refused to let in survivors of the holocaust, and that he could not get his boys to risk the gallows by telling them that it was all a misunderstanding, and the English were ultimately very nice people.

When the meeting was over, I realized how naive I had been in imagining that my arguments would have even the slightest influence. I had been close to Vladimir Jabotinsky, the founding father of the Irgun, some twenty years earlier* – but Begin and his men belonged to a different generation – hard, bitter and fanatical.

The meeting with Friedman-Yellin took a similar course. After that I decided to abandon these futile efforts and to write the book which for some time had been germinating in my mind. It was a novel, *Thieves in the Night,* its title derived from 2 Peter 3: 10: 'But the day of the Lord will come as a thief in the night.' The ambiguity of the quotation was a reflection of the ambivalence of my own feelings – and so was Joseph, the central character, whom I made to be half-English, half-Jewish. The main theme of the book is the birth and peaceful evolution of the kibbutz Ezra's Tower, and, as counterpoints, the growth, in the poisoned soil, of Jewish and Arab terrorism.

The central theme of the earlier trilogy – *The Gladiators, Darkness at Noon, Arrival and Departure* – was the ethics of revolution; the central theme of *Thieves in the Night* is the ethics of survival. If power corrupts, the reverse is also true: persecution corrupts the victim, though in subtler ways. In both cases the dilemma of noble ends begetting ignoble means has the stamp of inevitability.

The novel was written in Jerusalem, in the harrowing, poisoned atmosphere of three-cornered terrorism, savagery and mourning. The year was 1945; Auschwitz and Belsen had yielded their obscene secrets; there was hardly a family of European origin which had not contributed close relatives or friends to the death-chambers. . . .

Whatever its artistic merits and demerits, *Thieves in the Night* had certain political repercussions. Thus I learned that several members of the United Nations Palestine Commission of 1947 (which made the historic recommendations for partition and the establishment of a Jewish state) had gone to the trouble of reading the book, and that it had even to some extent influenced their decisions. The Chairman of that eleven-nation Commission, Judge Sandstrom of Sweden, repeatedly teased members of the later Israeli Government by telling them that the story of Ezra's Tower had made a stronger impression on him than their official memoranda; and though this was no doubt

* See *Arrow in the Blue,* ch. 13.

said tongue in cheek, I was more moved by it than by the praise and abuse of the literary critics.*

After my return from Palestine to London in August 1945, I wrote two long articles for *The Times*,† putting both the Arab and the Jewish case as objectively as I could, and advocating, once more, partition of the country as the only viable solution. *The Times* published the articles anonymously ('From a Special Correspondent lately in Palestine'), which created quite a stir for it was the first time that the old Thunderer had lent its implicit support to partition.

6

This duty discharged, and *Thieves in the Night* delivered to the publishers, I felt free to turn to a subject for a book which had been in my mind for several years: a theory of humour, which also seemed to provide some insights into the psychology of creativity in general. It was an ambitious project which, I thought, would take me a year (it actually took two and a half‡) and, to carry it out, I would have to retire to the country far from the hectic activities of London. Mamaine loved London, but she loved the country even more and, during a visit to friends in North Wales, we had found a farmhouse to let which seemed ideally suited for the purpose. It was a wildly romantic place in the hills of Snowdonia, completely isolated, with no other human habitation within sight, nor any living being except the sheep grazing on the surrounding pastures. Even the postal address sounded exotic: Bwlch Ocyn, Blaenau Ffestiniog, Merioneth, North Wales. The farmhouse – dating from the seventeenth or eighteenth century – was built on top of a hillock of large rough-hewn blocks of sandstone, in the style which architects call random rubble masonry. Its proprietor was the manager of the fabulous Port Meirion Hotel, Jim Wyllie, who had modernized

---

* *Thieves in the Night*, postscript to the Danube Edition, pp. 335f.; see also *The Invisible Writing*, ch. 35.
† 26 and 28 September 1945.
‡ *Insight and Outlook*, London and New York, 1949.

the interior of the house and provided it with rustic period furniture – but also, most incongruously, with a minstrels' gallery, which was put up in the former barn during our tenancy. Wyllie had acquired a taste for such 'amusing' experiments from Clough Williams Ellis, the eccentric architect who had designed Port Meirion – an Italian village, complete with campanile, piazza and pastel-shaded villas dumped on the shore of Cardigan Bay, at a driving distance of twenty minutes from us. Port Meirion and its luxury hotel provided a striking contrast to Blaenau Ffestiniog – a primitive slate-mining town with a high proportion of miners suffering from silicosis and a single cinema for entertainment which consisted mainly of B Westerns. The home-made advertisements were projected by lantern slides, and on the rare occasions when we ventured to the cinema we somehow always managed to come in at the moment when the screen displayed a photograph of a thoughtful-looking lady with the caption: 'NURSE DREW – COLONIC IRRIGATIONS'. On Sunday mornings, when the miners indulged their well-deserved hour of relaxation over a couple of pints, the Methodist ministers of the town used to do the rounds of the pubs reminding the customers that alcohol was the shortest way to perdition. It was definitely not a town for hedonists.

Thus Bwlch Ocyn* was situated midway between grim, puritanical Ffestiniog and the bogus Mediterranean village of Port Meirion; while the house itself, with its forbidding stony exterior and the minstrels' gallery inside, symbolized the contrast – and so did the life we led in it. Weeks of spartan living, of solitude and intense work alternated with periods when the stream of guests seemed never to dry up. Altogether we spent almost two and a half years in Bwlch Ocyn, interrupted only by occasional visits to London, and two trips to Paris. But Mamaine, who suffered from asthma, also spent some weeks in Switzerland and the South of France; and during those periods I had to hold the fort alone with our three dogs. Domestic help was only available, if at all, when

* A Welsh expert suggested that the name meant 'the yoke, or perhaps saddle, of Joacin' – but I could not swear to it.

Mamaine was in residence: Mrs Lloyd or Mrs Jones could not risk their reputations by setting foot in a house inhabited by a grass widower. Funnily enough, Cyril Connolly and his girlfriend Lis came to stay for a weekend (in February 1946) during one of these absences of Mamaine's; so I had to cook for the most notorious gourmet among English littérateurs. Surprisingly, our friendship survived the ordeal.

Four or five miles from Blaenau Ffestiniog there is the village of Llan Ffestiniog, where Bertrand Russell lived at the time with his third wife, Peter, and their small child, Conrad. Russell was in his mid-seventies – impish, waspish, donnish and, for a champion of so many humanitarian causes, from Pacifism to Free Love, strangely lacking in human warmth. (But much the same paradox applied to George Orwell, and it may not be a paradox at all.) In trying to recall his face, I am able to see it only in profile – the sharp, narrow silhouette of an aggressive jester – rich in wit but devoid of humour.

Towards the end of 1945, George Orwell and I had jointly embarked on a project which I had suggested to him, and for which we were anxious to enlist Russell's support. The idea was to revive, under a different name, the ancient League pour les Droits de l'Homme, which, before the war, had enjoyed great international prestige, but since the war had been taken over by the Communists. Over the Christmas holidays George stayed with us in Bwlch Ocyn; I have never seen him so enthusiastic as when we discussed the projected League. After his return to London he wrote a draft programme, which he showed to various people, among them Michael Foot, who was all for it, Barbara Ward and Tom Hopkinson (editor of *Picture Post*), who, George reported on 2 January, 'were both a little timid because they realize that an organization of this type would in practice be anti-Russian, or would be compelled to become anti-Russian. . . . ' A few days later I reported to George:

I had two long talks with Russell. He fully agrees with our aims but not with the method of approach. He thinks it is too late to start any sort of ethical movement, that war will be on us soon, and that more directly political action is necessary to prevent it. He suggests that a conference should be called with no more than a dozen people who are all experts – one expert on the Far East, one on Science, Propaganda, etc., to work out a programme of action. He himself is ready to read a paper but not to act as a convener. He is tired and overworked, but at the same time very anxious to do something. . . . I believe his idea for a Conference can be fitted into our plan and that the people at such a Conference would be in favour of initiating an organization on our lines.

So we set about organizing the conference. It was to be held in Snowdonia, over the Easter holidays. We were to put up three or four people in Bwlch Ocyn, and another eight in hotels in the vicinity. We also found a sponsor willing to provide the expenses. But at the last minute the sponsor got cold feet and the conference was off. The original League project, however, was still on, and Russell was still willing to support it – until a grotesque episode occurred which is the point of this tale. By the end of April Orwell's original draft had been subjected to various modifications to satisfy the objections raised by prospective signatories. Russell, in particular, had raised two objections to the following passage in the draft:

Since the end of the war, some of the victorious nations have raised certain territorial claims. Great Britain, who has no territorial claims, should table the demand for a general psychological disarmament, the first step of which would be an agreement between Great Britain and the USSR, based on the following points:

(a) Free access of British newspapers, periodicals, books and films to the general public in the USSR and territories occupied and controlled by her; and vice versa;

(b) Such modifications of existing censorship regulations as to permit the free circulation of information about the outside world throughout both countries and territories occupied and controlled by them;

(c) The conclusion of an agreement between the Reuter and Tass Agencies, according to which each of the two Agencies will compile a news summary of 500-1000 words per day which the other Agency undertakes to distribute for internal consumption. The news summary should be confined to a factual presentation of items relating to developments in internal politics, economy, the arts and sports, and its publication should be encouraged in the newspapers of both Government Parties and in the national Press. . . .

Russell objected that the first paragraph sounded like 'using psychological disarmament as a quid pro quo for territorial concessions' and 'that the section about Reuter and Tass appeared [to him] as unworkable'. Both objections could easily be met by changing a few words, but Russell had to leave for Cambridge and over a friendly dinner at Bwlch Ocyn we agreed that Peter, his wife, should redraft the disputed points. But when Peter came for dinner a few days later, instead of having reformulated those two outstanding points according to Russell's wishes, she objected to the term 'psychological disarmament' which had come to assume a central position in the draft after Orwell and I had rewritten it three or four times. Peter wanted to have the whole programme redrafted from scratch. She was an attractive and strong-willed redhead, who could be charming, but could also act as a troublemaker, and on this occasion she assumed the latter role. When I saw that we were getting nowhere I suggested that we postpone the discussion until Russell's return. A week or so later (on 3 May 1946) Russell wrote to me from Cambridge:

I was amazed to hear from my wife that you had refused to accept her as my plenipotentiary [sic], after having yourself suggested that she should represent me, and had accused her of not accurately reporting my opinions as to the draft.

I hope that on reflection you will realise that co-operation is impossible if such incidents are to be expected, and that an apology is due from you, both to my wife and to me.

I wrote back that if I had unintentionally hurt Peter's or Russell's feelings I was very sorry about it, and after that social relations became more or less normal again (except for a complaint by Mamaine to twin Celia: 'Arthur has asked Russell to dinner just when we had nothing to eat'); but the episode had made it clear – as others were to find out during other campaigns – that close political cooperation with Russell was impossible. After some more disappointments the project petered out – it had in fact been an abortive attempt, predating by several decades Amnesty International and the Western approach to the Helsinki Agreement, but aiming in the same direction.

Four years after the stillborn League project, I became one of the midwives of the successful Berlin Congress for Cultural Freedom – which also was endangered by the temperamental illogicality of the prince of symbolic logic.

7

To celebrate the first anniversary of our settling in Bwlch Ocyn, Mamaine wrote a doggerel which cannot claim great artistic merit, but conveys something of the atmosphere of the house. Here are some extracts of it, with some unavoidable explanatory footnotes:

> Bwlch Ocyn, Manod, Blaenau Ffest-
> Iniog, Merionethshire – you've guessed,
> 'Tis the abode of ARTHUR K.
> One year ago this very day
> K, who from sunnier climes had come,
> To make in CAMBRIA his home,
> Arrived with MERMAID* to begin
> With her a life of carefree sin.
>
> The antique House a little room contained
> New-built when K his needs to JIM explained;
> Here K did work; and, seeking not prosperity
> Nor fame, penned volumes destined for posterity.
> Often at evening, with his trusty Hounds
> JOSEPH and DIANA, K would tour the grounds
> And from some pinnacle or knoll inspect
> Th'autumnal hills with crimson fern bedeck'd.
> Or, if in sorrowful mood, he'd take the car
> All cares to banish in PORT MEIRION's bar.
> Apricot brandy, orange curaçao,
> Gin, rum and whisky there did freely flow;

* My nickname for Mamaine.

The Sage LORD RUSSELL would with K rehearse all
The arguments against the Universal,
While gentle PETER too would sometimes beaut-
Ifully speak about the Absolute.
And when, the evening over, he did wing
His homeward way, K to himself would sing:

> Biology, neurology
> Aesthetics and psychology,
> Ethics, epistemology,
> The art of terminology
> I'll study, and with them I do resolve
> The Riddle of the Universe I'll solve.

As time went by, attracted by its fame,
Many a Pilgrim to Bwlch Ocyn came.
ROTHSCHILD* and CROSSMAN, ORWELL, CELIA, FREDDY,†
BRENDA and WANDA, DOMINIQUE‡ and TEDDY;§
Many a cheerful evening thus was spent
In eating, drinking, music, argument.

So from now on each year will ARTHUR K
and MERMAID drink together on this day;
Where'er they be, they will this happy date
With wine and song together celebrate.

One prospective guest who never materialized was Dylan Thomas. We had planned to go with the Thomases on a holiday to Ireland, but for some reason I forget we had to cancel the project – which I did by telegram followed by a letter, inviting them to spend instead a few days in Bwlch Ocyn on their way. We didn't get any reply for a long time – until a letter arrived in Dylan's beautifully neat handwriting, which is worth quoting:

---

* Guy, head of the French branch.
† A. J. Ayer, the philosopher.
‡ Dominique Aury, French writer.
§ Teddy Kollek, later Mayor of Jerusalem.

Blaen Cwm
Llangain
near Carmarthen

26th August '46

Dear Arthur,
I'm so sorry not to have answered your wire, or written, or anything.
I lost both your London and Wales addresses, and have only just
found them in my best coat: the one with arms. And we were very
very sorry you couldn't come to Ireland with us: we ate and drank
and walked and climbed and swam and sailed all the time. Perhaps
next spring, if we see to all the permits long beforehand? I do hope
so. We couldn't, anyway, have stopped for a couple of days to see
you in Wales as we didn't go by boat via Holyhead but flew over
from Croydon. . . .

Yours,
Dylan

8

In spite of the swarms of visitors, the League and a lot of
other diversions, *Insight and Outlook* made steady progress; it
was finished by the end of 1947, and a few days after the last
page was corrected, Mamaine and I went on a rampage on
the Continent. Paris, Burgundy, Provence, Milan, Florence,
Rome, provided quite a change from Blaenau Ffestiniog. *Darkness at Noon* and *The Yogi and the Commissar* had been much-
discussed bestsellers in both France and Italy, and my various
publishers were lavish in their hospitality to us. There were
also the reunions with prewar friends whom, during the war,
I had given up all hope of meeting again – Silone, Malraux,
Leo Valiani (the Mario of *Scum of the Earth*), Manes Sperber
– and new friendships, short-lived but intense, with Camus,
Sartre and Simone de Beauvoir – about which later. So we
had a hectic and, on the whole, very enjoyable time until, in
the spring of 1948, I went on an even more hectic lecture
tour in the United States to raise funds for the IRRC: the
International Rescue and Relief Committee for refugees from
Eastern Europe.

On my return to Mamaine and Bwlch Ocyn, we had hardly settled down when, in June, the Arab–Jewish war broke out and Israel proclaimed its independence. So it was once more farewell to North Wales and off to Paris, whence a chartered plane took us to the newborn state – the dream of my Zionist years come true. Mamaine had been issued with visa No. 5 by the Israeli Consulate in Paris,* mine was No. 6.

The ostensible reason for the journey was to act as war correspondent for the *Manchester Guardian, New York Herald Tribune* and *Le Figaro*. But my personal motives were more confused. I was vaguely hoping to be able to make some positive contribution to the reborn nation's struggle for survival. Mamaine wholeheartedly shared my feelings in spite of being a blue-blooded Gentile, and in spite of the fact that most of her friends with the same background sympathized with the Arab cause. We even, half seriously, discussed the possibility of settling in the Promised Land if some creative opportunity for being useful offered itself – for instance, in education or public relations. A few months later when the war was over, and we were back in Europe, I realized how naive this idea had been. I admired the heroism of Israeli youth, which had won a war against seemingly impossible odds, but at the same time I realized – as I had realized twenty years earlier, after my first protracted sojourn in Palestine – that I could never settle in that country however much I admired its people. Had I been an architect or a scientist, this might have been possible, but I could never become a Hebrew writer, and by my upbringing I was a stranger to Jewish tradition. I was a political Zionist, but culturally rooted in Europe, and felt almost equally at home in London or Paris, Berlin or Vienna – but could never feel at home in Tel Aviv. Once more, Mamaine agreed. Being British, *and* Gentile, *and* having worked for a semi-hush-hush set-up during the war, she was treated with distrust – if not hostility – by the newborn Israeli politicians and bureaucrats, who had a tendency to behave like *nouveaux riches* – not in terms of money but of power. Anti-Semitism had been totally alien to her nature,

* There was as yet no Consulate in London.

but now she had to experience its reverse and she frankly loathed it. I in turn disliked the influence of the benighted rabbinical orthodoxy and its secular equivalent – a cultural chauvinism which affected even the socialists and trade unions. It was a state of mind, understandable, and perhaps unavoidable, in a country in a more or less permanent state of siege, but understanding did not make it a more attractive choice as a place to live in.

9

On our return to Europe in the autumn of 1948 we gave up our tenancy of Bwlch Ocyn and settled temporarily in one of the lodges of the ancient chateau of Chartrettes in the Fontainebleau region. The chateau was owned by a Hungarian friend, Paul Winkler, who had become a French newspaper magnate, and the lodge was ideal for work. The book I wrote there was *Promise and Fulfilment – Palestine 1917–49.*★ It consisted of three parts. The first, 'Background', contained a brief history of the country from the Balfour Declaration to independence. The second, 'Close-up', consisted of my war diaries and dispatches for the *Manchester Guardian*. The third part, 'Perspective', was, as explained in the preface, 'an attempt to present to the reader a comprehensive survey of the social and political structure, the cultural trends and future prospects of the Jewish State.'

Today, more than thirty years later, the forecasts of 'future prospects' turned out to have erred mainly on the side of optimism. But the most controversial part of the book is its epilogue which involved me in polemics for years to come.†

I finished *Promise and Fulfilment* in January 1949. What next? I was in my middle forties, and free to choose the country I

★ Macmillan, London and New York, 1949.
† In the four-page epilogue, Koestler argued that, with the formation of the State of Israel, Jews must make a choice between settling there or renouncing their religion – Editor.

wanted to settle in. Israel had dropped out from the list of possible choices. America had, on my first visit, inspired me with mixed feelings. Since 1940 I had lived in England (and Wales), wrote in English, and had become to some degree anglicized. But once the war was over, and the Continent liberated, England gave me a feeling of claustrophobia. Ruled by the Labour Party under the uninspired leadership of Clem Attlee, it had become a 'land of virtue and gloom', as I described it while London correspondent of *Partisan Review* (a non-paying job bequeathed to me by George Orwell). The government plastered walls with posters which threatened 'Work or Want' – a slogan more apt for a borstal home for delinquent juveniles than for a victorious socialist country. Eventually Mamaine and I would return to England, but for the time being we felt like paraphrasing St Augustine: Lord, give me austerity – but not yet. And what was wrong with France, anyway – except that the Communists were the strongest party in the National Assembly, the *intellectuels* were fellow-travelling in a body, and my name was mud in the Café Flore?

While still quite undecided about the future, we got in touch with an estate agent, just for the fun of it. He showed us a hideous villa built in the French 1920s style, but in an incomparably attractive position directly on the Seine, with a large landing stage and facing the Forest of Fontainebleau across the water. I fell in love at first sight with Verte Rive, and bought it virtually on the spot. We moved in as soon as the contracts were signed, in the spring of 1949.

The first thing I wrote in Verte Rive was a contribution to *The God That Failed*, an anthology by six ex-Communist intellectuals – Ignazio Silone, André Gide, Richard Wright, Louis Fischer, Stephen Spender and myself, with an introduction by Richard Crossman.* Dick Crossman had been among my closest friends; the idea of the anthology was conceived one late evening when he and his wife Zita were staying with us in Bwlch Ocyn. They were also among our first weekend guests in Verte Rive, together with Michael Foot – another

* Hamish Hamilton, London; Macmillan, New York, 1950.

close friend of the period – and his wife, Jill. Dick was a brilliant, outgoing and warm personality, but he was also an incurably opportunistic politician, as his diaries while a Cabinet Minister quite plainly reveal. Thus it is amusing to read in his introduction to the book, after describing that evening in Wales when the project had been hatched: 'We were not in the least interested . . . in swelling the flood of anti-Communist propaganda.' That of course was precisely what we were interested in, but for a Labour MP in those days it just wouldn't do to say so in as many words. At any rate, *The God That Failed* (the title was invented by Dick) became a kind of household word and seemed to have been quite effective in 'swelling the flood of anti-Communist propaganda', to judge by the number of reprints and foreign translations.

When I finished my piece for *The God That Failed*, I thought I had at last done with writing on political subjects for the rest of my life. I had been labouring under the same illusion when I fled London for Wales to write *Insight and Outlook*. In the preface I had promised the reader a second volume 'which is in preparation and will, it is hoped, appear twelve months after the first'. But all I had to show for volume II was a chaotic jumble of notes, the mere sight of which gave me indigestion. After a hopeless struggle I had to shelve volume II 'for the time being'. In actual fact, it never saw the light of day. Its place was to be taken by *The Act of Creation*, published fifteen years later. In 1949, I was obviously not ready to embark on that rather ambitious undertaking and so I was left freewheeling in a vacuum as it were. This is when – in July 1949 – a new arrival from Pretoria unobtrusively entered my life.

2

How Unpleasant to Meet
Mr Koestler

by C.K.

I

I was born in South Africa on 9 May 1927. Towards the end of January 1948 I left Cape Town for the last time to join my mother in Paris. As the boat sailed away, I stayed on deck, watching the land recede until all that remained looked like a small plum pudding swathed in mist on the ocean's horizon. I knew I would never return.

In Paris I joined the Alliance Française to brush up my French. Although I had spent a long summer holiday in Normandy in 1938, I had never been to Paris before. When spring came I was infected with the euphoria one never feels with the end of winter in the southern hemisphere. I found a secretarial job at the film company, Warner Brothers. The work, contrary to expectation, turned out to be boring as it had to do merely with the distribution of films. I worked for two American executives who were of German origin and had to correct their rather bad English in the letters they dictated. Perhaps I would not have been so scornful of this task if I had realized that they had probably been among the lucky ones who had escaped from Germany before the holocaust.

After a couple of months I saw an advertisement in the *Herald Tribune* which appealed to me. A writer was looking for an English secretary, and I eagerly applied for the job. I was a little disappointed when I found out that he was not in my naive view a 'real writer' but a psychologist writing a book on Pavlovian theory. His name was Dr Ishlondsky, he was a White Russian with an American passport, and he lived with his brother in the top-floor flat of a house in the Avenue Georges Mandel, overlooking a sea of chestnut trees which were then in flower. I worked for him every day for a month, typing his book and learning all about Pavlov and his dog-and-bell experiments.

After three weeks he gave me a week's notice, explaining that he was leaving Paris for the South of France. This was a bolt out of the blue, as he had not told me that the job was a temporary one when he engaged me. After work I walked down to the Trocadero and bought a copy of the *Herald Tribune*. Turning immediately to the 'Jobs Vacant' section, I found the following advertisement: 'Author, Fontainebleau area, seeks part-time secretary. Write Box. . . . '

In an instant I was transported from a state of gloom to one of wild excitement. I hurried to the Rond Point where a Rumanian friend of mine had a flat, so that I could borrow his typewriter to type out my application. For about an hour I struggled with the wretched machine, but it was an ancient one and, being continental, all the keys were in the wrong place. In the end I gave up and wrote my application by hand as clearly and neatly as I could. Name, date of birth, nationality, education and jobs. I was quite proud of the long list of jobs: a firm of solicitors, an art gallery, Warner Brothers and Dr Ishlondsky. This curriculum vitae was enclosed with a short letter.

What I did not say in this summary of my life was that it had long been my ambition to work for a writer. As a child I was happiest when reading and my favourite people were the imaginary heroes of books rather than those living around me. At twelve, I decided to write a book, a historical romance rather like Georgette Heyer's novels which we were all reading at school at the time. I got away from the other girls by shutting myself up in the loo with a pencil and notebook. The first paragraph would describe the hero – a dashing Regency buck – and the clothes he was wearing. I got as far as his 'sky-blue waistcoat', but the words which I expected to flow from my pen never came and I had to give it up. At fifteen I was inspired to write a play: the characters galloped about on their fiery steeds, using expressions like 'egad', 'methinks', and 'forsooth'. I tore it up. The closest I could get to writing would be to work for a writer.

About three weeks passed before I had a reply to my application. It was a letter asking me to come to an address in the 17ième arrondissement for an interview and was signed 'Daphne Woodward'. For some reason which I cannot remember I arrived there half an hour late, much to my mortification. Mrs Woodward told me that the name of the author was Arthur Koestler, that she was his secretary, but was going back to England. To test my shorthand she dictated a passage from *Darkness at Noon,* which I typed out. It was all right, except that I got one word wrong: I wrote 'effix' for 'ethics'. She then said that Mr Koestler was going to interview some of the applicants at the Hôtel Montalembert in a few days' time; I was to be there at 5 p.m.

After the interview with Daphne Woodward I went to see my Rumanian friend to ask him about this author. 'Ah, Arthur Koestler . . . ,' he said and I could tell from his expression that he was greatly impressed.

I wondered what he looked like. With a name like Arthur, he must be very tall, with a red face. I imagined his study, under the eaves of a house, lined with books and, beside the small window, his writing table with a lamp on it.

The most suitable clothes to wear for the interview would be clerical grey, so I put on my grey coat and skirt, a paler grey pullover and a grey beret. A bus took me from the Right to the Left Bank. As it crossed the Seine, I wondered what the outcome would be and was filled with excitement. I was determined to get the job. I got off the bus in the Boulevard St Germain and walked to the Hôtel Montalembert. In an effort to make up for having been half an hour late for the first interview I was now half an hour early. I went to the reception desk at the hotel and explained that I had an appointment with Mr Koestler but was early. I asked which of the two lounges he was in and the receptionist pointed towards a room which led off the entrance lounge. Relieved, I sat down at a table next to the entrance doors to wait.

The room was nearly empty at that hour of the afternoon. I looked at a couple facing me on the far side of the room. The woman was dark and attractive; she looked intense and leaned towards the man, who looked bored. I began to wonder about them. They obviously did not know each other well; perhaps he was taking her out for the first time. I thought they were talking English, which made it even more interesting. The woman had an American accent. I became engrossed watching them. After a while one or two words floated across the room – 'Melun', 'Fontainebleau', 'train'. I realized with horror that I had been staring at Mr Koestler while he was interviewing another applicant. In the same moment he became aware of me and called across the room to the reception desk: *'Concierge'* – his voice carried easily – *'est-ce que quelqu'un m'attend?'* The accent was very French.

I got up and went across. 'I'm awfully sorry,' I said, 'I'm early and I thought you were in the other room. I'll go next door and wait.'

When the other woman had left it was my turn. I sat down at the table with Mr Koestler, and saw a tired-looking man with red rings under his eyes. He did not say any polite, reassuring words. He explained that Mrs Woodward was going to be away for the summer and he needed somebody to take her place. It would be a temporary job. The summer seemed an interminably long time, so I was quite content with this arrangement. His manner was unnervingly direct. All conventionalities were brushed aside; he only said what he meant.

'Do you think you'll be able to do the job?' he asked. 'You don't seem to have much self-confidence.' I silently agreed with him. I blushed easily, an annoying trait that had afflicted me from the age of seventeen. He asked me if I would like a drink, but I said no. He urged me again, but I was adamant, so he ordered one for himself. He looked displeased. I had done the wrong thing, I could see, but it was too late to change my mind. I always refused hospitality when I was feeling shy. He seemed doubtful whether I would be the right person for the job and decided to try me out for a day. He was driving back to his house at Fontaine-le-Port, near

Fontainebleau, the following morning. I was to meet him at the flat of friends and we would drive there together. He would give me some letters to type and decide if I would do.

I went home to the solid, bourgeois Rue Copernic where I lived with my mother. I myself had no doubts about my suitability for the job. I had a high opinion of my secretarial abilities – in fact I thought I was the best secretary in the whole world.

I spent a sleepless night with a bout of hayfever, and whiled away the time trying to think of topics for conversation on the drive to Fontaine-le-Port. I was in the habit of carrying on endless imaginary dialogues with myself, but these never helped me in everyday life when I most needed them and I remained dumb. I struggled in vain to think of what I could talk about and dismissed every idea as banal.

In the morning, clutching my handkerchief and benzedrine inhaler to keep the hayfever at bay, I went to the flat near the Opéra. Mr Koestler was there with his friends, Paul Winkler, the head of Opéra Mundi, and his wife. We started at once, but, before leaving Paris, Mr Koestler had some shopping to do in the Galeries Lafayette, which was nearby. He strode through the shop at great speed, heading for the garden furniture department upstairs, where he asked for two rubber lilos in dark blue. These were produced and he bought them. We charged out of the shop in a matter of minutes and headed for the car.

The sun was shining and the countryside looked like those idyllic paintings I had seen in the Jeu de Paume. I could not think of a single word to say and he remained silent. He drove very fast along those straight, empty French roads, lined with trees sometimes forming a green tunnel. At last I said 'This car goes well,' and he replied tersely, 'It's got good brakes.' I wondered vaguely, as one sometimes does, what he would be like in bed; but such a thought seemed beyond any stretch of the imagination.

Before we arrived he told me that he had unexpected guests for lunch – a former girlfriend, Daphne, and her husband. His house, Verte Rive, was set back a little from a narrow road. Trees shaded the gravel drive. As we walked round to the front, I wondered if he had any children. I knew that his wife was away at the time, in England. To my relief, there was no sound of childish voices, only the welcoming bark of his magnificent boxer dog, Sabby, in his outside kennel. The garden sloped down from the house to a landing stage on the Seine. The river looked wide and peaceful. On the opposite bank the forest stretched endlessly as far as one could see.

In the garden above the landing stage a Canadian canoe lay on the ground keel-side up. Made of wood, with long flowing lines and graceful curves, it seemed to give out a gentle glow in the hot sun. Mr Koestler frowned as he looked at it. He muttered something about that damn woman letting it lie out there in the sun. I gathered that his housekeeper had committed this offence. Surely, I thought, it would come to no harm in a little sun, not realizing that the wood might shrink, making the canoe leaky. He appeared to be quite enraged and hurried into the house.

Soon the guests came. Daphne had dark eyes with a slightly melancholy expression. Her manner was matter of fact, a little brusque, and she did not hesitate to speak her mind. She was a sculptress. Her husband, Henri Henrion, was an industrial designer, an attractive, likeable person with easygoing ways. They had just returned from Italy and the conversation during lunch was all about art – Italian churches, painting and sculpture. The food was brought in by a grumpy old woman dressed in black, called Madame Grandin. We had black pudding, followed by a black stew and a salad of greasy, dark green lettuce leaves. The guests raved about the food, particularly the salad, and Madame Grandin was pronounced a treasure.

After lunch, we climbed into a large rowing boat and Mr Koestler rowed us across the river to the Forest of Fontainebleau on the other side. We walked through the trees until a clearing was found, spread out rugs and sat down in the shade. Nobody said very much. After a few minutes, Mr Koestler fell asleep. He lay on his back, his eyes tightly closed, breathing quietly. I did not feel sleepy at all and neither did the Henrions. They asked me questions about myself, where I came from and where I was living in Paris. As quickly as he fell asleep, Mr Koestler was awake again. We returned to the house and the guests departed for Paris.

Mr Koestler did not feel much like doing letters. He dug a few out of a file and dictated six short, one-sentence replies. His study was on the first floor, his desk by the window, looking onto the Seine. When I had typed them, he read them through and signed them. It had not been much of a test of my abilities. He said so too, and reluctantly decided to take me on. I was to come out by train for two days a week. The next date was arranged and he drove me to the nearby railway station of Fontaine-le-Port. I sat on a bench on the platform, waiting for the train. It was a tiny French country station, deserted, with a row of pollarded trees on each side of the line. From where I sat I could see the bend of the river. The hayfever bout was worse than ever and frequent sniffing of the benzedrine inhaler did not help much. I felt uneasy about my new job. Mr Koestler startled me. I did not know what he would say next. Every time he addressed a word to me I nearly jumped out of my skin. But it was only for two months after all. Nevertheless, I began to wish that it was over.

2

Twice a week I got up early, leaving at about seven o'clock. I travelled by Metro on the Neuilly–Vincennes line to the Gare de Lyons, where I got on a train for Melun. The depressing suburbs rolled by; they had picturesque names like Maisons Alfort (the grimmest) and Villeneuve St Georges. After Brunoy came Combe-la-Ville-Quincy and the landscape began to look like one of those heartbreaking country scenes painted by Pissarro, hazy in the sunlight. The train rattled on endlessly until at last it reached Melun. The wooden benches in the third-class compartments were very hard. At Melun I got into a little local train which criss-crossed the Seine, stopping at Livry, Chartrettes and then Fontaine-le-Port.

Verte Rive was an ugly French villa, but it seemed quite harmless compared with the one next door which belonged to a dentist. Luckily it was not visible from Verte Rive itself, being screened by thick hedges and shrubs. But glimpses from certain vantage points in the garden revealed a monstrous little bright yellow cube which the French in those days would describe as '*très coquette*'. Arthur had bought Verte Rive, including its furniture, at the beginning of the year. What appealed to him about it was its proximity to the river with its landing stage, the Forest of Fontainebleau on the opposite shore, and his study on the first floor, overlooking the Seine. It was essential to him to have a good view from his desk while he worked and the flowing current had a soothing effect, he said. The sitting room, with its red matting, gave on to a verandah with tables and chairs, where one could have drinks in the evening, watching the sunset colour the river. There was an archway in the sitting room leading into the dining room, in the corner of which was a bar with loops of heavy rope adorning the sides and bar stools trimmed with the same rope to give a nautical air. The bar was the source of much amusement to English friends, though some were too horrified by it to be amused. The main guest room was on the ground floor. Upstairs there was Arthur's study, the study of his wife, Mamaine, their bedroom, and two spare bedrooms. I worked in one of them, which was called the Purgatory because of its bright pink walls.

There was plenty of work to be done when I arrived. In the morning I took down replies to letters – letters to publishers, to literary agents, to friends and to readers. In the afternoon I typed them and, when I left about 5 p.m., took them with me to post in Paris.

One day, to my surprise, Arthur asked me to stay on for dinner; he was expecting friends from England who were going to spend the night, and he needed 'moral support'. I wondered how my presence could possibly give support of any kind. The friends were Hamish Hamilton, the publisher, and his wife, Yvonne, their son, Alastair, an enchanting little boy of eight, and a nanny or governess.

We sat down to an orgiastic meal at the candlelit dining table. Soup, followed by fish and entrée, were brought in by Madame Grandin – that old scarecrow, as Arthur called her. White and red wine were in abundance. The conversation was animated – it seemed like a dream to me, as if I were actually taking part in an exciting novel. The guests were enjoying the kind of food and wine which could not be had in England, where food rationing was even more severe than during the war. After the meat course they began to feel that they could take no more and apologetically explained to their host that they were no longer in training after living in puritan England. At this point Arthur said he would give them something which would miraculously dispel the feeling of overeating; it would burn a passage into their gullets and they would be able to enjoy the rest of the meal. He paused dramatically: it was called, he said, a *'trou Normand'*. He then produced four little glasses and filled them up with calvados. He urged everybody to follow his example and swallow the drink in one gulp. The effect would be immediate. It was impossible to resist such gentle persuasion and the guests, no doubt in trepidation, did not try to do so. I am sorry to say that the *trou Normand* had the promised effect only on the host, who continued alone to eat and drink with relish. At the end of dinner (Fontainebleau ice cream and champagne) the Hamiltons quickly retired to bed.

The next morning I was entertained by young Alastair about the prep school he was going to in the autumn, and thereby missed a memorable sight which Arthur has often described:

After breakfast I asked Jamie Hamilton to try out my single sculler as a hangover remedy. I was very proud of my proficiency as an oarsman and boasted to Jamie that by assiduous training I had brought down the time it took me from Verte Rive to the lock in Samois from thirteen to eleven minutes. He agreed to have a go, went upstairs to change and came down in rowing shorts. This should have made me suspicious – publishers do not usually travel with rowing dress in their luggage. We got into the sculler – I acting as cox – and to my utter mortification he did the stretch in nine minutes without visible effort. But I was somewhat comforted when he confessed that he had once won the Silver Medal for singles at the Olympic Games.

The summer of 1949 was a glorious one and it produced one of the great vintages of wine. In my memory it never seemed to rain; the pale, northern European sun shone, and the visitors to Verte Rive – English, American, Central European and French – sat around on the landing stage, talking and drinking champagne, which was cooled in the river; they swam in the Seine or took Sabby for walks in the forest. I often heard Arthur speak, during political arguments over dinner, with a passionate clarity which, I fervently felt, could move mountains. My train journeys to Fontaine-le-Port were light-hearted ones, and the return trips to Paris sad. Arthur's Canadian canoe had a sail and he taught himself to sail it with a book in one hand and the other on the rudder.

My Rumanian friend asked me if he carried a gun and was surprised to hear that he did not. Surely, he said, there must be an electrified fence round the house. There was none and the front gates were always open. But I did notice that when I came into his study after lunch to wake him from his short siesta, he always woke with a start.

The reason for my friend's concern was, of course, that Arthur Koestler had become a very controversial name in France. *Darkness at Noon,* which was first published in England in 1940, was only published by Calmann-Lévy in France, under the title of *Le Zéro et l'Infini,* after the war. The Communists bought up all the copies they could find in bookshops and burned them. Bravely Calmann-Lévy decided to reprint. The result was that, between editions, the book sold at black market prices. It made a tremendous impression, and everybody in France knew about the book and the name of its author. That was why I had to post all the letters in Paris. Nothing was ever posted in the village of Fontaine-le-Port as the clerks at the little post office were said to be members of the Communist Party. Only letters to personal friends were typed on writing paper headed with the address. All other letters bore the address, 'c/o A. D. Peters', who was Arthur's literary agent.

Arthur often used to play on the gramophone Mozart's Piano Concerto in C Major. Sometimes he would sit alone at night when everybody had gone to bed, playing it over and over again. When I hear the C Major concerto now I feel I am back again in that magical midsummer: the Seine with its smell of *la vase* and Arthur's three boats bobbing up and down on their moorings; hayfever (which is like breathing up water through your nose); the sensation of drinking Pernod for the first time; and knowing that, though this existence would soon be a thing of the past, I did not care and lived only for the moment.

Fontaine-le-Port was in the Brie country. Nearby were le Châtelet-en-Brie and Brie-Comte-Robert, a very pretty village. Alas, all the good Brie went to Paris and only shrivelled old stuff could be found in the region. Arthur was fond of cheese, particularly *chèvre,* and he was quick to notice that there was never any cheese on my plate.

'Have some,' he said, pushing the board towards me.

'I never eat cheese,' I said, feeling rather proud of my strange taste.

'Come on,' he urged impatiently. 'Try it.'

'But I don't like it,' I replied confidently.

It was a great mistake to say that, because he now became determined to convert me. How could anybody not like cheese? I must try it because he knew I would like it. In the end I had to give in and from then on I always ate cheese. I suffered from this disarming bullying when it came to sausages too, which I used to hate.

One evening in Paris my Rumanian friend told me that friends of the poet, Supervielle, had talked about Arthur with him. 'Koestler,' he said to me sternly, 'has a very bad reputation.' I said nothing. Anyway, it was too late.

He did little writing that summer and I was occupied with typing letters and filing. But one afternoon he read me a couple of pages written on lined manuscript paper. He decided to try dictating them into a new machine called a wire recorder, precursor of the tape recorder, for me to type out. But as he dictated, he wanted to make corrections, which proved to be a fiddly job, upsetting his concentration. In the end he gave up and I took it all down in shorthand. He stuck to this method and another use was found for the wire recorder: it became a sort of guest book, with guests giving their names and making comments – silly, witty or wise – into the machine.

The work Arthur had started on and which I began typing

that afternoon was the beginning of his autobiography, *Arrow in the Blue*. Chapter 1, 'The Horoscope', and chapter 3, 'The Pitfalls of Autobiography', which together amounted to twelve pages, were the only writing he did in July and August. 'The Horoscope' describes a visit to *The Times*, where he looked up the issue which appeared on the day of his birth – 5 September 1905 – in order to cast his 'secular horoscope'.

3

During August, Arthur's wife, Mamaine, returned from England. I did not see her in the morning when I arrived. Arthur dictated a mass of letters in his study. I met her for the first time when I came down to lunch, though I had seen a photograph of her so I knew what she looked like. I sensed in the first moment that Arthur had briefly studied my reaction and that he was proud of her looks. She had pale brown hair which hung down straight on to her shoulders. Her eyes were blue and her nose turned up a little. I could not decide whether I preferred her in profile or not; she had a small oval face and when it was serious she had a slight pout. I was overawed by her perfect French as she gave instructions to Madame Grandin.

She had been very ill in Verte Rive in June, and Arthur had taken her to London for treatment for her asthma. She and Arthur seemed so different. He had an energy which was almost superhuman; he was so quick – if you thought he was going to do something, you discovered that he had done it ten minutes before. She was thin, after her illness, and tired easily. But I saw her come wonderfully to life one Sunday when a crowd of her English friends descended for lunch at Verte Rive. She had a musical ear and was an unerring mimic. I once heard her taking off the Italian-born wife of a friend who was a great chatterbox. Mamaine kept up a flow of chatter, catching every nuance of accent and expression, until we all collapsed with giggles.

She often told me stories of her childhood. Her mother, who was a Paget, had married a Paget. They must have been distant cousins, but they met for the first time while on holiday in Switzerland. She never knew her mother, who died when the twin sisters were born, and her father died when they were only eleven. An uncle, whom she loathed, became their guardian.

On 5 September 1949, I came out to Verte Rive in the late afternoon. The house was in silence when I arrived. I went up the stairs and opened the door of Arthur's study, where he sat at his desk. 'Happy birthday,' I said. He looked surprised, dashed to the door and shouted, 'Darling, it's my birthday.' Mamaine came out of her study and ran across the landing. 'O-o-oh, sweetie,' she cried, giving him a hug, 'it's your birthday and I forgot all about it.' I was filled with admiration for such a nonchalant attitude to birthdays – the more so when I discovered that Mamaine's was two days later; no doubt that would have been forgotten too.

Mamaine's twin, Celia, came to stay at Verte Rive after a holiday in the Mediterranean. I looked from one twin's face to the other, trying to find a feature which differed slightly, but could find none. Celia was high-spirited, Mamaine was more serious, though this is not to say that they did not change roles sometimes. Celia's slender, sunburned arms looked quite plump compared to Mamaine's. 'Celia, you look positively Rubensian,' exclaimed Arthur.

The twins spent hours together walking in the Forest of Fontainebleau. I imagined them talking about birds, about music, about their friends (both were extremely loyal and prized friendship above all else), about past loves and about present loves too, for there were quite a few who were hopelessly in love with the twins.

Arthur and Mamaine had been living together for about five years. People who were married that long, I was sure, must be quite bored with each other. This was not the case with them. But in between the long, peaceful and happy times there were occasional rows.

The first row I witnessed took place during lunch. I can only remember wanting to sink beneath the dining-room table. I could not bear to see them quarrelling.

One morning I arrived at Verte Rive to find a blast being turned on me. An important letter had been wrongly addressed and returned to the sender. Arthur produced the envelope. I could see it had not been typed by me and said so. As Arthur went off to find Mamaine and vent his feelings on her, I realized what I had done. I should have taken the blame – how could I have been such an idiot? But Mamaine did not hold it against me.

After the sybaritic summer, Arthur went on a diet for the first time in his life. This made work all but impossible. The hours dragged by and he kept glancing at his watch with a woeful, half-guilty smile. I could not help laughing at him and he liked being mocked. On a beautiful sunny day he declared we should all have a treat and go on a picnic. We climbed into the boat and headed up river. On a grassy bank we unpacked the picnic. Mamaine and I had some terrine, chunks of bread and *cantal* – the sort of French food which tastes so delicious when you eat it out of doors. Arthur's lunch, according to the diet, consisted of radishes. There was not even any butter to go with them and he was particularly fond of that cheap, prix fixe hors d'oeuvre, *radis au beurre*. He looked at the radishes and frowned. Were they supposed to be for him? He turned to Mamaine and gazed at her accusingly. The countryside looked golden in the sunlight and the birds were singing to split their throats. 'But how on earth can you expect one to eat nothing but a lot of radishes!' he cried in exasperation. We ate our picnic and rowed back to Vert Rive in gloomy silence. The rows always seemed to be on trivial matters and my sympathies were always with Mamaine. Paradoxical as it may seem, this in no way changed my feelings towards Arthur.

3

Sartre and Simone

by A.K.

I

The first impression I gained of the young applicant for the job of part-time secretary during that interview in the lobby of the Hôtel Montalembert was one of extreme shyness. In her written application she had given her age as twenty-two, but she looked and behaved rather as if she was eighteen. More important, from my professional point of view, was a quality in her of unobtrusiveness, almost of self-effacement, which promised well for putting me into the relaxed state of mind I have always needed for dictating letters or editing versions of rough manuscript drafts. To achieve that relaxed state, I must have a certain rapport with the person who takes the dictation. She must look neither bored nor too keen, nor impatient when I get stuck (which happens all the time, for I am a painfully slow writer). Miss Cynthia May Jefferies, from Pretoria, South Africa, had, I intuitively felt, the necessary qualities to establish such rapport. And anyway, it was only a matter of two months. (As of today, the 'matter' has lasted for thirty-three years.)

But before continuing the story of life at Verte Rive, I must fill in some gaps left in the previous chapters relating to earlier visits to France while Mamaine and I were still living in Bwlch Ocyn. The first of these visits took place in 1946, and had all the makings of cheap melodrama. In 1939 I had been interned in France as an 'undesirable alien', and had fled the country as an outcast; now, six years and a world war later, I was returning as a literary celebrity – pariah dog transformed into social lion. To add the final touch to the melodrama, on my first night in Paris I was taken out by Guy and Alix de Rothschild to dinner at the Grand Vefour, top of the three-star restaurants in Paris, and fed on caviar, steak and wild strawberries.

Guy de Rothschild had a distinguished war record – Croix de Guerre with bar. When France collapsed, he escaped to the United States, but shortly after embarked on a convoy to Britain to join de Gaulle's Free French army in the making. His ship was sunk in mid-Atlantic; when the U-boat torpedo hit it without warning, he was reading *Scum of the Earth,* which had just been published. He spent five hours in the oily water before he was rescued; some time during those five hours he promised himself that, if he survived, I would be the first person he would look up in London. Thus started a long and intimate friendship which included his wife Alix, who was of Austrian origin, a great charmer and patron of struggling artists.

The first few days of this first postwar visit to Paris passed in a kind of alcoholic whirlwind. After a week of it I wrote to Mamaine (who was in London and was to join me some days later):

Hôtel Montalembert   9th October 1946

. . . The first three days were heaven, but then I got rather depressed. To be a lion is only fun for a very short time, or if one is younger, or if one's vanities are of a simpler nature. I got so utterly fed up with it that I cancelled a big press-reception, refused all interviews, radio, etc., and shut myself completely off. The real trouble is that my friends of the old 'scum' crowd are partly dead, and with those who are still here I can't recapture the old contact and warmth. I have so much looked forward to seeing —— and —— and two or three others again – but it is all rather ghastly. They live in greater misery than ever and I have become an *arriviste* for them. That kills everything. I always comforted myself when feeling lonely that these people are there in the background to fall back upon, and now I feel more cut-off than ever.

Camus is charming – but to make real friends one has to start at twenty. I am dining with him tomorrow and with Malraux tonight. . . . I had dinner at the [British] Embassy which was perfectly ghastly, and Dunstan gave me dinner with Merleau-Ponty and some communists present which was in a way amusing, and there was a chain of luncheons and parties given by my four publishers – but none of it is the real thing. As for scarlet women, they are mainly literary sluts from the Café Flore, etc., and they give one a cafard worse than after getting tight at Port Meirion. If I weren't ashamed, I would go back at once to our house, which seems paradise from here. Of course all this is tainted by the frightening political situation – no words can describe the economic and social jungle which this country has become.

Perhaps in a day or two this depression will pass. The funny thing is that I more or less foresaw that this was going to happen when I came here; that's why I was so frightened of it. I left France with a kick in my pants and now they receive me like Frank Sinatra, but the gold somehow turns into *merde*. . . .

However, after the initial shock, things got brighter and the hangovers lighter. In spite of the pessimistic remark that to make real friends one has to start at twenty, I seem to have managed to replace the vanished buddies of the scum days with new friends during those visits in 1946 and 1947. Apart from Guy and Alix, the most remarkable among them were Malraux, wnom I had known only slightly before the war, Camus, Sartre and Simone de Beauvoir. Some episodes of the encounter with the last three mentioned found their sadly distorted echo in de Beauvoir's third volume of memoirs *Force of Circumstance,* and her *roman à clef The Mandarins.*

One would hardly dare to invent two figures in a drama of such contrasting physical appearance as Sartre and Camus. Sartre looked like a malevolent goblin or gargoyle, Camus like a young Apollo. Sartre's goggling eyes had a disconcerting squint, his whole body was misshapen with stumpy arms and legs; the young Camus had been a football star in his native town, Oran, idolized by maidens of all ages. He had some Spanish blood, which gave his countenance an added dash, and he was known to suffer from TB, which added to his romantic aura. There could be no sexual jealousy nor any sublimated version of it between the ugly *professeur de lycée* and the *beau garçon d'Oran*; nor was their friendship tainted by professional rivalry. They were the twin stars at the zenith of the Marxist-Existentialist firmament of the French postwar intelligentsia – with Simone de Beauvoir as a fainter third, more like a planet shining with reflected light. When Sartre and Camus finally fell out, that whole universe collapsed, and the French extreme Left never looked the same again: in France, the intellectuals and their quarrels are taken seriously.

I admired both of them as novelists and playwrights, though not as philosophers (I never got through Camus' *The Rebel* or Sartre's *Being and Nothingness*). However, the quality of the relationships with each of them was different. With Camus, an easy camaraderie developed from our very first meeting; we tutoyed each other and shared much the same tastes in wining, dining and running after women. But in spite of the use of the fraternal 'thou', the relationship was more intimate than deep; we were in fact *copains* – chums rather than friends. This may have been due to a trait in Camus' character which prevented him from entering into deeper human relationships – which he himself had exposed in *The Fall* with such shattering honesty.

It was quite a different matter with Sartre; although politically much farther apart, there was a warmth of feeling and affection between us which had all the making of a genuine friendship. It is reflected in a curious little episode which took place in 1946 – shortly after we had first met. The unwitting cause of the episode was a rather nice American journalist whom I shall call X, and the occasion was a picnic dinner at the Camus'. Apart from Mamaine and myself, the other guests were Sartre and Simone (de Beauvoir), X and his wife, and Celia (who then lived in Paris). We all had a lot to drink, and later in the evening, after X and his wife had left, Sartre started attacking X in violent terms as an American enemy of freedom, while I attacked Sartre for defending Stalin's reign of terror. The next day I sent Sartre a note of apology for the vehement language I had used, and received in return a long letter in his small, neat hand, which was both endearing and characteristic. Here are translated extracts from it.

. . . I never took this broil seriously, for the good reason that a broil can only arise if there is an embroiled situation, just as a revolution needs a revolutionary situation. If that exists, incidents will occur as a mere matter of contingency. There exists no profound reason whatsoever for such an imbroglio between us; quite to the contrary I am very fond of you and you yourself must be aware of this. As far as I am concerned, I fully realize that I was wrong in proclaiming my dislike of X to his friends. You had invited him, you vouched for him, I had nothing to say and it is only natural that you felt offended. By the way, I know the reason for my outburst: as I felt hostile towards X, and as for two years I have rigorously avoided him* I was exasperated by having to spend an evening with him at Camus' and, without admitting it to myself, I felt irritated by you because you had invited him. I do not consider this irritation as a valid excuse; on the contrary, I am just trying to explain. Also, I was thoroughly bored by that evening where nobody had the time to talk to anybody (except for the twenty minutes during which I talked to the sister of Mamaine, who is charming) and I wished for something to happen. The immediate cause of a lynching is always boredom. In a certain sense, both you and I were acting as if in a comedy. The *reality* at the bottom of all this is a certain fairly fundamental difference between us, which guarantees that there will be other occasions when we shall feel exasperated by each other, but which, to my mind, cannot prevent us from being friends: you have been moulded by *a Party*, you have learnt to consider personal relationships as *part* of a shared operation. And certainly, for a member of the Communist Party any psychological assessment of a comrade in arms must appear as a *denigration*. I, on the other hand, was brought up in that individualistic culture of French bourgeois society which considers personal relationships as primary and thereby makes room for psychological considerations. We have already come face to face with that difference at the Scheherazade [night-club], when I offered you my friendship (for reasons of a psychological appreciation which is the exact opposite of denigration but of the same nature), and when you deferred its acceptance (because I was not a priori committed to a shared operation which could provide the foundations of our friendship). I don't believe that my point of view is superior to yours, or yours to mine: I think that both are incomplete and that this is neither your fault or mine As long as a concrete society – where the individual and his operations will become truly indistinguishable – does not exist, this type of conflict will continue. I may add that it has no profound importance whatso-

---

* 'This is not quite exact: I had dinner with him once, but it didn't improve matters.'

ever for us, and that, quite to the contrary it might be useful. . . .
All this is said to bury the incident. It only remains to laugh at it
together. . . . I shall telephone you tomorrow morning at the Pont
Royal to suggest a drink. . . .

Believe in my friendship and rest assured that I am *very happy* that
this incident is over. . . .

The irony of this episode is that it was Sartre who some
years later broke off relations first with myself and later with
Camus – on purely political grounds. I did believe, and still
believe, that friendship can transcend politics – but not when
'politics' means commitment to a totalitarian ideology, be it
Nazi or Stalinist. This is the crucial point which the Sartres,
for all their sophistication, never understood – as shown by
Sartre's affectionate but confused letter and Simone de Beauvoir's less affectionate comments on Camus and myself in her
memoirs. On the breach with Camus she wrote:

Everything was over between them. As a matter of fact, if this
friendship exploded so violently, it was because for a long time not
much of it had remained. The political and ideological differences
which already existed between Sartre and Camus in 1945 had intensified from year to year. . . . While Sartre believed in the truth of
socialism, Camus became a more and more resolute champion of
bourgeois values; *The Rebel* was a statement of his solidarity with
them. A neutralist position between the two blocs had become finally
impossible; Sartre therefore drew nearer to the U.S.S.R.; Camus
hated the Russians, and although he did not like the United States,
he went over, practically speaking, to the American side.*

As for the reasons for the break with me, she writes that I
have 'erroneously attributed' the initiative for it to her.† In
the same passage she relates an absurd episode as the real cause
of the break: a Gaullist friend of mine, given to outrageous
jokes, met her with me in the Pont Royal bar and was pulling
her leg by pretending that Sartre was a secret supporter of the
General – while I just laughed instead of rising indignantly to

* *Force of Circumstance,* Penguin Books, Harmondsworth, 1968. pp. 271-2.
† *Force of Circumstance,* p. 151.

her and Sartre's defence. The story was too silly to be taken seriously, let alone as a *casus belli*; but Sartre, out of loyalty to Simone,* was forced to terminate our friendship. That he did so only reluctantly was shown a few years later, on the last occasion when I met him. This, oddly enough, happened on a night train, which took Mamaine and me to the Berlin Congress for Cultural Freedom in June 1950. By pure coincidence Sartre travelled on the same train to a conference in Frankfurt, and his sleeping compartment was next to ours. The compartment on our other side was occupied by our bodyguard who, at the insistence of the French Sûreté, accompanied us in view of the vehement attacks in the Communist press on the forthcoming congress. As there was no restaurant car on the train, we were equipped with a basketful of food and drink and invited Sartre to share supper with us – which he accepted with visible pleasure, regardless of the break in diplomatic relations. Had *la Simone* been with him this would not have been possible, but minus her he behaved like a schoolboy on holiday, keeping forbidden company, and the old affection between us was restored for a night. The occasion was made even more hilarious by the bodyguard whom we also had to invite to supper, introducing him to Sartre as a former member of the International Brigade. A further touch of absurdity was added by the bodyguard telling us in confidence that whenever he got excited he was liable to suffer an epileptic attack.

It would be pointless to try to refute Simone de Beauvoir's rather vitriolic caricature of myself in her books; a single, relatively harmless example may suffice. In describing an evening in a nightclub run by Russian émigrés, she writes that I 'insisted on letting the *maître d'hôtel* know that he was accorded the honour of waiting on Camus, Sartre and Koestler'. In fact I was a habitué of that nightclub (which was called Troika 22 and appears as the Kronstadt in *The Age of Longing*); the maître d'hôtel, who was also the proprietor, was

---

* Somehow it came about that we called Simone by her first name, Sartre by his surname.

my friend, and I had as a matter of courtesy to introduce him to my guests – whom he had recognized anyway.

There were some private reasons for Simone de Beauvoir's later hostility towards me which are too trivial to go into; but the main reason, I think, was intellectual jealousy. She resented Sartre's repeated offers of 'unconditional friendship' and such influence as my anti-Stalinist arguments and experiences might have on him – particularly as they otherwise only saw people who belonged to, or sympathized with, the French CP and Stalin's Russia. Simone's own influence on Sartre aimed in the opposite direction, towards the extreme Left. At times she reminded me of the *tricoteuses* – the worthy housewives who sat knitting through the murderous sessions of the revolutionary tribunals.

However, I also had my share of the blame for the guillotining of this friendship. For I must confess that in early middle age I was still to some extent what is now called a male chauvinist, unable to take women who set themselves up as political philosophers altogether seriously. It was not a conscious attitude, and if accused of harbouring such reactionary sentiments I would have hotly denied it. Yet it may have played a part in the row with Peter, Bertrand Russell's wife, and on some other occasions.

On the other hand, the Sartres did break off one friendship after another. On that evening in the sleeping car Sartre complained that they hardly went out in the evening because there were so few people left with whom they agreed about politics. The tragic end was the falling out of Sartre with Simone before his death.

2

I have almost forgotten to mention – perhaps because it is too painful to remember – the immediate reason for that first visit to Paris in 1946; it was to attend the rehearsals of my play *Twilight Bar* (*Bar du Soleil*),* produced by Jean Villar in the Théâtre de Clichy. It was a play without literary pretensions

---

* See *The Invisible Writing,* chs. 14 and 38.

which I had written as an escape from depression in 1934 in Moscow. It was lost, with the rest of my unpublished manuscripts, when in 1940, I had to flee France; but I wrote a second version of it in 1944 – again as an exercise to fight depression when details of the holocaust became known. The basic idea was, I think, not bad: two glamorous scouts arrive from outer space in search of suitable planets to colonize; they explain that only happy planets have a right to live, and give humanity three days to organize its happiness – or else. Faced with this ultimatum, the government resigns, the opposition refuses to take over, and an anarchist poet called Glowworm is appointed Dictator of Happiness. Strangely enough, the experiment is successful and everybody is happy, but on the third day it transpires that the scouts are impostors, and mankind, with a sigh of relief, returns to its erstwhile miseries. However, a lingering doubt remains: perhaps the scouts are genuine after all? The last words before the curtain falls are spoken by Glowworm: 'We'll soon know, Sam. It's eleven now. In an hour it will be midnight.'

As I have said before, I had no illusions about the literary qualities of the play (I called it 'An Escapade in Four Acts'); but Cape published it in 1945, and a French translation was published a year later and caught the eye of Jean Villar – at the time a hopeful young producer whom Malraux recommended to me, and later director of all nationally owned theatres. Villar proposed to produce the play; I was in two minds about it but vanity got the upper hand over critical judgement and I consented. During the rehearsals I became convinced that the play would be a flop, but by then it was too late. All I could do was to warn everybody not to go to see it. Even so, the front row on the first night was occupied by André Gide and other aged luminaries, huddled in their overcoats and scarves, for the theatre was unheated and we were at the end of a blustering Paris October. I felt too discouraged to take a curtain call either on the first or any of the successive nights – of which there were few before the play folded.

A similar sad fate befell the American production. Only in Scandinavia – Oslo and Gothenburg as far as I remember –

does it seem to have been favourably received, and later there have also been some sporadic revivals in Birmingham, on German television and as a BBC radio play. Leafing again, after so many years, through this 'escapade', I feel mostly embarrassment. Its atmosphere is perhaps easiest to convey by an extract from the opening scene of Act III when Glowworm has become dictator. The scene is a crowded square, its centre occupied by a merry-go-round which turns to the sound of a barrel organ; backstage there is the imposing façade of a public building with the inscription 'MINISTRY OF SWEAT AND TOIL' crossed out and replaced by 'MINISTRY OF HAPPINESS'. The Chief of Police (whose secret ambition had always been to become an opera tenor surpassing Caruso) turns the handle of the barrel organ and sings:

> Hark, ye people, lend your ears,
> Blow your noses, wipe your tears.
> Gods on Olympus are your kin –
> Who told you pleasure was a sin?
> Who told the maidens to be chaste?
> Each unkissed kiss is a deadly waste.
> For Man is good and full of cheer,
> When no policemen interfere.
> Arise from your long penitence –
> Long live Homo sapiens!

> Hark, ye people, lend your ears,
> Wipe off your face those salty tears.
> You were deceived, it is a lie
> That things must always go awry.
> This earth has room for all of us
> Enjoy yourselves, don't fret and fuss.
> Where gifts abound, all envy pales,
> Full stomachs make for empty jails.
> A world of plenty knows no thieves –
> Who cares for last year's fallen leaves?
> For Man is good and full of cheer,
> If no policemen interfere.
> Arise from your triste penitence –
> Long live Homo sapiens!

Laughter and cheers

74

3

As I have already indicated, the first summer in Verte Rive was a period of indecision and false starts, but that came to a sudden end when an editor of the Canadian branch of Macmillan came to visit us – a nice man whose name, I think, was Mr Gray or Grey. He suggested over a drink, rather apologetically, a theme for a novel: a love affair between Russian agent and American girl. I said somewhat scathingly that variations on that theme have been around since *Romeo and Juliet*; but after he left, the idea sounded more and more attractive, just *because* it carried archetypal echoes. So the girl, Hydie, became a lapsed Catholic, symbolizing the West's loss of a universal faith, and Fedya a devoted Marxist, whose attraction for her lies in his absolute faith in the Party. The setting was Paris in the middle 1950s – that is to say five to ten years ahead of the time (1949–50) when I wrote it. The novel ends with the funeral of Monsieur Anatole, the last representative of a bygone generation of liberal men of letters, to the accompaniment of an air-raid warning. 'The sirens wailed but nobody was sure: it could have meant the Last Judgment, or just another air-raid exercise.'

Needless to say, the book was intended as a warning, not a prophecy. Twenty years after it was first published, I wrote a new preface for the Danube Edition, reminding the reader of the political situation in Europe in the early postwar years:

Soviet Russia had turned with dramatic brusqueness from an ally into an enemy. The Cold War was at its peak. So was Stalin's reign of terror. That he was suffering from paranoia was still a well-kept secret, revealed much later only, in his daughter's memoirs and his successor's speeches. But it made life both in the East and West full of unpredictable hazards. Inside Russia a dangerous lunatic was in absolute power. It was impossible to foresee against whom he would strike out next, and with what fantastic charges. The patent absurdity of accusations and confessions turned them into a kind of esoteric ritual: the boundary between the credible and incredible had long been eroded. It was the world of *Nineteen Eighty-Four*. . . .

Outside Russia it was a time of equally unpredictable confrontations, conflagrations, capitulations and containments. The Berlin

Blockade. The Korean War. The series of *coups d'état* which transformed Poland, Hungary, Czechoslovakia, into one-party 'popular democracies'. The series of purges and show trials, re-enacted in one after the other of the satellite countries, each rigidly conforming to the same formula, like a television serial by Kafka's own hand. And each ending with the liquidation of former prime ministers, Resistance heroes, Spanish War veterans: Rajk, Clementis, Slansky, Katz.

It was also the time of the World Peace Movement which, under the banner of Picasso's dove, succeeded in persuading millions of innocents that the world could only be pacified by Iron Curtains, mine-fields and barbed wire. The chapter 'Witches' Sabbath' describes a typical 'Peace Rally' of the period.

While the Peace Front was primarily aimed at progressive middle-class intellectuals, the Cominform applied itself to organising the 'revolutionary struggle of the working class' in Western Europe. In Italy, and in France, the Communists had emerged from the War as the strongest political party, and pursued a militant revolutionary policy. In 1947-8, waves of political strikes and armed riots shook both countries with intimations of civil war.

Fear breeds potential collaborators and mutual suspicion. France at the time was riddled with it, and its intelligentsia was riddled with fellow-travellers of all shades, from misguided innocents to cynical opportunists. The situation was epitomised in Jean Paul Sartre's dictum: 'If I have to choose between de Gaulle and the Communists, I choose the Communists.' Sartre's Marxist-Existentialist magazine *Les Temps Modernes* was the monthly gospel of French intellectuals. One of its guiding spirits was Professor Merleau-Ponty, successor to Henri Bergson's chair at the Collège de France, who, in a series of articles, defended Stalin's purges and his pact with Hitler in the name of Historic Necessity, condemned Anglo-American policy as Imperialist Aggression, and denounced any criticism of the Soviet Union as an implicit act of war. Incidentally, the title of the series was '*Le Yogi et le Proletaire*', a polemical paraphrase of *The Yogi and the Commissar,* which had turned me into a Fascist hyena in the eyes of French intellectuals. A few years later Merleau-Ponty saw the light and broke with Sartre; but at the period in question the Witches' Sabbath was in full swing. . . .

Later in the fifties, when American financial aid, combined with the beginnings of the Common Market, produced their stabilising effect, the triumph of Communism in Western Europe became unthinkable without direct Russian intervention; but at the time when the action of the novel takes place it was a distinct possibility. Hence the intimations of doom at Monsieur Anatole's funeral. . . .

In the novel it is Hydie, the lapsed Catholic, who sums up that funeral mood:

. . . Her thoughts travelled back to Sister Boutillot standing in the alley which led to the pond, where the autumn breeze swept the leaves towards her feet. Oh, if she could only go back to the infinite comfort of father confessors and mother superiors, of a well-ordered hierarchy which promised punishment and reward, and furnished the world with justice and meaning. If only one could go back! But she was under the curse of reason, which rejected whatever might quench her thirst, without abolishing the urge; which rejected the answer without abolishing the question. For the place of God had become vacant, and there was a draught blowing through the world as in an empty flat before the new tenants have arrived.

Thus *The Age of Longing* could be called a parable, but it was also a *roman à clef*. Most of the characters were mosaics composed of bits of living models which I had broken up and put together into fictitious combinations (a technique perfectly legitimate to my mind and used by many novelists, though some are reluctant to admit it). Thus the reader could amuse himself by detecting features of some French and British intellectuals in the characters of the novel, like components of an identikit – a bit of Sartre here, of Malraux there, a dash of Ehrenburg's cynicism or of the Webbs' touching naiveté.

Of the six novels that I have written, I like *The Age of Longing* the least. I think it has good chapters in it, but a few good chapters do not make a good novel. It had excellent reviews in England, lousy ones in the USA (the American critics could not stomach Hydie as a representative of American womanhood) but climbed up nevertheless to fourth place on the bestseller list. Its reception in France was mainly hostile, as was to be expected.

But one reader, at least, was following the story with baited breath: the shy, new part-time secretary from Pretoria. She even used to dream, she says, of Hydie and Fedya. Though she never felt bold enough to comment, I could feel her involvement, and this acted as a stimulus and encouragement.

4

Guests at the Wedding

by C.K.

I

Autumn descended on Verte Rive. The days were drawing in, and as the sun set the mist would rise over the river.

Madame Grandin, the old cook, was replaced by a Polish couple. One stormy night in 1949 a car slowly came to a standstill at the front gates, its headlights shining in the darkness. Then it moved on. The Polish couple had been frightened by rumours in the village that Verte Rive was being watched by the Communists and that it was unsafe. The episode with the car was the last straw and they gave notice.

Their place was taken by a French couple, Maxim and Anna. Maxim came from Nevers on the Loire. He would collect snails in the countryside around the house and subject them to the usual revolting treatment which is practised in France before they can be cooked. His *escargots* were the best in the world. He had a daily allowance of four litres of rough country wine – 'Château Maxim', Arthur called it. He adored Arthur.

In the mornings I now left home in the dark, and Maxim picked me up in Melun in Arthur's black Citroën. In the evening he would drive me to the station in Fontaine-le-Port to catch the train back to Paris. Often we missed the train: Maxim would draw up at the little station just as it was pulling out. This did not bother him; we would race the train to the next station, Chartrettes. He would be in the right mood for it, too, having downed a few glasses of his famous wine before leaving. On the straight stretches Maxim drove hard, the train running effortlessly beside us; then it disappeared into a little tunnel and we swerved round a few bends. The sun was setting and its colour was reflected in his ruddy, good-natured face. It was good sport and he beamed with pleasure. We arrived at Chartrettes; Maxim braked hard and I was ready to get out and make a dash for it. But no – again we had missed the train by a hair's breadth. Sometimes this chase would go on all the way to Melun, but we always caught up with the train in the end.

Arthur settled down to writing again. There was peace in the house. He put aside the autobiography which he had begun in the summer. The new book was *The Age of Longing*. Every week I came out to Fontaine-le-Port and typed a new instalment. I could hardly wait for the next one. It reminded me of my childhood when every Thursday my father used to bring home my favourite comics – *Tiger Tim, Bubbles* and *Puck*. In no time I had read them all and then had to wait another whole long week to see, for instance, whether Pat the Pirate would have to walk the plank. But now I was wondering what would happen to Fedya and Hydie. Whilst waiting for the next instalment I used to dream about them. In chapter 7 – 'Calf's Head and Champagne' – they dined together for the first time. Soon after typing this chapter, I saw Arthur's manuscript book lying open on his desk. My eye caught the heading at the top of a page: 'Love in the Afternoon', and before I could stop myself I had read the first sentence: ' "Wait," cried Hydie, "wait! You are tearing my blouse to pieces." ' Though these two chapters were written consecutively, that is not how they appear in the novel. I was kept in suspense for a long time and was only given 'Love in the Afternoon' to type in its proper order, which turned out to be a hundred pages after Fedya had first taken Hydie out to dinner.

Daphne Woodward intended to return to Paris at the beginning of September, but Arthur had a letter from her to say she had been held up for another month. When she did come back, it was decided that I should stay on as Arthur's secretary. She had a busy life and could not manage to put in the amount of time that Arthur required. I was overjoyed – if only life would go on like this for ever!

My mother decided to leave Paris and go to Vienna. I took a room in the 17ième arrondissement at the apartment of a Madame de Faudoaz. Arthur nicknamed her Madame de Foutaise. His French was colourful with a generous use of argot. Madame de Faudoaz disapproved of slang and I was constantly corrected when, in my efforts to express myself, I used it. Arthur would come bounding down the stairs at lunchtime, saying, '*Qu'est-ce qu'on bouffe aujourd'hui?*' *Bouffe* – that was an unusual word. I had never heard it before. I would try it out on Madame Faudoaz. She would no doubt be impressed by my flair for French. But it was met with gasps of horror and that word was never again used under her roof.

2

When I came out to Verte Rive after Christmas, I noticed that Arthur, as he sat at his desk giving me letters, had a bruise on his left cheekbone.

'What have you done to your face?' I asked. He brushed aside my question, muttering that it was too boring to go into. But before long the whole story was out: the press cutting agency sent clippings from the French press with head-lines that said: 'KOESTLER CHARGED WITH HITTING POLICE CHIEF', 'KOESTLER ON DRINK CHARGE', 'YOGI SOCKS COMMISSAR'. Some news agency reports alleged that he was found lying in the gutter. Of course, I had often seen Arthur drink a great deal but had never seen him drunk and was full of admiration for his strong head. I knew he had hangovers, and sometimes he would ask me if he was looking piggy-eyed. This made me laugh, but he never believed my denials.

With every post more cuttings came in: French, Belgian, Dutch, German, English, then Canadian and American, with the usual bitchy paragraph from *Time* magazine. A new file was started and Arthur called it 'Painful Incident'.

What had happened was that he had gone to Paris just before Christmas, without Mamaine, to see friends and to buy presents for the children of the local doctor, who had looked after Mamaine in the spring when she had been so ill. In the early hours of the morning he began the drive home, the car laden with toys, but he got no farther than the suburbs of Paris. Apparently he felt too drunk to continue and parked the car to sleep it off. Two policemen on their beat found the car, the front door open and a pair of legs sticking out. They took Arthur to the police station nearby.

One can imagine how he felt when he finally awoke in broad daylight to find himself in a cell. In a half dreamlike state he was back in prison in Seville. He was taken before the commissaire for questioning. When he asked to telephone his wife to let her know what had happened to him, his request was refused. At this point he punched the commissaire in the eye and was punched in return by one of the *flics*. He was finally released after about eight hours but he had to go through the horror of appearing at court in the spring, when he was fined. In France, getting drunk was looked on with tolerance, and apparently hitting a *flic* was every Frenchman's dream wish. Maxim's expression said it all: M'sieur was a hero.

3

Arthur's dog, Sabby, was a particularly fine, fawn-coloured boxer. Powerful and rather unruly, he was devoted to his master, who was the only person able to control him. Arthur and Mamaine had acquired him as a puppy in Palestine when they were there during the 1948 war. One day I took him for a walk in the forest. He bounded ahead of me, looking back in my direction from time to time. My thoughts were elsewhere when I suddenly noticed him coming towards me, an odd, greenish light in his eyes. He caught my wrist between his teeth and shook it vigorously. The next thing I knew was that Sabby was engaged in a glorious tug-of-war, the object of which was my wrist. Luckily I was wearing a thick jacket which protected it. I managed to bend down and pick up a stick, which I threw. Sabby raced after it. The rest of the walk was spent throwing sticks to keep Sabby amused. Like his master, he was easily bored.

In due course a bride was found for Sabby. She belonged to Professor Mimault, a schoolmaster in Melun. Poor Lily was no beauty – she looked old and ugly beside the handsome Sabby. For her confinement she came to stay at Verte Rive, where she gave birth to twelve puppies. Two of them died; two were kept by Arthur and Mamaine, who called them Romeo and Juliet; and the remaining eight were returned with their mother to Professor Mimault, who augmented his salary by selling Lily's offspring. This, however, led to international complications – and another favourite afterdinner story of Arthur's.

To sell the puppies Professor Mimault needed their official pedigrees from the Société Centrale Canine – the French equivalent of the Kennel Club. Lily's pedigree was in order, but Sabby was an alien. He was born in Tel Aviv on April 29 – the date is important because at that date Palestine was still British mandated territory. Israel only came into being a fortnight later (on May 14).

Professor Mimault wrote to the Société Centrale Canine enclosing Lily's pedigree and also Sabby's from the Palestine Kennel Club which I had obtained before leaving Tel Aviv. It was a remarkable document. The breeder, a German Jew called Hillel Goldrath, was internationally known for his Boxers. Sabby's ancestors included such proud Teutonic names as 'Sigurd von Dom', 'Gretl von Hoheneuffen', 'Alex von Uracher Wasserfall', and so on. But then Hitler came to power, the Goldraths emigrated to Palestine, and history was reflected in the different kinds of name which appeared in Sabby's more recent ancestry: 'Barak me Beth ha Meginin', 'Zaakan ben Satan' and 'Goliath me Beth ha Giborim'.

The pedigree was in English and Hebrew and bore several impressive stamps. But the French Kennel Club was not impressed and refused to recognise the Palestine Kennel Club's pedigree because the latter had ceased to exist. Professor Mimault was in despair. Without a pedigree the eight puppies were unsaleable. So I wrote to the British Kennel Club explaining the situation and pointing out that Sabby was born while Palestine was still under British Mandate:

'I presume therefore that a pedigree issued by the Palestine Kennel Club under British Mandate would have legal validity in England. If this assumption is correct, could I ask you to send me a letter to this effect which I could pass on to the French Kennel Club? The

French Kennel Club told me that if you would be willing to recognise the authenticity of my dog's pedigree, they in turn would recognise it. As my dog has just begotten 10 puppies out of a French pedigree boxer bitch, the matter is of some importance to the future of the offspring – and incidentally, also of considerable pecuniary importance to the owner of the bitch, Monsieur Mimault, a professor of Latin in Melun.'

But even this heartbreaking appeal failed to move the British Kennel Club who wrote back that they were unable to help because 'it would appear that the dog has never been domiciled in this country'.

Then I discovered that there existed an international organisation of kennel clubs, the 'Fédération Cynologique Internationale', presided over by the Baron Albert Houtart in Brussels. I wrote to Baron Houtart, explaining to him the situation and mentioning in passing that if I failed to obtain satisfaction I would feel obliged to appeal to the International Court of Justice in the Hague. To this discreetly blackmailing letter I had a reply from Madame la Baronne, informing me that her husband was ill and would I have a little patience. To my surprise, a few days later Professor Mimault received a letter from the French Kennel Club, dated February 28, 1950, which showed that diplomatic ingenuity is not unknown in the dog world. The decisive paragraph in the letter said:

'Bien que la Palestine ne soit pas en relation de reciprocité avec la F.C.I. en accord avec cette dernier, nous reconnaissons courtoisement "de facto" cette Société.'*

And that was the happy ending which saved the ten puppies from the stigma of a one-parent family.

4

For some time my mother, who was in Vienna, had been trying to persuade me to spend a holiday with her at St Anton in the Austrian Alps. I was not in the least bit keen on going away, but at last I reluctantly agreed to join her for a week.

---

* Although the Palestine [Kennel Club] does not maintain mutual relations with the Fédération Cynologique Internationale, we have, in agreement with the latter, decided as a matter of courtesy to recognize de facto that Society [i.e. the Israeli Kennel Club].

Since my mother left Paris, I had had a struggle to keep body and soul together. My job with Arthur being part time, I only earned enough to pay for my room and breakfast, with a pound over per month for food. I spent this pound on *rillettes de porc,* a greasy, delicious kind of pâté. Charcuterie was expensive even then – something like eggs would no doubt have been cheaper; but because *rillettes* consisted mostly of pork fat, I was under the romantic illusion that I was eating the food of the poor. Not that I could afford this food of the poor too often: my main meal of the day was breakfast, a gastronomic feast of *café au lait, baguette,* butter and jam.

The Swedish girl who had the room next door to mine also lived on breakfast. However, rather than waste the little money she had on food, she spent it on drink. Sometimes Ingrid and I dined together in her room on Vieille Cure, a sweet liqueur which, together with Parfait Amour, were her favourites. She used to buy red wine at a shilling a bottle. If you put a lump of sugar in it, she said, it improved the taste. Each morning, her wastepaper basket overflowed with empty bottles.

At lunch at Verte Rive twice a week, it was an effort not to fall too eagerly on the food. It never occurred to me to tell Arthur and Mamaine of my sorry plight.

At the end of January, I went on my holiday to St Anton. Mamaine had left for Switzerland for a few weeks – the Seine valley in winter was the worst place for an asthma sufferer. Arthur was working hard on the book, leading what he called a 'monk-like existence'.

In the splendid hotel dining room at St Anton, with its maître d'hôtel in black tails, gargantuan meals were served three times a day. But I was unable to eat and was pining away. I recently came across a pathetic postcard I sent to Arthur: 'Having a lovely time . . . dancing every night,' it said. But it ended: 'I'll phone the moment I get back which will either be Monday night or some time Tuesday, then I can work Wednesday and Sat.[?] or whenever you like.' The long, boring days never seemed to end. I counted the days and hours until I could leap out of that claustrophobic valley and wing my way back to France.

Spring came and Arthur hoped the book would soon be finished. But the weeks passed and still the end was not in sight. 'It's like a tapeworm,' he complained. 'It just goes on and on.'

5

There was a file in Arthur's desk drawer which I had not seen before. It was blue and written on the cover was the word 'Divorce'. Arthur explained that he and Mamaine were not really married because he and his former wife, Dorothy, had not yet got their divorce. But he expected it to come through soon and while he was dictating a letter to the lawyer who was handling it, Mamaine came into the room. Her face fell when she saw the secret file out on the desk, but Arthur reassured her. Cynthia had to know sooner or later, he said.

On the day of the wedding Arthur and Mamaine came up to Paris. They intended to return to Verte Rive in the late afternoon, and Arthur told me to meet them at the Café Flore at drink time so that I could get a lift out with them. He was keen to get back to work early the next morning.

The black Citroën was parked in the Boulevard St Germain just outside the Café Flore. Arthur and Mamaine were sitting on the terrace outside with some other people, including Stephen Spender – who had a boyish face, curly blond hair and a diffident manner. As we sat drinking, Arthur noticed a scruffy, shabbily dressed man and brought him to our table. It turned out that he was a former comrade of Arthur's in his Communist cell in Berlin at the beginning of the thirties. He told Arthur the story of how he fell into the hands of the Gestapo and was tortured by them and made to eat his own excrement. Arthur did not really seem to like the man (I think he was still a member of the Party), but these ghastly stories seemed to stir up old memories. He kept offering his former comrade drinks and knocked back quite a few himself.

It was getting late and eventually, to everyone's relief, the German left. It was decided that we should drive back to Verte Rive after dinner. In the restaurant there was a second unpleasant incident. One of the guests – a man who had tagged

along with his wife and whom Arthur had never met before
– thought that Arthur had been rude to him. It all happened
suddenly and, for a moment, it looked as if there might be a
fight, but the couple departed, leaving Arthur looking somewhat bewildered.

In my memory the evening ended when Mamaine refused
to let Arthur drive. He sat at the wheel of the black Citroën
and, when Mamaine refused to get into the car, he slammed
the door. The last we saw of him he was hurtling away into the
night alone. Mamaine and I were left with Stephen Spender. It
was too late for me to go home, for the bar across the front
door of the apartment was put up at eleven. Stephen Spender
offered Mamaine the spare room in his flat and I slept on the
sofa in his sitting room.

Early next morning I made my way out to Fontaine-le-
Port. Arthur looked pale and asked where Mamaine was. I
told him where we had spent the night. Why doesn't she
telephone me, he kept asking guiltily.

The wedding night had hardly been a conventional one, but
I thought nothing of it. For Arthur and Mamaine, weddings,
like birthdays, were simply not celebrated. A few days later,
when Maxim picked me up at the station at Melun, he was
beaming. '*Monsieur et Madame sont mariés,*' said he in his
homely Nivernais accent. I looked noncommittal but was in
fact horrified. How had the secret got out? Maxim proudly
produced some French newspaper with their photograph
spread across the page.

6

Arthur's mother came to stay for a week. During lunch on
the first day, there was little conversation and I noticed that
any remark made by her was acknowledged coolly both by
Arthur and by Mamaine. I knew Arthur's opinions about
mothers: mine was hell, he had told me many times, though
he had not met her then; but I had to admit that we rarely
saw eye to eye. Arthur's mother seemed a charming old lady
and I wondered why Mamaine appeared so actively to dislike
her.

She was Viennese and her blue eyes and the bone structure of her face looked remarkably like her son's. But perhaps a gene from his paternal grandfather, who was Russian, had made his eyes more slanting and the cheekbones more pronounced. In *The Age of Longing* there is a description of Fedya: 'Between the wide temples and wide cheekbones there was a marked stricture like the waist of an hour-glass, which gave his features a slightly Mongolian touch'; and later: 'his light, somewhat slanting eyes . . .'. I once asked Arthur if the physical appearance of Fedya was a self-portrait. But he said he was only describing one type of Eastern European face.

˙ That evening I played canasta with Arthur's mother. As the game progressed, I became all too aware of her strong-willed character. A transformation had taken place: she took advantage of every sign of weakness and I was demolished quite ruthlessly. Later, when I told Mamaine about my débâcle, she said she hated Arthur's mother because she had made his childhood such hell.

Almost weekly, Arthur would write to Messrs John and Edward Bumpus, the London booksellers. Here is a selection of books he ordered between January and June 1950:
Concise Oxford Dictionary – 'the edition with the cut-in alphabetic finger holes'
Freud, *Gesammelte Werke,* Volumes I, XVI and XVIII
C. E. M. Joad, *Decadence*
Charlotte Haldane's autobiography
Sir Maurice Powicke, *Ways of Mediaeval Life*
R. M. Graves, *Experiment in Anarchy*
B. Ifor Evans, *The Use of English*
Stephen Spender's autobiography
Gurdjieff, *All and Everything*
Eliot, *The Cocktail Party*
Hemingway, *Across the River and into the Trees*
Antonia White, *The Lost Traveller*
Fred Hoyle, *The Nature of the Universe*
The 'new Aldous Huxley'

An English translation of Alexander Block's *The Twelve* –
'new or secondhand'
Joyce Carey, *The Horse's Mouth*
Sir Charles Sherrington and others, *The Physical Basis of Mind*
Silone, *The Seed Beneath the Snow*
Schwarzschild, *The Red Prussian*
Sartre, *Iron in the Soul*
Mary McCarthy, *A Pier and a Band*
Henry Green, *Nothing*
Hoyle's Games Modernised
Simenon, *Poisoned Relations*

7

An enormous cupboard in Verte Rive was filled with the files
Arthur had accumulated in the last ten years, since he escaped
from France in 1940 and settled in England. I was given the
task of arranging them in more or less chronological order,
or by subject and putting them into file storage cases. On the
spines of these cases I wrote what was contained in them and
today I still see that familiar, unformed handwriting.

I sat on the bed in the Purgatory, with its Schiaparelli-pink
walls, surrounded by old files. One file haunted me. It was
called simply 'Jews' and contained snapshots, rather blurred,
of concentration camp victims; some were of thin, skeleton-
like figures standing to attention, waiting to be shot.

There were endless correspondence files. Most letters were
filed away – one might need to refer to them some time – and
once filed, stayed there for ever, for the job of weeding them
out would have been too time-consuming.

He was conscientious about answering fan mail. Here is a
letter to a little boy in Africa, who had asked Arthur if he
would be his penfriend:

Dear Ebenezer,
It was very kind of you to write to me. I am sending you enclosed
a picture and hope you will like it. If you want other pen friends
you could write to:

and to:
Mr Kingsley Martin
10 Great Turnstile
London WC1
Mr Andre Malraux
19 bis, Avenue Victor Hugo
Boulogne s/Seine
France

They both like coconuts and are very nice people.
Many good wishes to you and your friends.

In January 1950, he answered a letter from Professor Dennis
Gabor, a fellow Hungarian who was later to get the Nobel
Prize in physics:

Methodologically your objections to the quality of evidence re telepathy are certainly valid, but there are a number of buts which it
would be too long to discuss by mail. Maybe some day we will
meet after all – at any rate, if you happen to visit France, will you
let me know?

Soon after, Dennis Gabor did come to France and their long
friendship began, though they never did agree on ESP. There
is a long letter to Vita Sackville-West, again on the subject of
telepathy. She had written an article on a telepathic experience
and had asked her readers to communicate with her if they
knew of any explanation. Arthur began his letter by
explaining:

(a) that I am convinced that telepathy and clairvoyance are
empirically established facts;
(b) that over 90% of the reported cases of telepathy and clairvoyance
turn out to be based on self-delusion;
(c) that the power of such unconscious, bona-fide self-delusions is
sometimes quite astonishing – as I found in two cases which I had
occasion to investigate in detail, and one of which was rather similar
to yours;
(d) that I believe you are a victim of an unconscious and bona-fide
self-delusion of this kind.

As the incident also involved the fallibility of memory, he
suggested: 'There is a relatively easy way to check it: any

89

reliable hypnotist could make you recall in three or four sessions what exactly happened. . . .'

In reply to a letter from a young writer, he said:

I liked the poem, and it made me feel that you can write excellent prose. I do think you should try to write that novel. If it doesn't come off, write another one. Perfectionism is death to the creative impulse. And the only way of writing a book is to write it. This sounds like Hemingway, but it was actually James Burnham who once said it to me. If it's any comfort to you, let me tell you that my first two and a half books were never published.

In January 1950, shortly before George Orwell died, Arthur had a letter from Malcolm Muggeridge, to which he replied:

I wonder what could be done about George. I know that all available specialists have already been consulted and that you and his other friends have explored all possibilities. Yet I still wonder whether the risk of getting him to Switzerland in an air ambulance should not be reconsidered. When Mamaine was very ill last year I made enquiries about air-taxi ambulances and found that the service is reasonably cheap and very efficient. But as I don't know the exact details of his present condition, all this is just thinking aloud.

When Orwell died, Arthur wrote his obituary for the *Observer*. Soon after, he replied to a letter from its editor, David Astor, who had been a close friend of both Orwell and Arthur:

I was very moved by your letter. Curiously enough the evening before it arrived I sat at my lonely fireplace (Mamaine is in Garmisch and I live like a hermit in the forest) and wrote a long handwritten letter to you about George which however the next morning looked too sentimental so I threw it away. Now I can't write it again.

Sometimes I made a mistake in typing a letter. When this happened, an expression of irritation would flit across Arthur's face; he might even bring his fist down on the desk with a little rap. Surely, I thought to myself, having typed so many letters faultlessly, he can't mind a small mistake like that? If there was an error in the typescript of the book, he would let out a cry, not of exasperation but of pain.

When Mamaine was away during the winter in the Bavarian mountains, Arthur wrote to her frequently and sometimes he sent her typed reports of his activities:

I am working furiously on the novel and haven't been to Paris since you left, nor do I intend to go for several weeks. . . .

I still haven't been to Paris and had a heroic haircut in Melun which makes me look like a shorn poodle. . . .

He was to appear in court on 1 March, he wrote Mamaine, in connection with the Painful Incident, and

would like you to be here for moral support. . . . Don't worry as I have ceased to care about the whole thing. It will just be an unpleasant half-hour with photographers, reporters, etc., and afterwards we will offer ourselves an exceptionally good champagne lunch.

The last phrase is an example of the gallicisms which appeared at that time in Arthur's writings; it was the price he paid for living in France. The text of *The Age of Longing* was exotically coloured by them, but he eradicated them in the final draft.

He worried about Mamaine and wrote:

Your last letters gave me the impression you are slightly bored or depressed. If that is so, maybe you would prefer to spend February somewhere else where there are more people and life? Haute Savoie for instance? You didn't say anything about that ear trouble. . . .

Later in February he wrote:

The weather is still lovely and everything is all right but I am very overworked because apart from the novel which is coming along fine I have to revise the French translation of *The God That Failed* and the German translation of *The Yogi*. This sort of thing is really hell but in the end it pays – morally I mean.

At that time Arthur still insisted on revising the French and German translations of his books, which was a frustrating and time-consuming task. He only gave it up about five years ago. How strongly he felt on the subject of translations is reflected in the following extracts from a letter to a young Hungarian writer:

I have read your MSS carefully and I have no doubt that you are a very gifted writer. . . . Under normal circumstances in Hungary I don't think there would be any difficulty in getting them published by a literary magazine. But I don't know of any translator who could translate from the Hungarian into English. The few people in London who do this are hacks. The strength of your short stories is in the atmosphere and in the flavour of your style, both of which would be lost in translation. I have some experience in trying to help young writers and I know that it is almost impossible to find a market for translated short stories.

If you want to make a career as a writer the only way I think is to learn English. Read English day and night, both you and your wife, and try to talk English to each other, and seek the company of English-speaking people. I wrote my first book in English at the age of thirty-five; for you who are so much younger it should be so much easier. And then try to write an autobiographical type of novel. Nobody who has had your type of development has done that; if it is done sincerely – with a fearless and ruthless sincerity – it should not be impossible to interest an American publisher.

This is the hard way, but the only way that I can see. To write in a language which has no literary market means writing for one person only – the translator, and being entirely at his mercy. . . . Don't hesitate to write again whenever you feel like it.

Vita Sackville-West was to spend a holiday in Provins and wondered if they could meet. 'Do I connect Fontaine-le-Port with Chateaubriand and Mme Récamier, or am I mistaken?' she asked. Arthur replied:

We would be delighted if you and your friend would come over for a day or a meal. Fontaine-le-Port is a few kilometres from Provins; we live on the river facing the Forest of Fontainebleau. I haven't found any trace of Chateaubriand or Madame de Récamier and our only claim to be a historical site is I am afraid contained in this phrase from the guide book: '*Le peintre royal, Martin de Fremines, y fut inhumé en 1619.*'

In due course, Miss Sackville-West and her friend, Violet Trefusis, came over for lunch at Verte Rive. I heard that

Arthur found them rather overwhelming, and I believe they were shocked by the nautical bar in the dining room.

There was correspondence with the sister of Arthur's old friend, Paul Ignotus, the Hungarian writer. Paul had lived for many years in England, but in 1949 he decided to revisit Budapest for the funeral of his father. He would be a fool to go, Arthur had told him, he would be put in prison. Paul thought Arthur had persecution mania, but this prediction came true. Sari, Paul's sister, was afraid that if the British press took up the case, Paul's life would be in danger. Arthur was sure that, on the contrary, only a public campaign could save him. At last Sari agreed to this and the details of his case were printed both in England and abroad. Paul was eventually released in 1956 at the time of the Hungarian Revolution.

8

At the end of May 1950, Arthur finished the first draft of *The Age of Longing*. He wrote it by hand; every time I came out, he dictated to me the pages he had written, making corrections as he went along. He then read through the pages I had just typed out, making a few further corrections and putting a wavy line under passages he was doubtful about. He now began to read through the whole book, making the final corrections and sometimes using scissors and paste. He expected this to take him two months. The first typed draft had to be retyped and there were always plenty of pages waiting for me whenever I was there.

From the middle of June, most of his time was occupied with preparations for the Congress for Cultural Freedom, which he and Mamaine were to attend at the end of the month. He thought that the congress should end with the issuing of a manifesto on intellectual freedom, which he dictated to me. Normally when he dictated letters, he would pause frequently, trying to find the right words and sometimes ending a sentence as if it were a question – will that do, he seemed to be wondering. But now he seemed sure of what he wanted to say as he walked up and down the room. He won't need to make any corrections, I thought; the style was simple and clear.

Sentences like 'Deprived of the right to say "no", man becomes a slave' stuck in my mind.

On the day before Arthur and Mamaine left for Berlin, I was at Verte Rive typing last-minute letters, as Arthur wanted to clear the decks. The following morning the three of us drove up to Paris. On the journey, Arthur gave me instructions about things to be attended to in his absence. And, he said, if anything were to happen to Mamaine and him, I was to send the typescript of *The Age of Longing* to A. D. Peters in London. A. D. Peters was his literary agent and an old friend.

Over the next twenty-four hours I could hardly bear to look at a newspaper. To reach Berlin, Arthur and Mamaine had to fly over part of East Germany. Supposing someone were to take a pot shot at their plane. I tried to push such melodramatic thoughts out of my mind.

A few days later, the Korean War began and I was assailed with new fears. It was the beginning of the Third World War, I was sure; its shadow, which looms over *The Age of Longing*, was about to become reality, and Arthur and Mamaine would be trapped in Berlin. They were supposed to be away for just a week. Three more days passed and there was no sign of them. But at last my gloom was dispelled by a telephone call: they were home.

The summer was at its height. Outside the sun blazed and the Seine seemed to beckon, but we sat indoors working. As I typed the last lines of *The Age of Longing* I was filled with melancholy. For Arthur it was much worse. His vitality seemed to have ebbed away. He was subdued, almost apologetic.

5

The Congress for Cultural Freedom

by A.K.

I

In March 1950 I wrote to Hermon Ould, secretary of the PEN Club:

> . . . I was somewhat shocked to find in the *P.E.N. News* for February on page 5 a report on 'Culture in the Soviet Union' which sounds as if it had been written by a man in the moon. I don't want to involve you in any polemical correspondence knowing how busy you are but I do wish to register my protest. You probably remember that I used to be one of the more active P.E.N. members and then ceased to be so; the reason for this estrangement is to be found in this kind of neutrality towards the most grotesque and dreadful persecution of art, science and literature, from geneticists and musicians to circus clowns.

Neutralism was indeed the most refined form of intellectual betrayal and perhaps the most contemptible. It showed a forgiving attitude towards totalitarian terror but denounced with unforgiving venom any failing or injustice in the West. It equated the Hollywood purges of suspected Reds in the film industry with the purges which had decimated the Soviet population.

This perverse attitude of the postwar intelligentsia derived its strongest mental and moral support from the various peace appeals, international congresses and pacifist movements, launched by or exploited for their own purpose by the Comintern's front organizations. By the same semantic sleight of hand which referred to one-party dictatorships as 'popular democracies', 'Peace' was turned into a slogan which somehow implied benevolent neutrality towards tyranny and terror; while those intellectuals who protested were branded as warmongers and tools of imperialist aggression. What was needed under these circumstances was a powerful demonstration to clear the intellectual atmosphere in the West. Thus was conceived the project of the Berlin Congress for Cultural Freedom in June 1950. It was an ironical coincidence that Sartre, the arch fellow-traveller, and I, the cold warrior, became literally fellow-travellers on the same train which took us both to Germany – for diametrically opposite purposes.

The Congress for Cultural Freedom, an international meeting of writers, scholars and scientists under the patronage of Bertrand Russell, Benedetto Croce, John Dewey, Karl Jaspers, and Jacques Maritain, was held in June, 1950, in Berlin. Its opening session coincided with the beginning of the Korean war. It served a double purpose: as a kind of intellectual airlift, a demonstration of Western solidarity with the brave and battered outpost of Berlin, a hundred miles behind the Iron Curtain; and as an attempt to dispel the intellectual confusion created by the totalitarian campaigns under the slogan of peace. Out of the deliberations of the Berlin Congress arose an international movement with branches and publications in a number of European, American and Asiatic countries.*

In fact, the Berlin Congress turned out to be a dramatic success; and as every popular drama must have a villain whom people love to hate, the Communist and fellow-travelling press elected me to fulfil that role. A typical example was an article in *L'Observateur* under the headline : 'KKK – Koestler's Kultur Kongress'. The official Party organ, *L'Humanité,* went one better. It published a map of Fontaine-le-Port, with an arrow pointing at Verte Rive, and explaining : 'This is the headquarters of the cold war. This is where Chip Bohlen, the

---

* *The Trail of the Dinosaur,* London and New York, 1955; Danube Edition, p. 112.

American Ambassador, trains his para-military Fascist militia.'
It was surprising they didn't call my sailing canoe a battleship.

The grain of truth in this hate campaign was that, as a
member of its five-men steering committee, I had indeed taken
an active role in planning and steering the congress. I also
delivered an opening address, read a paper to the political
panel session, and read at the closing session the congress
manifesto that I had drafted and which somewhat to my
surprise, was adopted unanimously by the audience of some
15,000 people, packed in the Rundfunk Garden. The manifesto
ended:

We hold that the theory and practice of the totalitarian state are the
greatest challenge which man has been called on to meet in the course
of civilised history.

We hold that indifference or neutrality in the face of such a challenge amounts to a betrayal of mankind and to the abdication of the
free mind. Our answer to this challenge may decide the fate of man
for generations.*

There was no heckling, no interruptions, nor any sign of
frontier hysteria, in spite of the recent blockade of the town's
lifelines to the West. Berlin, AD 1950, had learned its bitter
lesson and was immune against the opium of neutralism in
spite of being an isolated enclave, surrounded by the potential
enemy. The people knew that they could not have survived
the blockade without the allied airlift; and they understood
that the Congress was intended as another kind of airlift, to
prove that the intellectuals of the West did care about their
fate. When the manifesto had been acclaimed, and I called out
'*Die Freiheit hat die Offensive ergriffen*' – 'Freedom has taken the
offensive' – nobody in the audience mistook this for a cold-
war slogan, except those determined to misunderstand.

---

* The text of these speeches is reprinted in *The Trail of the Dinosaur*, Danube
Edition, pp. 112-27, and in *Bricks to Babel*, Hutchinson, 1980.

2

In the autumn of 1950 I was back in New York on a more protracted visit than the hectic lecture tour two years earlier. Macmillans were preparing to launch *The Age of Longing*, Sidney Kingsley was working on the stage version of *Darkness at Noon*, but beyond these immediate concerns, Mamaine and I were still undecided where to settle, and I was vaguely toying with the idea of spending part of the year in the United States, part in France. As I explained in an interview in the *New York Times*:

I would like to divide my time between this country and Europe. A political writer of our time can only hope to get a balanced picture of the world if he knows America not as a visitor but as a resident involved in everyday life. And the same goes for Europe. The hopelessly one-sided and distorted view which the European holds of America and the American of Europe is one of the main sources of the political and cultural confusion of our age.*

So an additional purpose of the trip was to look out for a flat or cottage where we could spend part of the year; Mamaine was to follow in due course.

But I was too busy – and also too undecided – to do any serious house-hunting. The country places to which I was occasionally invited for weekends did not appeal to me and would have appealed even less to Mamaine – they were all lacking in privacy, with no hedges or fences or bits of old wall to enclose them; they seemed to stand in the open landscape naked and exposed, and they made one long to live on an island. So an island it was that in a rather crazy venture I bought in the end.

The island was in the Delaware river in Bucks County, Pennsylvania. It was oval-shaped, a mile long and half a mile wide at its widest point. It had once been called Hooker's Island but was now known simply as Island Farm. It was connected to the mainland by a single, eighty-yard-long steel suspension bridge which belonged to the property and could

* 1 April, 1951.

be locked. Here was privacy indeed. 'In the peaceful seclusion of this island,' the auctioneer's brochure enthused, 'the rest of the world might well be thousands of miles away. Here you can live the way you want to in complete privacy and seclusion, with nothing to disturb you but the breeze in the trees.'

I had come to stay for a weekend in October 1950 with friends who had a place near Flemington, New Jersey. (Jupp Loewengard was a banker, his wife Kathrin wrote under the pseudonym Martha Albrand.) During dinner on Friday they mentioned that on the next day – Saturday, 6 October – an island in the Delaware was to be sold by public auction just a few miles away, and we tentatively decided to have a look for curiosity's sake. But on Saturday we lingered over lunch and by the time we arrived on the island the auction had already started on a secluded lawn at the end of an alley. There were perhaps twenty sleepy-looking people standing on the lawn, forming an irregular semicircle around the auctioneer. The whole scene looked somehow unreal, and the most unreal aspect of it was my hand shooting up at I don't remember what figure. But I do remember that the whole affair was over in a few minutes, and the sum for which the island was regretfully knocked down to me by the auctioneer: $41,000. My host Jupp, who knew about real estate, thought it would fetch $80,000. I was later told that by a sheer fluke the real estate agents and speculators were on that particular afternoon attending a crucial baseball game.

My feeling of disbelief in having in a few minutes become the ruler of an island kingdom was intensified by the fact that its price was almost exactly the sum that Macmillans, my American publishers, were holding for me in accumulated royalties. But as a British citizen, subject to the complicated exchange control regulations still in force in 1950, I was not allowed to have an American bank account: my foreign earnings, except for personal expenses, were supposed to be converted into sterling. So when the auctioneer asked me for the usual deposit of 15 per cent, I had to explain that I had no bank account and that I would have to ask my publishers to send him a cheque in a few days.

'Do you mean, mister,' said the bemused auctioneer, 'that you have *no bank account?*'

I guiltily admitted that this was so, expecting him to call the cops and have me arrested as an impostor. But then he would have to start the auction again and by now the prospective bidders had gone. 'You go to the house, mister, and speak to Mrs King,' he said at last. Mrs King was – or, rather had been – the proprietress of the island, which she had to sell because of her husband's sudden death.

'OK,' I said, 'but could you kindly tell me where the house is?'

The auctioneer seemed close to a heart attack. 'You mean to tell me you haven't even *seen* the house which you just bought?' I again pleaded guilty and tried to explain that I was so bowled over by what I had seen of the island while driving down the lane that I had not noticed the house. Fortunately at this critical moment the Loewengards, who had kept discreetly in the background, intervened and Jupp wrote out the cheque for the 15 per cent deposit.

When at last I did see the house I was enchanted. It was built in the last century in the Pennsylvania Dutch style and carefully modernized, spacious but compact, with plenty of guest rooms, servants' quarters, wide porches and a solarium with views of the river from three sides. The auctioneer's brochure also informed me that 'the island comprises about 112 acres in all. There are approximately 65 acres tillable, 40 acres of valuable tall timber and 7 acres of gardens and lawns' – not to mention outbuildings, barn, garages, '150 apple trees, 100 pear trees, a number of pecan trees and poultry houses with a capacity of 2800 chickens'. What else can you wish for?

Mamaine arrived in New York after Christmas, and we moved into Island Farm at the beginning of January. It was exciting furnishing the house and looking after the lawns and gardens, but we both felt ambivalent about American ways of life. In my political outlook I was staunchly pro-American, but that did not help much to make me like American cooking, or popular culture, or spiritual values. This also applied to the literary scene.

In the interview that I quote above, I said:

The longer I live here the more I get the feeling that there is something radically wrong with literary life in America. I don't mean the
quality of the writers. You have, all in all, a greater number of first-
rate novelists here than any European country. What disturbs me is
something different. Let me put it this way. If you were to ask me
what a writer's ambition in life should be, I would answer with a
formula. A writer's ambition should be to trade a hundred contemporary readers for ten readers in ten years and for one reader in a
hundred years.

But the general atmosphere in this country directs the writer's
ambitions into different channels. However much innate integrity he
has, publishers, reviewers and editors focus his attention – consci-
ously or unconsciously – on immediate success here and now. Religion and art are the two completely noncompetitive spheres of
human striving and they both derive from the same source. But the
social climate in this country has made the creation of art into an
essentially competitive business. On the bestseller charts, this curse
of American literary life, authors are rated like shares on the Stock
Exchange. People open the Sunday book-supplements with the same
thrill as others look at the stock-market reports: how is General
Electric doing today? Is Budd Schulberg still on top of Hemingway?
You can pursue the parallel further. You can make speculative
investments – Robert Penn Warren, for instance, or play it safe with
widow shares and back Waltari or Taylor Caldwell.

This sounds merely funny, but the fact is that making literature
into a competitive game has a corroding effect on readers, writers,
publishers and reviewers alike. No writer is without vanity, the
artist's professional disease. But here is a difference whether your
vanity and ambition is directed at the reader in a hundred years' time
or at doing well on the bestseller chart. If you are a novelist living
in this country you may be a saint but you will be unable to resist
glancing at the devilish chart to see how you and your friends are
doing; and your friends thus automatically turn into competitors. I
know of a young American writer who once headed the bestseller
list and is now paralysed and on the verge of a nervous breakdown
because of the fear that if he does not repeat the performance he will
automatically be regarded as a passé novelist – and this very excellent
young writer is still under thirty. Can you fathom the whole horror
of what this implies? And can you fathom the grotesqueness of
Hemingway, America's greatest living novelist, talking of his books
in terms of 'defending the title of champ'? I know he meant it to be

funny, but it just isn't. It is a give-away; it betrays the basic assumption that writing is a competitive business like prize-fighting.

I am convinced that a century from now the historian will regard the degradation of art to the competitive level as one of the main aberrations of contemporary American culture and the bestselling chart as its grotesque symbol.

The *New York Times* printed a bowdlerized version of the interview which infuriated the interviewer, Harvey Breit – a nice chap, who made a speciality of interviewing writers visiting New York.* He wrote to me:

I have been in a great fight that has made me very angry. . . . The argument, to simplify it, was how can we run an attack on the very thing we do? . . . The editors here finally approved a version that has little reference, if any, to the best seller lists, but does refer to the commercial aspects of our literary life. Going along with the idea that half a loaf is better than no loaf, I acceded.

It was an insidious little example of literary censorship. 'How can we run an attack on the very thing we do?' One must let this sentence sink in, for it is the direct opposite of Voltaire's famous, 'I disagree with what you say, but I am prepared to die for your right to say it.' Incidentally, I could not be accused of pining after sour grapes, for *The Age of Longing* had, to my intense satisfaction, just climbed to fourth place on the bestseller list. And this incidental remark, incidentally, proves the point I have been making.

3

No sooner had we moved to Island Farm than Mamaine's asthma got worse and she had to stay in bed for several weeks. This had happened with distressing repetitiveness each time we moved into a new house: in Bwlch Ocyn and Verte Rive. The strain of moving might have been too much for her, or else there was some psychosomatic devilry at work, for

---

* See his collection *The Writer Observed: Revealing Interviews with the World's Most Famous Writers*, Collier Books, 1961.

though Mamaine loved travelling, the only place where she really wanted to live was London. In Verte Rive I had domestic help when she was ill, but on the wuthering heights of Wales and on the island kingdom in the Delaware I had to cook and do the household chores as best I could. It soon became evident, however, that the best was not good enough. For a week or two I had a black daily who came in her own car from Flemington, ten miles away, when she felt like it, but when the country lane which led to the bridge became icy, she petered out. To tell the truth, I quite enjoyed hoovering, cooking *pot-au-feu* and mowing the lawns as a holiday from the book I was writing (*Arrow in the Blue*) and from coping with correspondence; but as the red file marked 'Urgent' and the grey one marked 'Unanswered' kept swelling like jilted maidens in advanced pregnancy, guilt gained the upper hand. Luckily, there was an obvious solution to the problem: faithful Cynthia. She was not only the ideal secretary, but also a passionate gardener and as good with a hoover as with a lawnmower. In the middle of February, while Mamaine was still bedridden, I wrote to her:

This letter will be a big surprise. Mamaine and I have made up our minds to ask you whether you would like to come over and stay with us until we go back to Europe. . . . We very much hope that you will like the idea and that, as work is pressing, you will arrive yesterday.

In fact she arrived ten days after receiving this letter – the time it took her to get an American visa.

The crisis was over. As the pressure was lifted from her, Mamaine was soon on the way to recovery, and I could get back to work.

Apart from dictating some chapters of *Arrow in the Blue* in rough draft to Cynthia and writing some essays (reprinted in *The Trail of the Dinosaur*), my main preoccupation – soon amounting to an obsession – during that first spring on the island was the launching of an enterprise called Fund for Intellectual Freedom or FIF for short. I was only too familiar with the misery of fellow-writers -- Russians, Poles, Hungarians, Czechoslovaks, Rumanians – who had succeeded in saving their physical existence and spiritual integrity by escaping to the West, and were now struggling for bare survival. I also felt that prosperous writers in the free world had a special obligation to help their less fortunate colleagues – not by charitable alms but by constructive help to enable them to continue writing during the cruel period of transition before they found their feet on alien soil.

The trouble with charity is that your contribution is merely a drop in the ocean. But the number of creative writers among the refugees was limited – perhaps not more than two hundred. On the other hand, the exiled writer's existence is more difficult than that of exiles in other professions. Charitable organizations such as the International Rescue and Relief Committee (IRRC) could only supply the basic necessities to keep them above starvation level, but could not create the conditions which would enable them to continue to work. This is where the FIF came in. It did not hand out doles but provided constructive help according to each individual's needs, ranging from typewriters (some of them with Cyrillic keyboards); grants for finishing a book; the means for paying translators; arranging for publishing and radio contacts, and so on. But above all, the FIF provided creative outlets by publishing or subsidizing émigré magazines in several languages: Russian (*Literaturny Sovremennik*), Polish (*Kultura*), Rumanian (*Orizontori*) and Hungarian (*Uj Magyar Ut*).

The most ambitious of these enterprises, the *Literaturny Sovremennik,* was a monthly magazine of approximately 260 pages, published in Munich. It was in the classic format of the so-called 'fat' literary magazine, which since the beginning of the nineteenth century played such a central part in the cultural life of Russia – some of the masterpieces of the great Russian novelists were first published as serials in 'fat' magazines. The birth of yet another literary magazine is nothing to get excited about, but the launching of *Literaturny Sovremennik* was a symbolic event. Its significance is reflected in the following extracts from a letter to me by its editor, Boris Yakovlev:

People say that there are no miracles, and least of all among exiles. Hence the first news that a group of you English and American authors intended to make a miracle come true and give us back our lost voice was received with sceptical smiles. They could not believe that solidarity, this word which we have heard so often misused as a political slogan, could exist in the world of facts.

He then went on to explain how the Russian exiles were unable to find a market for their work because they had no money to pay translators and could not get publishers and editors to read a manuscript in Russian. He described how these men, who risked their lives to get out and make their voices heard, had one after the other given up writing in discouragement and despair. The letter concludes:

And now the miracle has come true. We have waited for it during twenty-five years 'over there', and during five years over here – for the miracle to be permitted to write what we think, and to see what we have written published. Now it has come true. I believe our people here have deserved it. You as writers will understand no doubt what it means to us writers and poets escaped from the USSR to have for the first time in thirty years, the chance of saying what we like in print.

Yours sincerely,
B. Yakovlev

The FIF had no overhead expenses; all the work was done by voluntary helpers – mostly in Munich and Paris, who were in close contact with refugee organizations and coordinated from New York by Agnes Knickerbocker* and myself. On starting this venture, my idea had been not to appeal for cash donations but to ask prosperous writers to assign to the FIF, by way of self-taxation, a percentage of the royalties from a book, or a foreign translation of it, or from a stage or screen production, etc. It sounded like a good idea (at least to me) but the response of American writers to the FIF appeal, published by the *New York Times, Herald Tribune* and *Saturday Review of Literature,* was dismal. One anonymous donor sent

---

* Widow of the writer, H. R. Knickerbocker.

a cheque for $5. A crank, who had invented an umbrella with an electric bulb inside which lit up when the umbrella was opened, proposed that the FIF should market his invention and retain 10 per cent from the proceeds. This letter, and the anonymous cheque, were the only spontaneous responses to the appeal. A few writers made promises when individually approached, but in fact only Aldous Huxley, Stephen Spender and Budd Schulberg lived up to their promises of financial help.

What kept the FIF going nevertheless was an ironic twist of fate. To get the venture started, I had assigned to the FIF, as my own contribution, all future royalties derived from the forthcoming Broadway stage production of *Darkness at Noon*. I disliked the play, which I considered to be verging on melo-drama and even started a lawsuit (which I lost) to regain control over its contents from the dramatizer, Sidney Kingsley. Yet the Broadway production turned out to be a great success, ran for eighteen months and brought the FIF some $40,000 – about the same sum that I had paid for the island, which at that time amounted to a modest fortune. I ought to mention, however, that when I made the assignment, I could not foresee how much my royalties would amount to. Anyway, the play provided 90 per cent of the FIF's budget throughout its existence, and enabled it to provide constructive help for a number of refugee writers at a critical period of their lives.

After a couple of years, however, the FIF had bitten off an inadmissibly large amount of my working time, and in 1952 I handed over the administration of the fund to the International PEN Club. But David Carver, who succeeded Herman Ould as the secretary of PEN, had second thoughts: by helping only refugees from across the Iron Curtain, and not from other dictatorial regimes – from Latin America for instance – the PEN would lay itself open to accusations of political bias. So the PEN, in 1956, transferred what was left of the fund to the Congress for Cultural Freedom.

This gives another ironic twist to the story, for the Congress for Cultural Freedom was at that time financed by the Central Intelligence Agency – presumably because the American government had no other established route for channelling funds to deserving cultural institutions in Europe – such as, for instance, the magazine *Encounter*. Thus while Communists and fellow-travellers insinuated that I was 'on the payroll of the CIA', the opposite was actually true: my hard-earned royalties from the stage version of *Darkness at Noon* went, via the Fund for Intellectual Freedom, to the Congress for Cultural Freedom and thus indirectly benefited the Central Intelligence Agency. It gives one a nice, smug feeling to know that – to use the language of my ill-wishers – the CIA was on my 'payroll' and not the other way round.

6

Life on the Island

by C.K.

I

When, at the end of September 1950, Arthur went to New York, he did not know how long he would be away. Mamaine was going to stay in London with Celia and join him later. I decided, sadly, to go to London too and find another job. Verte Rive and the dogs were to be looked after by Maxim and Anna.

When Arthur left, I existed somehow. In the morning I got up; at night I went to bed and cared not whether I slept or did not sleep. I was conscious only of a pain in my heart which seemed to radiate to my lungs, stomach and liver. Could a heartache be experienced not only in a figurative sense but literally as well? After a while, a boil appeared under my arm. I took the Métro to the American Hospital at Neuilly to have it lanced. The tiny scar reminds me of my sickness of the heart.

On arriving in London I found myself a job and a place to live. The latter was a little mews house behind Sloane Street, which I shared with two other girls.

The job was as assistant secretary to Sidney Bernstein, chairman of the Granada group. I took the job on the advice of Mamaine. I had had supper with her at 3 Stewart's Grove, the enchanting little house which belonged to Celia. Mamaine knew Sidney Bernstein who, she said, was charming. Because of the link between him and Mamaine and Arthur, I accepted the job.

The office was in Granada House overlooking Golden

Square. Sidney Bernstein had an engaging, informal manner and an untiring, restless energy, and working for him was great fun. Although I heard rumours of his quick temper and of the ensuing rows that rocked the building, I myself never came in for any displays of it. When his chief secretary was away on holiday I had to take over; in spite of my awful blunders, he was patient and good-humoured.

In November Mamaine came to see our little mews house. Arthur, she said, had just bought a whole island in the Delaware river with a farmhouse on it. Although I had wondered whether I would ever see him again, this news depressed me; now he had his island he would never come back to Europe. At the end of December Mamaine left, too, to join Arthur.

On a dreary morning in February, as I was leaving home to go to work, I found a letter addressed to me on the hall carpet. It had an American stamp and as I hurried to the bus stop I opened it and read:

This letter will be a big surprise. Mamaine and I have made up our minds to ask you whether you would like to come over and stay with us until we go back to Europe which, if all goes well, should be some time in April.

Of course this offer is not entirely unselfish. Out here where we live it is as impossible to find an efficient and nice secretary as in Fontaine-le-Port. I have now got seriously going on the autobiography and with your help I could have most of it done in a couple of months by dictating straight into shorthand. This being a non-fiction book it could be done the same way as letters and political pamphlets, but there is nobody else whom I am so accustomed to working with.

There followed a few paragraphs about the technicalities of the journey, air ticket, and so on, and it ended: 'Well I told you this would be a surprising letter. We very much hope that you will like the idea and that, as work is pressing, you will arrive yesterday.'

That evening I replied:

Dear Mamaine and Arthur,

This is all too wonderful for words. I JUST SIMPLY CAN'T BELIEVE IT! I have been so excited ever since I received your letter this morning and leaping round the streets like a mad thing – no wonder I notice people looking at me queerly! But, apart from my job, I shall try not to be a bother to you.

I realise that the sooner I come the sooner you will be able to get on with the book, so I am really getting down to things in a hurry. I went at lunch-time today to the Consulate to find out what I need. . . .

There were a lot of things to do and it took ten days to get my visitor's visa. At the American Consulate they looked solemn when I explained that the purpose of my journey was to work for Arthur Koestler and I had to swear that I was neither a Communist nor a Fascist. I would have sworn to anything.

Never having flown before, I was filled with excitement. Whenever I took a bus during those ten hectic days, I would go upstairs and sit right at the front. High above the street, I would look down on the cars and people below me; in a sort of daydream, I imagined that I was on a plane as the bus slowly moved along the street. Looking back on that childish game, it occurs to me that it was the source of a recurrent nightmare which plagues me: I am a passenger in a plane which has got out of control; it roars along a busy street, just above the ground, and the tall buildings on either side of it whizz frighteningly by.

The journey by air took twelve hours and I arrived at New York in the early morning. I had only a glimpse of the city as the taxi took me to Pennsylvania Station. The sirens of ambulances and police cars echoed with an eerie, hollow sound among the skyscrapers. At the station I took a train to Trenton, New Jersey. I had already had breakfast and lunch on the plane, but I now tucked into a second breakfast, my first American meal. The boiled egg had been removed from its shell and was served in a glass and there were strange things called corn cakes. As we got into the country, the long, brown, wintry grass beside the railway track reminded me of South Africa.

Life on the Island – C.K.

Arthur was at Trenton Station to meet me. I was struck by how foreign his accent sounded. Had I never noticed or forgotten it? I had not seen him for such a very long time, more than five months. To my surprise he used the short American 'a', though it sounded strangely un-American. He was wearing a brown leather jacket of the kind that motorbike riders wore. He had a black Cadillac convertible which looked streamlined and graceful compared to his old black Citroën. There were electrical switches to open the windows and to lower the hood. There were gadgets to do everything, he said, except to make mayonnaise.

It took threequarters of an hour to drive to the island. On the way, Arthur complained of the inefficiency of Americans. I was astonished. Surely Americans did everything better than anyone else in the world. That was a fallacy, I was informed. They were hopeless and he had come up against this in every field, from builders to ordering furniture and electric lamps.

We crossed a little canal. It was a perfect day, the sky cloudless. The river came into view, the current carrying it along its shallow, stony bed. You could not do any boating, nor swim in it, Arthur said. The narrow tract of land between the canal and the river was his, too. He made a right-hand turn on to a steel suspension bridge. It was only just wide enough for the car; the wooden blocks on the bridge made a terrible racket as the car drove over them. The bridge spanned an arm of the river and now we were on the island.

The Pennsylvania Dutch house, built about 1824, was of white weatherboarding. Verandahs ran along two sides of it and lawns sloped down to the river. A long straight alley led from the house, which was at one end of the island, to the far side, which was wooded. There were a barn and numerous farm buildings. In the spring, the fruit trees blossomed and there was dogwood everywhere, with its pretty, pale, single flowers. The house was built on three floors. The top floor, under the gable, was Arthur's domain and consisted of a bedroom, bathroom and his study. As in Verte Rive, his desk was under the windows, which overlooked the river.

When I arrived, Mamaine was in bed with bronchitis. On the floor beside her bed lay Nellie, a young St Bernard – a 'calf', Arthur called her. She barked ferociously at the stranger. Arthur and Mamaine had found her at a local lost dogs' home. She had been rescued from a house whose owners had simply packed up and departed, leaving Nellie, her mother and the rest of the litter alone, without food. Nellie was the only survivor. It was a typically American story, Arthur said.

In a saucepan in the kitchen was a stew, put together by Arthur; it was an inspired concoction, well laced with wine and brandy. The daily had not turned up, he said; her car had broken down. It was normal for dailies to have cars out here, he told me, and just proved how affluent the country was.

On that first day on the island Arthur taught me how to make an Old-Fashioned. It was essential for me to know this, I was told, and as he mixed the drink he glanced at me now and then to see if it had sunk in.

2

Arthur now began to dictate to me his autobiography. At the beginning it had no title; it was only much later that he called it *Arrow in the Blue*. He started with the chapter called 'The Koestler Saga', whose first paragraph reads: 'The family tree of the Koestlers starts with my grandfather Leopold and ends with me.'

Mamaine said Arthur was such a complex character that she did not know how he could write an autobiography which would bear a true, yet believable, resemblance to him.

He dictated for about two hours in the morning and for two to four hours in the afternoon from about four o'clock. I sat curled up in an armchair beside his desk, while he paced up and down the room. He never dictated fast and sometimes there were long silences; but I could have sat there for ever. I tried to be like Arlova, Rubashov's secretary. When I read *Darkness at Noon* in the summer of 1949, I decided that she was the kind of secretary Arthur wanted. She never spoke, never reacted in a distracting way:

It was nearly a month before he first spoke to her in a conversational tone. He was tired by dictating and walking up and down, and suddenly became aware of the silence in the room. 'Why do you never say anything, Comrade Arlova?' he asked, and sat down in the comfortable chair behind his writing desk.

'If you like,' she answered in her sleepy voice, 'I will always repeat the last word of the sentence.'

. . . Sometimes he added sarcastic commentaries to what he was dictating; then she stopped writing and waited, pencil in hand, until he had finished; but she never smiled at his sarcasms and Rubashov never discovered what she thought of them. . . .

It is awful to tear these sentences out of their context, but they illustrate what I was trying to be. I only wished that I was wearing an embroidered Russian blouse like hers.

The sitting room on the island gave on to the solarium. It was a large room with windows along all three walls and furnished with Mexican wickerwork tables and chairs and chests; the floor was covered with rush matting. This was where I typed. Sometimes I was interrupted by a scratching sound by a window: Miss Nellie – she was no longer called simply Nellie; Arthur said she was too dignified for that – was desperately trying to attract my attention. She gazed at me wistfully, hoping I would let her in. One of her brown eyes had a slight cast in it and this gave her an added appeal. However, Arthur had said that Miss Nellie was to be an outdoor dog and she was only allowed in in the evening after work. He had originally asked Mamaine if she would bring Sabby over from Verte Rive; but she could not bring him to England because of the quarantine regulations.

Mamaine had a music room on the ground floor, well away from everyone else so that she could practise in peace. But as yet she had no piano and the room was empty. In Verte Rive, her grand piano was in the sitting room and she would often spend her afternoons playing.

As always, there were many letters to type and Arthur was also revising the French and German translations of *The Age of Longing*. In a letter to his German publisher he wrote:

I suppose you want my frank opinion. The translator has done an honest job. But the style is old-fashioned, *langathmig,* verbose and lacking in crispness. . . . Furthermore, the translator apparently hasn't noticed that in the original Nikitin [the young Soviet Russian] speaks a peculiar, stilted and un-idiomatic language, not only because he's a foreigner but also because of his peculiar conditioning. In the German text Nikitin's talk is smooth and fluent. This would kill the individuality of the character.

Here is another letter on the same subject, written to Melvin J. Lasky, editor of the German literary magazine, *Der Monat:**

I have received the June edition of *Der Monat.* Will you *please* not omit in future to mention that the extracts from my novel were translated from the English, as many German readers assume that I still write in German and as it is very unfair to make an author responsible for the translator's style – regardless of the quality of the translation. I have made this request repeatedly and am furious. . . .

Mel Lasky replies to this blast:

You must realise that our readers are quite aware that you are an English writer and the German texts are translations. If we keep on repeating and insisting on it (and we *will,* if you care to have it that way) there may be some who think we protesteth too much.

Sidney Kingsley's dramatization of *Darkness at Noon* had opened on Broadway at the beginning of January. It was 'apparently a great success', Arthur said in a letter to his French publisher, Robert Calmann-Lévy. 'The opening night was a gathering of all New York celebrities including the Duke and Duchess of Windsor and excluding myself.' He and Mamaine saw it later in the month. Sometimes people would ask Arthur what he thought of it and he would sweep the subject impatiently aside, a look of distaste on his face.

In March Arthur and Mamaine went to a dinner party in New York and Arthur got a ticket for me to see the play. I tried to look at it with an unprejudiced eye, but could not help being put off by the glossy, Hollywood-type love scenes. However, the critics loved it; it won the New York Drama Critics' Circle Award.

---

* He left *Der Monat* in 1958 to become editor of *Encounter.*

By the end of March Arthur had dictated to me about 40,000 words of his autobiography.

In chapter 9, 'Portrait of the Author at Sixteen', I learned that Arthur suffered from timidity. Whilst feeling full of sympathy for this predicament, with which I too was cursed, it was an astonishing revelation. He was so natural, always said what he meant, was so forthright – could such a change for the better take place in me too? I felt pessimistic about it.

I particularly remember a passage he dictated to me as he walked back and forth across the room: 'Some twenty years later a shrewd Comintern agent said to me: "We all have inferiority complexes of various sizes, but yours isn't a complex – it's a cathedral." ' As he finished the sentence he swung round to study my reaction with an amused smile. Scribbling away, I gave a noncommittal smile at my notebook in return. What could he mean? I wondered to myself. An inferiority complex like a cathedral? He must be referring to something rare and strange, only to be found in psychology textbooks, some frightfully complicated phenomenon. Many years passed before the true meaning of the passage dawned on me. It was perfectly simple and straightforward. Somehow I had miraculously managed to turn a blind eye towards this side of him.

Perhaps because of the absence of self-pity in describing the agonies of his childhood, it seemed to me that Arthur had placed his youthful self on a dissecting board, where it became the object of a scrutiny which was both curious and dispassionate. Thus the young Koestler seemed to become a separate entity who was not really connected with the real Arthur I saw. I felt a warmth for this slightly comical young Koestler and though we often used to laugh at him, my laughter was affectionate. In that chapter 9 Arthur summed him up:

Adolescence is a kind of emotional seasickness. Both are funny, but only in retrospect. The youth of sixteen that I was, with the plastered-down hair, and the fatuous smirk, at once arrogant and sheepish, was emotionally seasick: greedy for pleasure, haunted by guilt, torn between feelings of inferiority and superiority, between the need for contemplative solitude and the frustrated urge for gregariousness and play. . . .

3

As Arthur intended to spend part of the year in America, a private Bill had to be introduced in Congress to give him, as an ex-Communist, the right to a permanent US visa. He had hoped that the Bill would be passed by April and that he and Mamaine would be able to return to Verte Rive for the summer; but it dragged on and on.

Bernard Berenson wrote to Mamaine from Ischia urging them 'not to remain in America'. 'Arthur's books will dry up,' he said, and 'he will find no subject-matter for his gifts.' Arthur wrote to him:

Mamaine showed me your letter to her. I understand only too well your warning about the dangers for a writer to live in this country. But Europe today has an equally stultifying effect of a different kind. Just look at the stuff which French novelists have been turning out during the last few years. . . . Before we left I had a feeling of near-suffocation.

Our plan is to live for seven or eight months every year over here and for four or five months in Europe. I don't think any political novelist can have a balanced view of our time if he doesn't live in both realities, the American and the European. So we are going to try this formula. . . .

Mamaine had many good friends in America and there was, as always, somebody who was hopelessly in love with her. But she was pining to return to Europe. Beside her place at the breakfast table was a jar of Cooper's Oxford marmalade – a symbol of her longing for home, I used to think.

Arthur and Mamaine had to spend a night in Washington and I was taken along too to see the capital. On the train Mamaine said she was looking forward to old age and to the peaceful and happy time she and Arthur would have together. The picture this conjured up of Arthur and Mamaine grey-haired, stooped, wrinkled, made me collapse with the giggles.

Mamaine said she did not particularly want to become a mother, but she longed to be a grandmother.

In Washington the trees which lined the streets were covered with blossom. I travelled in a bus which had piped music on it and spent a happy evening seeing the film of *The Tales of Hoffmann*.

At the end of March, Cornelius Ryan came to the island to see Arthur. He was going to edit a special issue of *Collier's Magazine* to be called 'Preview of the War We Do Not Want'. The contributors to this special issue were to write about life in 1961 – a decade hence – just after the end of the Third World War. Arthur's imagination was caught by the project and he agreed to be one of the contributors. He called his piece 'The Shadow of a Tree'. As he dictated it, I was plunged into a world of postwar Russia 1961, described in diary form which made it come intensely alive. In the diary entry 'Kharkov, July 5th (Election Day)' he listed twelve 'political parties' which competed in the elections to the Kharkov Municipal Council – the first free elections since 1917'. He went on:

The remaining 'independent candidates' – cranks, religious sectarians and world reformers – who, since the liberation, are sprouting like mushrooms after rain, might be classed as 'religious and miscellaneous'. They included:

The Pupils of Tolstoy (a pacifist and vegetarian group, rejecting religious dogmatism).

The Theocrats (followers of the Orthodox church, who hold that Russia should be ruled by the Patriarch Sergei).

The 'Old Believers' (a traditionalist sect of religious zealots).

The Servants of God (who refuse to have family names).

The Doukhobor (who refuse to wear clothes).

The Starosti (who preach and sometimes practise self-castration, because mankind is evil and should be brought to an end).

The Esperantists (who hold that introduction of a universal language would solve all problems).

The Pavlovites (who hold that the whole of mankind should be made to have uniform opinions through controlled reconditioning of their reflexes by Professor Pavlov's famous method of training dogs).

The Barankavitzi (have never been able to find out what they want). The remaining party, called *World Redeemers,* was founded by an escaped inmate of a mental home, who started raving and had to be locked up on the night before the elections.

Vast expanses of lawns had to be mowed. Arthur did this with a machine which he sat on. After the grass was mowed he had to rake it. It was great fun working away in the hot sun and we soon acquired healthy-looking tans. In bed at night I felt less healthy as I tried to keep the hayfever at bay; it was a bore, but it certainly would not keep me away from such pleasures in life as grass-raking.

Arthur had wanted to get a couple to do the housework and take care of the garden, but as he was unable to transfer money from England to America, and the money from the Broadway production of *Darkness at Noon* went to the FIF, he was rather broke and the couple had to be shelved for the time being.

Giant weeds, surging with life and vigour, had suffocated the rhododendrons in a long bed which bordered the drive. Arthur was furious when he saw the devastation. How could Mamaine allow such a thing to happen – the flowers were her domain? He brooded about it and there was no way of placating him. His mood was spoilt and, once spoilt, could not be changed. Later I saw Mamaine weeding a rose bed, the soil harsh and unyielding. To get anywhere needed a lot of strength. She gave an impatient tug at a weed in a fit of exasperation which seemed to express her frustration at living in a land so alien to her.

I was in for it too. After lunch one day I was brushing Miss Nellie outside the back door. Vain as a film star, Miss Nellie loved being brushed. Her coat was long and flowing and she had a pretty, feminine head. Suddenly Arthur appeared at the back door. 'What on earth are you up to?' he cried. Miss Nellie, pleased with her appearance, pranced about, flaunting her beauty. 'I've been yelling you for half an hour,' he said as he looked at me accusingly. For an awful moment I took his statement literally; but no, I realized with relief, he would never have the patience to yell for 'half an hour'. Filled with guilt at having upset him, I hurried back to work.

The sitting room carpet was pale blue and covered the entire floor. The sofa was also in pale blue and had been chosen by Arthur, though Mamaine had wanted a dark blue one. Arthur's efforts at redecorating his study in Verte Rive had been less successful. He was fond of stripes, checks, pentagons and hexagons; patterns with flowers on them, unless fairly geometrical, he called '*jeune fille*'. He had the walls of his study in Verte Rive papered with pale blue and white stripes and his divan covered in a material of dark blue and white stripes. The effect was one of prison bars; though anything but restful, it was at least Koestlerian.

He wanted to have a wooden bench made for a niche under the stairs in the sitting room. Fortunately he found an old carpenter who took a pride in his work. Together, with yardstick and pencil and paper, they worked out how it was to be done. The carpenter seemed astonished at Arthur's knowledge of his craft.

When the cooker broke down, an electrician was called in to repair it. Almost immediately after he left it blew up in a sheet of flames and Arthur had to set to and mend it himself. He spent a happy afternoon surrounded by spanners, screwdrivers and insulating tape, and like magic it worked again. Furthermore, he had had a valid excuse to take time off from writing.

On a weekend in April we took the train to Boston, where Arthur and Mamaine were going to stay with Arthur J. Schlesinger Jr and his wife.

At Trenton we got into a carriage which was not divided into compartments as on English trains. It was fairly empty and we found some seats which were away from the other passengers. On the journey Arthur examined the specimens of American wildlife in our carriage. Not a single person was reading, he exclaimed, surprised, nor was anyone looking out of the window at the landscape. I gazed around: some passengers looked bored, others were wrapped up in their own

private worries. I leaned forward to tell Arthur and Mamaine
something and began to talk softly.

'Don't whisper!' said Arthur in what I thought was an
incredibly loud voice. Whispering carried much farther than
speaking in a normal voice 'as I am doing now', he explained;
besides, it attracted attention. He had learned this in his
Communist Party days. I had noticed that when he was in a
restaurant or some other public place, he would sometimes
turn round and have a good look over his shoulder before he
spoke.

The Schlesingers lived in Cambridge, Massachusetts, and I
was put up at a nearby hotel for the weekend. Their house
was large and comfortable, with a slightly shabby, donnish
air. That night there was a dinner party and ten or twelve
people sat round the dining-room table. A lively discussion
was going on at Arthur's end. I tried to hear what he was
saying, but the hum of conversation made it impossible; too
far away to catch any of his scintillating sparks, I shivered in
the outer darkness. I liked my sympathetic neighbour though.
Handsome, with expressive eyes, he must have been very
dashing when young, I thought. His name was Thornton
Wilder.

The following day, the Schlesingers took a party of friends
to a restaurant for lunch. This entailed a drive of thirty miles
there and thirty miles back – which meant nothing to Americans, Arthur said; it was considered 'nearby'. Mary McCarthy
and her husband offered me a lift. The three of us sat on the
front seat, American style. The thought of driving thirty miles
with this formidable bluestocking appalled me; if only I could
sit in the back of the car and say nothing. Contrary to expectation, I enjoyed every minute of it; indeed I was sorry when
the journey ended. She had dark Celtic looks and took a
passionate interest in everything. She was curious about me
and asked questions, but was kind. Years later, in a review of
one of her books, she was dubbed a 'beskirted Koestler' (probably by Philip Toynbee). Perhaps that is why I liked her so
much.

★　★　★

Miss Nellie was growing up and had reached the rebellious adolescent stage. I looked out of the kitchen window as I was getting breakfast and there she was on the lawn with my nightdress in her mouth. I had hung it out on the washing line and that huge calf had torn it down. Furious, I chased after her. She trotted around, her neck proudly arched, halting now and then to give the nightdress a vigorous shake. After I had retrieved it and grimly noted the enormous hole in it, I decided she must be punished and gave her a hard whack on her rump. That'll teach her, I thought, but Miss Nellie appeared quite unmoved. Apparently I had not put enough effort into it, so I had another go. She was delighted; this was a new and exciting game and she was all for it, bounding around and laughing at me, quite unrepentant. I had to give it up.

Several times a week I bicycled into our village, Stockton, to post the letters. This meant crossing over three bridges. Once I had got off the island I began to feel I was in America. I rode along the little Delaware Canal, which was in Pennsylvania, crossed its bridge and then the main bridge over the Delaware river into Stockton, which was in New Jersey. A single-track railway line passed through Stockton; there were no barriers between it and the street – when the little train wended its way through the village its hooter would give out a melodious and romantic sound. On the way home, I stopped at Mary's Diner for a chocolate ice-cream soda.

Sometimes we went to Mary's Diner for a sandwich lunch. Arthur enjoyed these outings like a schoolboy playing truant, albeit with a guilty smile, and he liked to chat with the owner, the cosy Mary. Mamaine, though she gamely participated in the fun, was snooty about Mary's Diner; such lowbrow forms of entertainment were not for her and she would appear a little sulky – which only enhanced her looks.

Once when we were in the garden, Mamaine told me about her first meeting with Arthur in 1943. She was going to a party and someone had said that Arthur Koestler would be there. Mamaine groaned: 'Not *another* Central European intellectual,' she said. At the party Arthur had stared at her all evening until they were introduced.

Frequent visitors to the island were Johnnie von Neumann, the mathematician, and his wife Klara. Both were Hungarian and lived in nearby Princeton. Von Neumann was short and dark, with a round face and round, dark eyes, a warm-hearted manner, and a mind which seemed to race ahead in leaps and bounds. Listening to him and Arthur talking, I realized with surprise that I had understood next to nothing of a conversation which had lasted all evening in my native tongue. The exception was a spooky science-fiction story which Arthur told about an underground train which had set off from one station but had never reached its destination; it had got lost in the vast underground system and, together with its passengers, had never been found again. The point of the story, I learned later, was something to do with topology.

While we were eating dinner, I went into the kitchen for a minute and to my horror found Miss Nellie devouring the remains of a chicken which she had dragged off the kitchen table. I salvaged what was left of it. Since it was futile to try and spank her, I gave her a thorough scolding. Well, she won't do that again, I thought, as I left the room. But when I returned later, the criminal had removed a whole, uneaten chicken from the table and was wolfing it down. When I told Arthur and Mamaine what she had done, Arthur found it terribly funny. He doted on her.

In May I had my twenty-fourth birthday. We were having dinner in the kitchen when I broke the news. Twenty-four! Arthur seemed horrified; he had no idea I was so old. He could not think that I was still the same age as I had been two years ago when I first came to work for him; it seemed more likely that he had forgotten anything as irrelevant as my age.

Twenty-four did seem old to me and I was pleased. But it bothered me that I was often taken for a teenager, or even a schoolgirl. I longed to be thirty-five!

The heat on the island became unbearable. It was not a dry heat, but close, steamy, jungle-like. Arthur's study under the roof was like an oven. He took off his shirt as he paced up and down the room, working on the book. Occasionally he vanished to the bathroom to dip his head in a basin of cold water.

At night my hayfever kept me awake and during the day the hayfever pills made me sleepy. One day as Arthur dictated, walking back and forth, I yielded to the temptation of closing my eyes when his back was turned, quickly opening them when he turned round again. After a few minutes he looked at me and said in a quiet, laconic voice: 'You know, to dictate one's autobiography to someone who is falling asleep is rather putting off.' I was shattered. Black with guilt, I mumbled something like, 'I promise I won't do it again,' but I cannot swear that I kept my promise.

American guests never went for walks to the far end of the island for fear of the poison ivy and poison oak. Not being natives, we were still immune. Like Mamaine, Arthur began to pine for Europe. Whilst driving in New Jersey he often remarked on the dull, hazy colours of the countryside, which lacked the clarity of colour to be found in Europe. The whole American continent ought to be closed down, he would say; it was not fit for humans because the mountain ranges ran from north to south, causing climatic extremes, whereas in Europe they ran from east to west.

Although the private Bill had not yet been passed, we were able to leave for France at the end of June. Miss Nellie was being looked after by Cornelius Ryan and his wife, who spent the summer on the island. She watched us mournfully as we got into the car with our luggage. Doped with hayfever pills I never said goodbye to her properly, which still makes me feel sorry. She must have the last word in this chapter. Here is her letter, dictated by Arthur, to Nancy Hart, the wife of Arthur's editor at Macmillans:

I have been instructed by Miss Nellie to thank you for your refined gift. Pressure of work prevents her from thanking all her admirers personally. Rumours that her eagerly awaited book 'How to be an Author's Dog' is being dramatised by Mr Sidney Kingsley, are premature.

Yours truly,
Secretary to Miss Nellie

Part Two 1951-1956

by Cynthia Koestler

7

End of a Marriage

I

When we arrived in London, Arthur and Mamaine gave me an elegant grey Revelation suitcase. I had observed Arthur giving my battered old suitcase a rather pained look, but I had taken no notice. It seemed to me that a suitcase was a suitcase, and not a matter of aesthetics.

Soon I was living in Paris again and travelling back and forth to Verte Rive. I was no longer staying with Madame de Foutaise. In the spring of 1950 I had found a much nicer and cheaper room in the 16ième arrondissement in the apartment of Madame Hussenot de Senonge and on my return to Paris from America it was waiting for me. It was spacious and included a *cabinet de toilette,* though there was no hot water. The hot water system of the apartment had broken down during the war and Madame Hussenot, a rich old widow, was too mean to have it repaired; besides, she needed the bath to keep her hats in.

No sooner had Arthur and Mamaine arrived at Verte Rive than Arthur's mother came to stay for nine days. The following day (5 July 1951) Arthur recorded in his diary: 'Decide not to sell Verte Rive. Greatly relieved.' And on the 6th: 'Back to work.' Over the next three days every dinner engagement jotted down in his little Hermès diary is described as 'depressing' or 'even more depressing'. After a 'depressing' dinner in Paris on 9 July, a walk along the Boulevard Miche is despairingly described as 'more depressing'. And on 12 July the entry runs : 'Very depressed. Retreat?' That dreaded word 'retreat' crept ominously into the conversation every now and then. Like Leontiev in *The Age of Longing,* he suffered from a floating anxiety which would attach itself to a worry, whether major or minor, and this in turn might lead to an obsession. If he was obsessed by something trivial, one felt a regret for the waste of so much passion and time; but more often than not what had seemed outwardly trivial acquired an extra dimension which he had presumably sensed from the beginning.

On 13 July Mamaine went to London to have a medical check-up and spend some time with her twin and all her friends. Whilst on the island Arthur had taken her to the Johns Hopkins Medical Center for two days for tests, but the result had been disappointing as the doctors were unable to do anything about her asthma. She never seemed to put on any weight; Arthur would urge her to eat more, and she tried to comply just to please him.

Soon after her arrival in London, she wrote to say she had booked passages for five on the *Ile de France,* arriving in New York on 1 October. Anna, Maxim and I were to return with Arthur and Mamaine to the island, and Verte Rive was to be let during our absence. Anna's reaction to this new plan was one of polite reserve, but Maxim was as excited as a child – and so was I. I had childhood memories of life on board ship, having travelled eight times between South Africa and England. Arthur and Mamaine did not seem to relish the prospect of the journey by boat; on his first visit to the USA in 1948 Arthur had sailed on the *Queen Elizabeth* and had felt bored and trapped. Sabby was coming too – his fare cost £18.

Orwell said that 'the chink in Koestler's armour is his hedonism'. True to form perhaps, Arthur spent the Quatorze Juillet in Paris and wrote to Mamaine: 'I had a lovely Fourteenth of July at the Vallons'.' The first chapter of *The Age of Longing* is called 'Bastille Day, 195 . . .' and its mood is infectious:

He saw the rocket thrust like a golden comet across the stars, then silently explode into a shower of green and purple drops. A Roman candle burst somewhere above the Louvre, a Bengal light on the

Pont Neuf set the Seine on fire with blue flames. From the quays below rose the enchanted murmur of the crowd. . . .

Six revolving Catherine wheels were spluttering fire of six different colours from the balustrades of the Pont Royal. Hydie stared at them, colour-drunk and dizzy. Then a girandole of some fifty sky-rockets, released at the same time, ripped into the dark tissue of the firmament; and as they exploded, an enormous luminous peacock tail spread from the mansards of the Cité up to the moon.

The crowd down on the quays yelled in a frenzy. The guests on the balcony gave out a long voluptuous a-ah; several young women screamed with delight like children on a roller coaster. . . .

The fireworks were nearing their end, and the Catherine wheels, gerbes and lances, the pastilles, maroons and girandoles were fighting a losing battle against the first fat drops of rain. As the rain gathered momentum, the flame and colour gradually went out of the sky and gave way first to a dusty afterglow, with a smell of gun-powder, then to the normal darkness of night. The last attraction was to be an elaborate pyrotechnical model of the Bastille going up in flames, to be replaced by a lettered design featuring the three words which expressed the creed of the Revolution. But it got only as far as LIB . . . ; the rest of the letters, together with fixed suns, fountains and waterfalls, were smothered by the cloudburst. . . .

2

Arthur had said that Kingsley's dramatization of *Darkness at Noon* had been a 'competent job'. In spite of blunders, he had raised no objections to the Broadway production. Europe was another matter. Producers in Germany, France, Italy and Scandinavia were all keen to show it, but Arthur was determined to do all he could to prevent the play from appearing in its original form. His major objections are too long and complicated to go into,* but here are a few of his minor criticisms:

Page 3: Rubashov is an important political prisoner whom the guard would not dare to touch.

Page 4: Although the stage directions say that he 'carried himself very erect and with a fierce authority', Rubashov's first lines are

---

* Some of his objections are stated in the Appendix – Editor.

plaintive and self-pitying. They would start him off on the wrong foot. . . .

Page 117: Rubashov's attempt to convert Gletkin at the last moment is too naive.

Page 117: Gletkin cannot of course take out a pistol. Investigator and executioner cannot be the same person even taking poetic licence into account. It is the kind of technically wrong symbol which, before a semi-hostile audience, as is to be expected in France for instance, would threaten to bring the house down with laughter.

He had never actually read the finished play before it was produced. The story had really begun in 1950, when Sidney Kingsley wrote to Arthur saying that he would like to write a dramatized version of *Darkness at Noon* for the theatre. Arthur greeted the idea with enthusiasm : Kingsley was well known; his *Men In White* had won the Pulitzer Prize; it would be fun to collaborate with him. In August 1950 Kingsley arrived in Paris, and I was roped in to be his secretary during his stay. His light blue eyes had a rather cold look. I liked his beautiful wife, the former film star, Madge Evans.

When I went out to Verte Rive I found Arthur taken up with ideas for the play. He had drafted out a whole scene, which was ready to be typed. Back in Paris at the Hôtel Prince de Galles, Kingsley was busy too. As I typed his version I wondered why he wanted to make a play out of *Darkness at Noon,* and whether, as an American, he would be able to convey the feeling of the book.

Perhaps Arthur felt the same. On 20 August he wrote to Kingsley, who was by then back in New York, that he had read his draft of the second and third acts and that 'the marathon dialogue between Rubashov and Gletkin and how to lead it up to a climax' seemed to him to be 'satisfactorily solved'. But he added:

A number of other scenes – particularly the scenes with Arlova and with Little Loewy – I regard according to your wish as rough drafts. They haven't got the language and atmosphere of that exclusive club; but as we have discussed this problem at length there is no point in saying more about it at this stage.

'There was plenty of work to be done when I arrived. In the morning I took down replies to letters — letters to publishers, to literary agents, to friends and to readers. In the afternoon I typed them.' Cynthia and Arthur at work at Fontaine-le-Port after she got the job as temporary part-time secretary in 1949

Cynthia's first day at work, Fontaine-le-Port, 1949. 'After lunch, we climbed into a large rowing boat and Mr Koestler rowed us across the river to the forest of Fontainebleau on the other side.' Facing Arthur are Daphne Henrion (left) and Cynthia

Mamaine and Arthur playing chess and *opposite,* having tea by the window, and entertaining the Labour MP R. H. S. Crossman and his wife Zita in 1947 — all at Bwlch Ocyn

When Cynthia joined the Koestlers in 1949, they were living at
Fontaine-le-Port on the Seine where the photos on these pages
were taken. (*Top*) Arthur with Mamaine working on *The Age of
Longing*. (*Above*) 'Arthur's Canadian canoe had a sail and he taught
himself to sail it with a book in one hand and the other on the
rudder' — and sometimes with his new secretary on board

Arthur with Sabby, 'a particularly fine, fawn-coloured boxer. . . .
Powerful and rather unruly, he was devoted to his master, who
was the only person able to control him'

Arthur writes of his 'feeling of disbelief in having in a few minutes become the ruler of an island kingdom . . . a mile long and half a mile wide at its widest point.' Island Farm was in the Delaware River in Pennsylvania, and he and Mamaine made it their American home, where Cynthia joined them. Here is a page from the auctioneer's brochure

'The new girlfriend was Daphne Hardy, a young sculptress who had won a travelling scholarship to Paris; she appears as "G" in *Scum of the Earth.*' This photo was probably taken shortly after their reunion in London in 1940

Pictured above is
steel suspension
this farm with

Sale No

R

SAT., O
A

Open fo
Sunday,
from 9

'A friend who plays second paddle and who shall be called "Crew" ' was how Arthur referred to Cynthia in his canoeing essay *Drifting on a River*. 'The canoe is of British make, costs around £35, and answers to the name of *Blue Arrow*'

Acre "Island Farm"

ONE OF THE MOST UNIQUE FARMS IN THE U.S.A.

In The Delaware River

4½ MILES NORTH OF NEW HOPE

In Heart of the Beautiful, Convenient, Art Colony Section of

Bucks County, Pa.

WILL BE SOLD AS 3 PARCELS OR AS AN ENTIRETY, AT

ABSOLUTE
AUCTION

WITHOUT LIMIT OR RESERVE • CLEAR OF MORTGAGES • POSSESSION

> PARCEL No. 1—"ISLAND FARM", 112 ACRES WITH BUILDINGS.
>
> PARCEL No. 2—COTTAGE WITH AN ACRE ON THE MAINLAND.
>
> PARCEL No. 3—14 ACRES BETWEEN RIVER AND CANAL.
>
> *Live Stock, Farm Equipment, Furnishings in Separate Lots.*

Louis Traiman
AUCTION COMPANY

1315 Walnut St., Philadelphia 7, Pa.—Kingsley 5-2238

950

The house on Montpelier
Square which gives this
book its title and, as *envoi,*
a comparatively recent
study of Arthur and
Cynthia (with David)
in their sitting room

Kingsley promised to hire technical advisers to help him with his difficulty in portraying the Communist mentality and mannerisms but, as Arthur said, 'nobody, however much intuition he possesses, can acquire within a few weeks the feeling for a very elusive yet inbred milieu by the Berlitz method, as it were.'

Before leaving New York in 1951 he consulted a solicitor. The conflict had grown out of hand and he was no longer able to cope with it. His lawyer advised going to arbitration and Arthur felt relieved: it would bring the matter to an end one way or the other.

Back at Verte Rive, as he sat at his desk one morning opening the mail, he came across a parcel. It was obviously what, in a family joke, we all referred to as the 'daily book'. At least one book seemed to arrive with each day's mail. On that morning the 'daily book' was *Darkness at Noon* – A Play by Sidney Kingsley Based on a Book by Arthur Koestler. Arthur proceeded to remove the dust jacket. He stared at the spine, caught his breath and bit his lip as he read: *Darkness at Noon* by Sidney Kingsley.

His 'child' had been wrested from him. Later Kingsley was to write:

. . . The *Darkness at Noon* Koestler refers to is a novel which is a decade old. The *Darkness at Noon* we are discussing here is a drama written by me a year-and-a-half ago which has *proven* itself, and not unworthily. As a dramatist, my horizon is the world. My plays are designed for the world. They have proven themselves in the world. This play will do likewise.

Arthur had a less inflated view of his own play, *Twilight Bar*. In a letter to a German producer, he tore it to pieces:

I have read Mr Braun's adaptation of *Twilight Bar*. I think Mr Braun has done a good job. I have no objection to the alterations which he made. *But* I feel that they do not go far enough to compensate for the weaknesses of the play. It is not modesty which makes me say so, but the fact that wherever the play was presented – in the United States, in Paris, Oslo, etc. – it was a complete failure.

As I said in my first letter, the characters are puppets and the Third Act where Utopia is realised is a terrible let-down of the public's expectations. . . . I believe, therefore, that it will save both you and me a certain disappointment if I propose that we drop the idea. The play was a mistake of mine. . . . It's hardly worth while to bother about it.

3

When *The Age of Longing* was published in France – under the title *Les Hommes Ont Soif* – Malraux was apparently upset about the resemblance of one of the characters to himself. Arthur got wind of this and wrote to him:

Vallon told me that you were away, otherwise I would have tried to get in touch with you. Of course there are some Malrauxesque elements in the composite picture of St. Hilaire; but according to all who have read it, these are the most sympathetic elements in the whole book. If it amuses you to re-read the passages in question, they are in the chapters 'Une Soirée chez M. Anatole', 'L'Ombre de Neanderthal' (a terribly bad chapter), and 'L'Enterrement de M. Anatole'.

Ceci dit . . . shall we try to contrive an amicable dinner? It is at least a fortnight since we have met. I'll ring you on Monday to see whether it can be arranged.

The theme of that 'terribly bad' chapter, 'The Shadow of Neanderthal', was one which was to haunt him for many years: the convening of a meeting of intellectuals to find ways and means of saving the West from an impending war. This theme took the centre of the stage in his next novel, *The Call Girls,* which he was to write twenty years later, though here the intellectuals came from the other culture.

As for the Malrauxesque character, he was

a dark, slim man . . . every limb of his body in dynamic movement. His face kept twitching in remarkable contortions, his arms and legs moved forward gawkily like those of an adolescent but at the same time with utmost energy, his head was thrust forward as if he were preparing to ram it into an enemy's belly. The people who were standing about in little groups gave way as he advanced and engaged in hushed comments behind his back. . . .

'It is Georges de St. Hilaire, the novelist–knight errant,' whispered Monsieur Anatole. 'We call him Saint Georges because he is always engaged in spearing some dragon, Fascist or Communist or whatever other monster happens to be at hand. But he is a very esoteric and highbrow knight errant; compared to him, Lawrence of Arabia was a flat-footed philistine. When he talks to you, you will understand only one phrase in ten, which need not disturb you as you won't have a chance to put a word in anyway; but those ten per cent are worth listening to.

In a later chapter, St Hilaire refers to the 'language of destiny': 'Destiny's challenge to man is always couched in simple and direct phrases . . .'. Arthur has always held a 'perhaps superstitious, but deep belief' in the language of destiny. It cast its spell on many events in his life, always leading to a change of course. In *Arrow in the Blue* he wrote:

When major and minor calamities crowd together in a short span of time, they seem to express a symbolic warning, as if some mute power were tugging at your sleeve. It is then up to you to decipher the meaning of the inchoate message. If you ignore it . . . you may have missed a chance to remake your life, having passed a potential turning point without noticing it. It is not an altogether naive superstition if one concedes that such series are often produced by unconscious arrangement; that the warning may have been issued by that 'he in me who is more me than myself'. Later on I discovered that André Malraux holds a similar superstition – or belief; he calls that tugging-at-the-sleeve by apparent coincidence '*le langage du destin*'.

4

The atmosphere at Verte Rive that summer was hardly tranquil or conducive to work. Passports had to be obtained for Anna and Maxim; we all needed US immigration visas. I rushed around Paris doing what I could at the American Consulate and at various French bureaucratic institutions, but Arthur still had to write letters to friends such as Budd Schulberg and to his American publishers, asking them to sponsor the visas for Anna, Maxim and me, in order to satisfy the demands of the American immigration authorities. The nightmare hanging over him was whether the private Bill granting him US residence would be passed in time. And of course there was still the Kingsley case. These were soul-destroying preoccupations, but writing and his passion for sailing on the river had a stabilizing effect.

Oddly enough, on his return to Verte Rive from the island he had reached the stage in the autobiography where he was transferred, as a foreign correspondent in the Middle East, to Paris. During the month of July, whilst living at Verte Rive, he wrote the chapters on his first year in Paris as a journalist at the age of twenty-four.

Sometimes he went up to Paris for a night. There are jottings in his little Hermès: 'Dinner Voltaire, bad wine'; 'lunch Vieux Paris; dinner Dominique, Engels in new Boite "Chaplaine" ', ending up in Les Halles. On the day after the latter outing (a Sunday) he noted : 'Sailing; at last a day alone.' And there was the usual constant flow of weekend guests. Before retiring to bed, he liked to take guests for a row on the river. Drifting on the water in the dark was blissfully peaceful; the ripples faintly reflected the lights from the windows of the house.

Another worry was money. He had failed to get permission from the Bank of England to transfer his money abroad. Thus he was hard up in the two countries where he had chosen to live – France and America – and well off in England. As a result, instead of being able to buy clothes in Paris or New York, poor Mamaine had to dress herself in the austere shops of London. Arthur, however, was quite blind to these feminine difficulties. When Mamaine wrote that 'it will be impossible to buy any decent clothes here, because they do not exist', his reaction was none too sympathetic:

P.S. Sorry about the clothes, but you really must try to get what you need in England as what you say about the currency regulations means a very radical tightening of belts.

He himself had had no difficulty in buying what he needed on his way through London at the end of June. At the bottom of a file called 'Lectures and Various 1951' lie two bills which tell the story of how he dealt with his shopping in one fell swoop. On 29 June he went to Simpsons of Piccadilly and spent £13.18s. on twelve pairs of socks, one handkerchief, three pairs of underpants, two shirts and one pair of flannels. Buying clothes was a bore and furthermore a waste of money, he felt, when it could be spent more enjoyably on dining out in a restaurant, which he looked upon as an 'investment'. I liked the sports clothes he wore at home, but his awful suits with their hideous bird's eye pattern (as can be seen in some photographs of him) made me shudder, uncritical though I seemed to be.

Mamaine was worried, feeling that the passages to New York should have been booked on a later boat. She wrote:

I do think it is a mistake as it leaves us only just over two months to get all the papers through. . . . Besides there is your Bill, and you will go frantic with worry if it hasn't gone right through by early September. I do think that by insisting on our going so early you are taking a serious risk of spoiling your last working weeks in Europe by worry. . . .

But Arthur was against any alteration of the bookings 'as I cannot go on postponing the Kingsley arbitration date without spoiling my case'.

In his diary he wrote: 'Liverish and melancholy', but on the next day: 'Excellent sailing; servants out; alone; high spirits.' Soon he was 'immersed in Rousseau', adding in a note of despair: 'mail, mail – more kidney'. Kidney was his joke name for Kingsley, a sort of abbreviation of Sidney Kingsley.*

Then he noted: 'Work slowing down; still, 45 pages this month. Kingsley suit gets on nerves, sultry, sleepless.'

When Mamaine heard about his sleeplessness she quickly wrote to him:

I am so sorry you have had all this worry about Kingsley. I have never known anything keep you awake for more than a minute once you are in bed, so I can see what an obsession you must have got about it. . . . I can't bear to think of you worrying so much about the whole thing. . . .

* See Appendix – Editor.

The obsession with the Kingsley affair led to a crisis in work and over the next five days he noted in his diary: 'Depressed' and 'work near standstill; canoeing; mood improved' and 'more canoeing, no work' and 'more Kingsley trouble; no work'.

However, on 5 August he wrote : 'Alone; work restarted on "portrait at 25" chapter'; and the next day: 'Alone; good progress on same chapter'. As in 'Portrait of the Author at Sixteen', which he wrote on the island, he once again pinned an earlier self on to the dissecting board for a detached examination. But this time he would not let me witness it. When I came out from Paris, he shut himself up in his study, muttering that he wouldn't need me as he could only write this part 'alone'. Feeling hurt, I found myself relegated to the Purgatory to get on with the filing.

Eventually I was given the handwritten pages to type. When I came to the part about falling in love, I understood how off-putting my presence in the room would have been. Though I was not jealous of past loves – they served rather to deepen the spell I was under – nevertheless the aggrieved feeling secretly lingered for a while, try as I might to banish it.

Letters and telegrams went to and fro between Mamaine and Arthur every other day, sometimes two a day. She had been to see her doctor who said that 'nobody could possibly imagine there was anything wrong with me. Indeed I am in wonderful health, better than ever since I can remember (wonders will never cease). Hope I can find some way of putting on weight.'

Arthur asked her to 'let me know presto' the result of tests she was having. In the meantime she had been to a ball:

I'm a bit tired as I got back at 3.30 from the Hultons' ball. . . . The ball was quite prodigious . . . the whole thing took place in the garden, there were swings, a roundabout, all sorts of pretty decorations and illuminations, a vast dance floor in an elaborately decorated marquee, two bars, and a nightclub – all in the garden. The result was enchanting to look at and quite fun, but only moderately enjoyable from my point of view, since for each person I saw whom I like I saw about twenty I don't like. . . .

After hearing the results of her medical examination, she wrote to say she had been advised to stick to a diet for about a year and not drink any wine or spirits. Rather wistfully she added : 'Although the prospects of a year without drink are sad indeed, I feel very cheered at the prospect of eventually becoming normal, horse-like and FAT.'

Arthur had promised his mother several autographed copies of *The Age of Longing* for her friends. As no spare copies were available at Verte Rive, he wrote to Margaret Stephens at A. D. Peters, his literary agent: 'Could you be an angel and fake my signature and send the copies to my mother?' Each copy was to be inscribed with the name of the recipient in the same phoney handwriting. Stevie obliged without turning a hair, and in her next letter, beneath her usual signature, were typed the words 'DEPARTMENT OF DECEPTION'.

A week after Mamaine had gone to stay with her twin in London, Celia went to Greece for three weeks. Mamaine wrote: 'I've more or less seen the last of her. So I'm depressed at the moment.'

As the summer wore on, she could not decide when to return to Verte Rive. It seemed she was torn in two directions. Towards the end of July she wrote:

I feel I ought to say when I am returning, instead of drifting along like this, but can't make up my mind about a date. . . . Still, I don't want to leave you alone. . . . So let me know how you feel. Celia gets back the 9th; would it be possible for me to stay till say the 11th so as to see her once more before another 9-month separation? The fact that I lent her my camera and could then get it back is an added inducement. . . .

And Arthur replied: 'By all means stay until the 11th, or longer if you are enjoying yourself.'
We were expecting a visit from Hamish Hamilton and his

family, en route for Italy. Mamaine ended one of her letters: 'Enclosed note for Cynthia about dinner for the Hamiltons, which please okay.' She instructed me to

fix with Anna the following menu for when the Hamiltons come to stay next Tuesday. Corn on the cob (which they like), steaks, veg. (I promised Jamie), cheese: chèvre and carré de l'est; ice from Soupeault if available or macédoine de fruits with rum and whipped cream with some rum in. If no corn is available yet, anywhere, the safest thing in my absence would be to make Maxim get some fish, either trout (which is probably too expensive) or sole. We gave them langoustines last time they were there, I remember.

Arthur was hoping that the Hamiltons could bring with them a typewriter which had been repaired in London and was now in my flat there, but Mamaine had to send a wire to say the typewriter had been left behind:

So sorry abt the typewriter: it was the fault of Cynthia's blasted room-mates, who said they'd be there at a certain time so I cd collect it and take it on to the Hamiltons, & weren't.

On 8 August Arthur wrote in his diary: 'House votes Bill.' He went up to Paris for a couple of days to celebrate. On 14 August Mamaine came home.

The following day, a Wednesday, I found Arthur in a black mood; he was on edge, as if every nerve in his skin were exposed and raw. The most trivial things upset him. In the middle of dictating letters, he flung open his study door and shouted irritably down the stairs at Mamaine. His complaints seemed quite unreasonable. Mamaine, the target of his irritability, looked pale and tense. How could he, I wondered; after all, Mamaine had only just got back. Painful as it was, I was sure it would blow over.

I spent the night there and the next day typed the remainder of the letters. When I had finished I took them to him for signing. As I opened the study door I saw Mamaine sitting with Arthur and he said: 'Leave us alone for a while – we're having a council of war.' Mamaine gave me a reassuring smile.

Arthur seemed no longer in an irritable mood. They were probably discussing financial matters, I thought.

A little later, when Mamaine had gone, Arthur called me in. He told me Mamaine and he were breaking up; she was leaving him. I was stunned. They were so close to each other – almost as if there was a blood tie. To think of Arthur without Mamaine, and Mamaine without Arthur seemed wholly unbelievable. As I tried to take it in, he told me he did not know yet whether he would return to America and whether he would take Anna and Maxim with him. He could not take me now.

A pessimist by nature, I had all the time had a funny feeling that the boat trip on the *Ile de France* and the idyllic life I would lead on the island were all too good to be true. As I left the room I met Mamaine in the doorway. Life would never be the same again without her there. Like a devoted dog, I was happiest when I was together with both of them. I tried to control my emotions and she too caught her breath.

Mamaine began her packing. She was leaving for London the following evening, only two days after she had come back. Arthur asked me to spend the night at Verte Rive. The thought of their last night together must have seemed unbearable and the presence of a third person might make it a little less painful. I retired early. Later, perhaps out of despair and hoping for some sort of comfort, they came into my room. I heard the door open and Arthur urging Mamaine to come in. Perhaps they had come to a dead end in their dialogue. They sat on the end of my bed in the darkness for a few minutes. They can scarcely have derived anything from my feeble monosyllabic replies; I felt helpless and inadequate.

The following morning we had a farewell drink at the bar in the dining room before I went off to catch the train back to Paris. I wondered how Mamaine could bear the thought of a day passing without knowing what Arthur's opinions were on this or that topic. I was so deeply dependent on him myself – what he thought of a book, a film, a new sensation – and his reactions always surprised and impressed me. But Mamaine seemed somehow liberated and more independent than I had ever seen her.   ★   ★   ★

In Arthur's Hermès diary for 15 August, there is one sentence: 'Mamaine breaks news she's decided to leave me.' The handwriting is barely recognizable, the generously rounded letters changed into a thin little scrawl which makes one sense the effort of putting the words on paper.

Four days later he wrote: 'At home. Misère.'

When I came out he dictated a letter to A. D. Peters:

The private matter about which I wrote to you is unfortunately final. Mamaine will explain it to you. I am now going to simplify my life. I don't want to sell the Island but I would like to let it for five years or so. . . .

I haven't decided yet whether I am going to live in America or England. I am going to keep Verte Rive as a summer holiday place. . . . But as a permanent resident I can only live in an Anglo-Saxon country, because otherwise I would lose my English again. . . . In London I could live in a flat for a while. . . . I felt that the competitive, commercialised atmosphere in the States – bestseller lists and all that – is very bad for a writer. On the other hand, of course, the staleness of the English literary scene is also rather depressing. So I am weighing the pros and cons . . . and would have liked your wise advice over a bottle of wine. You have got lots of experience about conditions propitious for writers at cross-roads. If it's too inconvenient for you to spend a day in Paris or here, I would probably come over. . . .

In the postscript he spoke of the burden of possessions: 'All this is not in my style. I always used to travel with one handy suitcase.'

We walked round the garden while he tried to sort out his plans. He was going to settle in England, he said. How ironical, I thought; Mamaine always hoped they would live in England. In his diary he wrote: 'Played canasta with Cynthia. Atrocious depression.'

A. D. Peters flew over from London and spent a couple of nights at Verte Rive. Though he looked the sort of Englishman who is rather a cold fish, he had a disarmingly warm-hearted nature.* His visit, Arthur wrote to him, 'was not only a boon

---

* In fact, he was not English at all, as Arthur was only to discover after his death.

from the point of view of clarifying my plans, but I thought also great fun.'

He would return to the island in order to arrange to let it, and the Kingsley arbitration case was looming. He had decided not to take Anna and Maxim with him. Unable to bear the disappointment that Maxim would feel at the sudden change of plans, Arthur found an answer to his feelings of guilt and responsibility towards the ménage. He wrote in his notebook on August 25: 'The obvious solution was to build them a house here. On Monday arranged this w Maitre Guitar and felt much relieved, the more so as the plot we visited is charming.'*

<h1 style="text-align:center">5</h1>

Arrow in the Blue was threequarters finished, but Arthur was not in the mood for writing. He spent much of his time in Paris and when at Verte Rive was occupied with the revision of the German translation of *The Age of Longing*, which was published under the awful title of *Gottes Thron Steht Lehr* (*God's Throne Stands Empty*). On 28 August he wrote to his German publisher:

I am afraid the revision . . . will take a few days longer than I thought. . . . Of course for somebody who once wrote in German, no translation of his work into German can be entirely satisfactory. I realise this and therefore did nothing to change the style. But there is a great number of errors in meaning. . . .

A week later he had to write again:

I am distressed about the necessity of making so many corrections. . . .

To give you an idea first of the political distortions in the translation: in the English text I refer to the 'Nordic industry and diligence' of the people in Paris; this is translated as 'germanische Tüchtigkeit'. I repeat, we are talking of the people of Paris.

In Chapter Five the negro speaker at the Rally, who in the original

---

* A note from A.K. suggests to C.K. that she should 'insert details and peasant building methods.' Alas! This was not done. – Editor.

text is a naive and rather pathetic figure, is turned into a vicious caricature by the translator's gratuitous addition of derogatory adjectives. . . . As the negro problem had politically a significance similar to that of the question of anti-semitism, you will understand what this distortion implies for my political reputation.

There are further political slip-ups on practically every page. The translator . . . frequently turns the meaning, no doubt by inadvertency, into its direct opposite.

Secondly, the style . . . What [he] did was not to render my text in his own language, but to improve upon it by the addition of colourful adjectives and embellishments in every single paragraph. . . . [To give] a few examples: 'in love' becomes 'von ganzem Herzen liebt' . . . the single word 'threat' becomes 'das Domokles Schwert der Folterung'. . . . There is hardly a phrase in the text to which the translator has not added some ornament of his own, thus altering the entire character of the book from one of economy to one of bombast.

This cannot be helped at this stage. I wish you to believe that I am trying to confine my corrections to a minimum, regarding both correct meaning and a decent style.

Sometimes, however, I found it necessary to supress even apparently harmless words. . . . The reason for this becomes only clear if you read the whole paragraph or page in both versions; then you will see how a passage written with deliberate restraint becomes changed in character and atmosphere by such additions and becomes an overstated and artificially dramatised passage instead. . . .

On the day before Arthur left Paris for London, we had arranged to meet on the terrace of a café in the Champs-Elysées so that he could give me last-minute instructions. It was strange to see him on the Right Bank, and in the Champs-Elysées of all places. His haunts were on the Rive Gauche, his favourite being the Café Flore. Next to the Flore was the Deux Magots, where the more staid intellectuals gathered, sipping their drinks and contemplating the church.

On his first evening in London Arthur took Mamaine out to dinner at the Etoile. Apparently he was still in London when I arrived, for his Hermès diary says '1-2 Cynthia' on 19 September. I must have typed the letter he wrote on that day to his German publishers: 'Enclosed further corrected proofs (pages 395-428).

'I hope that I shall be able to airmail you the remaining twenty-six pages either tomorrow or Saturday from New York. . . .'

Heartbroken as I had been the year before when he went off to America, I have no memory of my feelings on this occasion. Perhaps farewells and the black voids which followed them were becoming commonplace. At any rate, he intended to return to London very soon.

8

The Montpeliers

I was living again in the mews house behind Sloane Square which I shared with two other girls. 'As far as jobs go,' I wrote to Arthur, 'I have not been lucky. Sidney Bernstein promised me a job but nearly three weeks have passed and I've heard nothing from him.' I took a temporary job and spent my days 'typing out reams and reams of envelopes'. It was 'all very boring and sordid, but actually I don't mind it nearly as much as I did this time last year because at least one knows it's only for a short while.' My friends and I moved into a new flat in Montpelier Walk with three other girls. It soon became a horrible slum. All except one of my five flatmates were ex-debs. Having lived in a whirl of parties during their coming-out year, they were now neglected and an invitation to dinner caused quite a flutter. Some took jobs as models. The most sluttish deb spent her time pacing up and down the sitting room in a state of frustration. She is now a duke's paramour.

Sometimes I had lunch with Mamaine and once she came to lunch in our new flat. She had bought a house in Hasker Street, near Knightsbridge, and was busy making it habitable. She gave me news of Arthur and regaled me, talking very fast as was her habit, with more stories of the twins' extraordinary childhood and of the short time they had spent at school in their teens.

Mamaine had taken a job in the publishing firm of Derek Verschoyle, in which she spent most of her time reading books and writing reports on them; a lot of the books were in French or German.

'Today Derek asked me,' she wrote to Arthur, 'if I knew anybody who liked reading about FISH, so I said Yes I do, whereupon he produced a massive German work on the subject; I look forward to reading this!'

Here is an unforgettable glimpse of history – her account of the funeral of George VI:

We had a magnificent royal funeral, it was prachtvoll. I had a fine view of the procession from the roof of my office, in St James's St. The crown on the coffin sparkled with huge jewels, some of which Henry IV (or whoever it was) wore at Agincourt. Gazing at it in rapture through some field glasses belonging to the man sitting next to me, I almost missed the royal Dukes marching mournfully along behind the gun carriage, followed by the Kings. The latter mostly looked like old clothes men, & their marching was lamentable. Lu★ said afterwards the King of Denmark was the cause of the trouble for he would march faster than the other Kings, who had to make a series of spurts to keep up with him. The B.B.C. was in its element commenting on the funeral: 'the royal chauffeur is putting his foot on the royal pedal of the royal car', etc., in sepulchral tones. . . . It was odd to see the 4 Russian officers who took part; they looked I thought somewhat drab in their ill-fitting uniforms; but no worse than the Kings, only different. . . .

Perhaps her feelings at the time are reflected in the cruel light of this dream, which she described to Arthur:

Last night I dreamed I was travelling in a tram (I go to my Greek lessons in a tram) & beside me was an open coffin in which lay my own dying body; the conductor said, any objection if I finish it off, it's dying anyway, then I can nail down the coffin and throw it out? I said all right, go ahead, but I knew it would be pretty awful when he did, for though I would go on living I would have first to go through the anguish of dying. Don't you think this is rather a fine dream? Or is it just as bad as the rest?

I had a new job, working for the Huxley Group, whose organizing secretary was a nice young man called Glyn

---

★ Prince Louis of Hesse, a great friend of the twins.

Seaborn Jones.* The most important project in the group, which had been started by Julian Huxley, was to set up junior universities in centres such as London, Paris and New York for exceptionally intelligent children, since these bright children were either made to feel insecure in classes with older pupils or became bored, lazy and conceited in classes with children of their own age. Once a month, a meeting of Huxley's 'Idea-Systems Group' was held, at which I had to do the minutes; among those who attended the meetings were Denis Brogan, J. Bronowski and Barbara Wootton.

I often wrote to Arthur. Reading through those letters now, after thirty years, I had no idea that I was being such a pest. I was aware of how harassed he was and even wrote: 'You must have a thousand things on your mind.' Yet I urged him: 'If and when you write, please let me know how the Kidney affair is progressing'; 'How I wish I were on the Island; I miss it most terribly'; 'I do hope you'll send the autobiography to me to type out'; 'I would awfully much like a copy of the American edition of *The Age of Longing*'.

I was longing for the past – for the days when I had worked for him and for the thrilling moments when we happened to be alone. I could not face the fact that life would never be the same again.

2

On the island, Arthur had been working on *Arrow in the Blue*, spending his evenings with neighbours, who included Budd and Vicky Schulberg and Johnnie von Neumann and his wife. On the sixth day after his return he wrote in his Hermès diary: 'Work. 1st evening home.' But soon he was 'hedge-clipping, rubbish burning, etc.' After the summer the island was a jungle, though Cornelius Ryan and his wife had done all they could to keep the garden under control. At the beginning of October there was a heatwave. Arthur had just got back after a two-day visit to Washington and wrote: '80° in shade. Got really to work. Tree cutting.' Every day he made a note of

* He now appears on television programmes as a psychologist.

the evening temperature in the shade; on 5 October it was 86 degrees. The rubbish-burning continued as well as 'dustbin scrubbing; etc.' After scrubbing the dustbins he had guests for the evening: the von Neumanns and Herbert Read, who was visiting Princeton. 'Still a neutralist,' Arthur wrote, 'he so hates USA.' Herbert Read wrote to say that he was 'glad to have had a glimpse of you in your island home & would have loved to take a hand in keeping the jungle back.'

On the following day (Sunday) Arthur coped with the mail: '18 letters; evening storm, heat breaks, river road blocked.' Two days later he was bothered with a kidney stone which he described as 'very unpleasant'. The next day he was given morphia, felt euphoric, and had the telephone repaired; but during the night he wrote: 'more kidney stone'.* On the following day the morphia made him feel depressed 'but good work done'.

Over the next four days Arthur was in intermittent pain, went to Doylestown Hospital for tests and felt dopy with morphia. He nevertheless managed to do some shopping (he often wrote his shopping lists in his diary): 'valve, sponge, teapot, haircut, candles, oil, ball bearings.' On 18 October he got rid of the kidney stone and was 'back to work'.

During November, he worked on the last chapters of the book. 'Finished boring Zeppelin part – at last,' he wrote in the diary. The weather was 'hot, steamy and damp'. His Sunday routine was: 'Mail, diary, accounts, housework'. Among other friends, James Burnham† spent a weekend, accompanied by his wife, three children and a dog. Arthur received a bread-and-butter letter from their little girl, Marcie: 'All of us had a wonderful time last weekend. Your island is really wonderful, and the dinner Saturday night was really something.'

On 21 November he 'finished first draft at 8.15 p.m. Got somewhat tight.' He now began to revise the book, which was to take three months. On December 10 he wrote to me:

---

* See Appendix – Editor.
† Author, among other books, of *Managerial Revolution*.

Bad news: the Kingsley business is going to arbitration after all in the second half of January, so I have to stay here until the end of that month, and probably even until the middle of February. I know the disappointment: I am doing the typing out of the book myself. As you know, it is partly written in longhand, and I have collected, cut and remodelled so much of the typewritten chapters that it is simpler for me to retype the second version myself. . . . I am terribly sorry about this as I know that you were looking forward to doing it. . . .

I am in mild despair about having again to waste my time and energy upon this Kingsley business. . . .

At about the same time Arthur wrote in his notebook that he would soon have to make up his mind where to live. He gave a list of considerations to be taken into account, including 'reconnoitring of new lands (Mexico, India) or digesting accumulated experience? I believe the former, while still time; and new vistas act as catalysers to digest the old ones.'

Edmund Wilson wrote from Massachusetts: 'Are you people back in New Jersey now?' They were going to spend a week in New York and 'we'd love to have you come back up here with us or visit us later.'

Sometimes the revision of the book went well, sometimes not so well and Arthur got stuck. According to the diary, he was quite frequently in a depression. Later, when he was to begin the second volume of the autobiography, he wrote it by hand. Most of the first volume, which he had dictated to me, had had to be rewritten, he told me later, and he was never to use this method again.

In the Hermès diary he wrote: 'First new year's eve ever alone – with Miss Nelly.' On 1 January 1952, he worked on a statement for his lawyer in the Kingsley case and answered letters. 'Working on the book,' he wrote, 'has become a luxury.'

In February he went up to New York to attend the arbitration case, which, as he wrote to A. D. Peters whilst awaiting the verdict, 'went rather badly. . . . Morally I won, legally I shall probably lose. But as I can't do any more about it, it has ceased to bother me.' Eventually he lost the case and Kingsley gained virtually complete control of the film and play rights of *Darkness at Noon*. A curious aspect of the case was that all discussion of the contents of the play in court was taboo.

In order to delve into his memory concerning an incident in his past which he wanted to write about, he went to see a New York hypnotherapist called Wollberg, hoping to achieve this recall through hypnosis. To his disappointment, he was unable to be hypnotized. The word 'depression' occurs so many times in the diary that, perhaps not surprisingly, he consulted Wollberg again. But after a few sessions he gave it up.

The following postscript to a letter to A. D. Peters bears more than a trace of these depressions and also of the *Galgenhumor* which seemed to accompany them:

P.S. If any more of your authors intend to write autobiographies the following best-selling title may be of help:

AN EMPTY LIFE
In Three Volumes

3

At the end of March I had a letter from him; he had now been away for six months:

Just a line in a hurry to let you know that I shall be back in London on or around April 20. This time it's true, cross my heart. But please don't give up your job, nor make any hint that you might be giving it up, nor slacken in diligence because I don't know yet how I shall divide my time between London and Paris and my plans are pretty much in the air. But I do hope that while I am in London you will help me out with mail, etc., at least outside office hours.

I have rented the Island for three years to a tenant with five children who adore Miss Nellie, so left her there for the time being. Everything else remains to be seen.

After a few days in Paris, during which he visited Verte Rive, which was still let, Arthur came over to London on the boat train. He arrived at Victoria Station on the morning of 22 April, had lunch with Hamish Hamilton⋆ at the Garrick,

---

⋆ Who, together with Collins, published *Arrow in the Blue*.

saw A. D. Peters in the afternoon, had drinks with friends, and dined with Mamaine.

On the following day after work, I went to see him at Athenaeum Court in Piccadilly, where he had a service flat overlooking Green Park. The winter had been long and drab. I had not led a lonely life, only a half-hearted one. I ought to get married, I felt. In May I would be twenty-five and what the French call a *vieille fille*.

I started working for Arthur at Athenaeum Court about twice a week for a couple of hours in the evening between six and eight. He paced around the brown upholstered furniture in his small sitting room, dictating one- or two-line letters. All his correspondents had to be answered – except the obvious loonies, though he would always give a suspected loony the benefit of the doubt and send a reply. During these sessions he was for ever consulting that Hermès diary of his and dashing off somewhere. As always, he was predictably unpredictable and this side of him, fascinating though it was, had the effect of scattering my poor feelings in all directions, as if a whirlwind had been through them. I was constantly receiving some sort of jolt, of which Arthur of course was quite unaware. Sometimes I felt happy, at other times I went home with a sinking heart.

In the middle of May, whilst occupied with the boring job of filing, I came across the copy of a yellow Athenaeum Court invoice. It was not made out in Arthur's name but in that of a friend of his, whom I shall call L. She did not live in London, but she had apparently recently stayed at Athenaeum Court. I had met her once in 1950, when she came with her husband to dine with Arthur and Mamaine at Verte Rive. A most unpleasant evening. I had been consumed with the blackest jealousy. Sitting directly opposite me on Arthur's right, L. had flirted with him outrageously and, though modestly discreet, he seemed all for it. She was blonde like my mother and I hated blondes. Though her face was boyish, when she flirted dimples appeared and then vanished again. She was dressed by Dior or one of the great couture houses.

I looked at Mamaine at the other end of the table. She appeared rather scornfully to ignore what was going on at our end and was conversing with L.'s husband. What I did not know at the time was that Mamaine had innocently made a remark at the beginning of the evening which infuriated Arthur (and which had led to a flaming row). He was doubtless both taking his revenge on Mamaine and deriving comfort from the flirtation. It was not in his character to play cruelly with feminine jealousy, for which I am eternally grateful.

For L. it was the beginning of falling in love; perhaps it was love at first sight. Apparently she was not averse to making her husband jealous, but possibly she could not help herself. That dinner party had all the ingredients of a melodrama.

Surely Arthur can't like her, I thought as I filed the wretched yellow invoice, trying to forget I had ever seen it. L. belonged to that category of women who are attractive to men and anathema to women. I was wildly jealous of her.

Arthur only intended to stay in London until the end of May, after which he was returning to Verte Rive for June and July. However, he was looking for a flat in London.

During the winter, before he arrived, I had rushed to work in the mornings, always late, taking the shortest route from our flat in Montpelier Walk to the bus stop in the Brompton Road. But one morning I was early and decided to take a slightly different route. Walking along Montpelier Terrace, I suddenly came upon a hushed, deserted square. It was not large. Through the bare branches of the plane trees the sky looked pale and wintry. A few lights glowed in the windows of the Georgian brick houses. Something about the atmosphere of the place gripped me. It struck me as the most beautiful square I had ever seen. Little did I know, as I glanced up at the street sign which said 'Montpelier Square', that I would spend most of my life there. Looking back, it seems that for an awestricken moment my present came face to face with my future.

It was by sheer chance Arthur came upon Montpelier Square during his flat-hunting. He would certainly have forgotten that I lived in Montpelier Walk. On his way with a Harrods estate agent to look at a flat one day, he noticed a Harrods 'For Sale' sign outside a corner house in Montpelier Square. In his unpredictable manner he stopped.

'Why didn't you tell me about *this* house?' he exclaimed.

'But, sir,' stammered the poor estate agent, 'I thought you said you wanted a flat.'

Arthur looked over the house, which belonged to a Scottish laird and whose sole occupant was the butler. Some walls were covered with crimson wallpaper embossed with silver fleurs-de-lys. Other rooms had a different wallpaper on each wall: pale blue with white dots and, next to that, green and white Regency stripes. Despite the interior decoration, it was again love at first sight. Arthur made an offer on the spot.

During the wars of religion, the town of Montpellier had been a Huguenot stronghold. When a colony of Huguenots fled to London they established what Arthur calls a 'French ghetto' in an enchanted *quartier* off Knightsbridge. There is Cheval Place, Beauchamp Place, Beaufort Gardens, and above all the Montpeliers (somehow one of the l's in Montpellier got lost, under the eccentric influence of English spelling). Montpelier Square is the grandest member of the family. Galsworthy set Soames Forsyte, a rich patrician, in a house in Montpelier Square, where he held sway in *The Forsyte Saga*. The house is a few doors away from the George IV pub where Arthur spent Sunday mornings with Henry Green. Poorer relations of the Square are Montpelier Place and Montpelier Street. Even lower in the hierarchy is Montpelier Walk, where I lived, the miniature garden in front of each doll's house planted imaginatively with flowers and ornamental trees, though now these gardens of Lilliput are somewhat neglected. An old magnolia tree would fill the tiny Montpelier Terrace, were it not ruthlessly kept in check. The lowliest member of the family, Montpelier Mews, is the ugly sister and discreetly hidden away.

In June, soon after Arthur's return to Verte Rive, he learned that the house was his. Eight months earlier he had made a list of 'Resolutions' in his notebook, one of which was 'freeing myself from responsibilities'. The paragraph ended: 'DON'T BETRAY OR WHITTLE DOWN RESOLUTION THIS TIME – IT MAY BE THE LAST CHANCE.' He now had three houses.

★   ★   ★

During June and July, whilst Arthur was at Verte Rive, I had a number of temporary jobs, including working for a friend of his, Dr Egon Plesch, also a Hungarian. Egon was a Freudian analyst and lived in a large house off Sloane Square. On the first day he warned me that I might think I had the same symptoms as the patients whose cases I was taking down, but this was a common fallacy and I should beware of it happening to me.

He was writing an article on 'morbid blushing'. As I was in the habit of blushing myself, I was in a state of worry, in spite of his warning. I wondered if my kind of blushing was morbid; it sounded very much as if it was. The article was illustrated with the dreams of his patients and his interpretations of them. For hours I was steeped in Freudian symbolism. As I left Egon's house after work and walked past an old pub called the Antelope, the street – quite an ordinary street – changed incredibly before my eyes into a jungle of phallic symbols. 'He is terribly kind and gives me hayfever pills,' I wrote to Arthur. But on the following day I had to write to tell him that I had been sacked because 'my typing is bad and doesn't make sense; also my spelling is bad.'

I was obviously unfit for the job with Egon (with whom Arthur had a brotherly bond, despite their totally different views on Freudianism), though hayfever was partly to blame. Arthur found me several other part-time jobs over the next few months and Mamaine gave me a lot of typing jobs for her publishers.

9

'Sad Adieux from Cynthia'

At the beginning of August Arthur returned to London, having sold Verte Rive (to the sister of Antoine de St Exupéry), and moved to his almost empty house in Montpelier Square. At first his study was on the second floor, but soon he moved it to the top floor, the walls of which he had covered with eighteenth-century pine panelling and bookshelves.

Soon the house was filled with ladies. In the bedroom was a huge Civet nude in pastel colours, bending over her wash-basin in the grey Parisian light. She did not grow on me, though I tried to like her. Over the mantelpiece in the kitchen, Leda reclined, the swan's neck curled around her, which shocked the charlady. But the loveliest lady of all was in Arthur's study. She lay asleep, the light shining on a breast and on her face which somehow looked both innocent and voluptuous. As soon as the room grew dark he switched on her picture light.

In the sitting room hung a Courbet portrait of a cow called *Vache Perdue de Maizière*. She stood before a bluff of chalky Jura rocks, lifted her head and seemed to be giving a loud, bewildered moo. '*C'est mon âme,*' said Arthur, sometimes adding a deep and doleful moo as well. Later, he became bored and got rid of her.

I was working for Arthur in the afternoons, as I had a morning job with a stamp collector in Bond Street, which I rather enjoyed. But Arthur said that working for him in the afternoons was really impossible, since that was just when he needed to be alone. He always took a long time to warm up and his best writing time was in the late afternoon. The little bedroom where I typed was next to his study and he could hear every sound I made. Luckily my stamp collector was quite agreeable about the switch.

The house was full of painters, carpenters and electricians, and sometimes Arthur would send me downstairs to the kitchen to see if they were still having their teabreak. I would walk down a flight or two of stairs, guiltily wait a minute or two, and then climb up again to tell him the white lie that they were back at work, in order to spare him a fit of anger.

He recorded in some detail the first months in Montpelier Square. He spent the first night on a camp bed. Four days later, he 'moved from 2nd to 3rd floor of empty house to get the feel of future study.'

'Five weeks passed as a day,' he wrote. 'Didn't read a book, hardly glanced at the paper. The builders have been working for the last four weeks.'

He had never done up a house from scratch, but he soon got rid of the interior decorator. There was 'no friction' with the builders, though he had trouble with a 'particularly bloody electrician' whose own views on how his job should be done clashed with Arthur's.

He spent much time in antique shops, buying furniture, and was out every night. He saw a lot of Mamaine: they dined together, went to Whipsnade Zoo and to Hampton Court and Epping Forest. One evening, after a party at the Gargoyle, he took Dylan Thomas and another friend home and 'listened to music and his poems till 5 a.m.' Dylan, he wrote, was 'drunk, sweet, cherubic'. Of another poet he remarked that he had 'become a father and was losing his Shelleyan looks'.

One evening after work, he took me to the cinema. As we got into the car I was struck by the almost intoxicating smell of perfume that filled it. One could only associate such a heavy scent with a dark-haired woman and I was sure that the person was Sarah (not her real name). I had met Sarah several times and was enthusiastic about her. She impressed me as being an intellectual and I was sure that she and Arthur had a lot in common. She had been chatting with him in his dressing room one evening as I came downstairs after work. He was in a dinner jacket, struggling with his bow tie in front of the mirror. I said goodbye and left, feeling rather sorry for myself as one eye was swollen with a hideous stye. During work that day Arthur had been unable to look at me; he had even let out a cry of horror and half-shuddered at the sight of the stye which made him feel quite sick. How could he write about torture and the gas chambers, I thought, when he cannot bear the sight of a mere stye? I had noticed before how incredibly squeamish he was.

That autumn of 1952 he wrote to a friend in America: 'Life in London makes me very happy and New York makes me very unhappy. I am just a hopeless European.'

He was hard at work on the second volume of the autobiography, which he called from the beginning *The Invisible Writing*. He also found time to take a subscription to the *Journal of the Society for Psychical Research*. And he started a new file called 'Suicide of a Nation'. In it were newspaper cuttings illustrating the state of the country, such as one titbit that the royal yacht was undergoing repairs in a foreign dockyard, rather than in Britain, where it would take twice as long.*

The books ordered from Bumpus at that time included: *The Physical Phenomena of Mysticism* by Father Thurston; *The Devils of Loudun* by Aldous Huxley; and *Selected Prose of Hugo von Hofmannsthal*.

Mel Lasky of *Der Monat* wrote from Berlin: 'Just a quick question to ask are you writing anything on the Prague Trials? Did you know Otto Katz et al? Would you drop me a line if we could get anything from you.'

It was the time of the Czech show trial in 1952. When his former comrade Otto Katz was hanged in November, Arthur was considerably shaken.† But he sent Mel Lasky a one-sentence letter: 'Sorry, nothing doing.' He had not yet reached that part in the autobiography when, in the thirties in Paris, he had worked in the Western propaganda headquarters of the

---

* This eventually became a book, *Suicide of a Nation?*, written by twelve hands and edited by Arthur.

† See the chapter 'Darkness at Noon' in *The Invisible Writing*.

Comintern. The chapter was to be called 'Red Eminence' after Willi Muenzenberg, whose chief lieutenant had been Otto Katz, the anonymous author of the *Brown Book of the Hitler Terror*.

During the same autumn Arthur also revised the French translation of *Arrow in the Blue* and asked the translator, Denise van Moppes, if she could spend three days in London so that they could work on it together. 'The translation is in patches brilliant,' he wrote, 'and always good where a personal story is told. When it comes to theory and abstraction the result is less satisfactory and there are some parts which have to be gone over thoroughly.'

The *Daily Mail* published a review of *Arrow in the Blue* by Peter Quennell with whom, for a short while in the early forties, Arthur had shared a house, together with Cyril Connolly. But whereas his feelings of affection for Cyril Connolly never wavered, he and Peter Quennell had never got on. This review prompted him to write a letter to Harold Rubinstein of Rubinstein, Nash & Co., the literary lawyers:

Enclosed a clipping from the *Daily Mail*. Do you think it is actionable? I realise that a book review would not normally be actionable, but the headline, Three Koestlers, followed by Clown, Careerist, etc.,* seems to me more personal than usual. I would love to have a crack at the *Daily Mail*.

Having not so long ago burned his wings in the Kingsley arbitration case, was he now going to start another lawsuit? Harold Rubinstein was away, but Arthur received a prudent reply from his son, the wily Michael Rubinstein:

I have read the review of your book most carefully. . . . Bearing in mind that the *Mail* would be only too happy to be able to defend proceedings in the guise of champions of free speech, I could not advise you that in this case it is wise to enter the lists. You will I am sure realise that the review is by no means wholly hostile, and the critic would invoke his more appreciative passages in proof of the critical balance he has sought to maintain. When you add to this that the critic is himself a writer of great distinction and a prominent

* The third Koestler in the headline was 'Philosopher'.

literary figure, our difficulties become even greater and wisdom, in this case, I think decrees a dignified silence until you are vouchsafed an opportunity of reviewing Mr Quennell's memoirs.

2

One of the façades of the house in Montpelier Square looked grim with its blind windows which had been bricked up at the time of the Victorian window tax. The whole exterior was painted in battleship grey and the house was known to Arthur's friends as Bachelor's Fortress, or BF.

One morning as I came in I was taken aback by the same smell of perfume which had filled Arthur's car. I felt as if I had been transported from Bachelor's Fortress to a *salon de couture*. Voices speaking in French came from the sitting room and I realized that L. was there. I walked upstairs in a state of gloom. My belief that it had been Sarah who used that scent could hardly have been more mistaken. As I reached the bedroom landing, the scented air was even more suffocating, but it vanished when I reached Arthur's study on the top floor which just smelt of old Gauloises.

After work I came downstairs and found Arthur and L. in the alcove on the first-floor landing. They were studying samples of material for curtains. I noticed that they called one another *vous* in my presence. Surely they couldn't believe that I was quite such a fool, I thought rather scornfully. L. slipped up once and said *tu*, correcting herself a little impatiently.

There is a brief mention of the occasion in Arthur's diary: 'L. back again; Cynthia en crise.' And I thought I had hidden my feelings!

Tempted by longings to lead the life of a hermit at the time when Mamaine left him, the pendulum now seemed to be swinging the other way and he was embracing the life of the flesh. In October he wrote: 'When, oh when, am I going to change back from Life of Decoration to Life of the Spirit.'

After he had finished the 'gruesome task' of revising the French translation of *Arrow in the Blue,* he began 'with trembling insecurity' to write a play about a psychiatrist, called *Dr Icarus.* One might have thought he would return to the neglected autobiography, but for the past month *Dr Icarus* had taken possession of him. Obsessed, he even worked at night till one or two in the morning, which was rare.

When the play was finished he 'celebrated alone w. bottle of Beaujolais'. It had taken six weeks to write, though at one stage he had left it in suspense for a short while and worked on the autobiography. Soon he was to have 'grave doubts' about it and later decided it was 'no good'.

After *Icarus* he had an idea for a science-fiction story, to be called 'The Gulf Stream', but gave it up. One evening he discussed another idea with a solicitor friend, Anthony Lousada, who wrote to him:

I was intrigued with your question about your projected work concerning the trial of Stalin in 1957. I have ascertained that it is a Common Law Misdemeanour for anyone to defame a Foreign Potentate and irrespective of whatever position Stalin may hold in Russia I think it quite clear he would fall within this description. . . .

In your case however, I am not at all convinced that you would be libelling Stalin at all. You would not be holding him up to hatred, ridicule or contempt. The whole thing would obviously be a fictitious forecast. . . .

But nothing came of this either, perhaps because Stalin died about a month later.

3

In the late autumn or early winter a change occurred in my life. It took a week or two before the truth finally sank in, for Arthur said nothing to me about it. I came to work for him every day, as usual; but trips to the pub together for a sandwich lunch or outings to the cinema when he was feeling depressed ceased altogether. Worst of all, the brief illusion of being at times close to him faded, died and was supplanted by a fathomless void.

He might have told me, I thought in despair. Perhaps an instinct warned him not to. I knew he did not want me to be his 'slavey' for ever and that he thought I should find a husband

and lead a life of my own. Unable to derive comfort from reading or to bear listening to music any more, I was confronted by my empty self from whom there was no escape even for an instant. At last I found a solution to this intolerable existence. Why had I not thought of it before since it was so simple? I would kill myself.

A great weight lifted from me. I no longer cared. Obviously I could not do it at home – I hated to think of one of my poor flatmates finding my body. The best place was Kensington Gardens. I would sit on a bench at night after the gates were closed and take an overdose of sleeping pills. I would not write a suicide note; perhaps my body would not be identified and I could slip out of life unnoticed. There was a doctor in Montpelier Place whom I would ask for a prescription of sleeping pills. Even without pills I could always end my life somehow if I was desperate and determined enough. And so, buoyed up by thoughts of suicide, I continued to live what I believed to be a temporary existence.

Sometimes Arthur recorded in his notebook an 'inventory', with comments, of his harem. I see that my name was included, with four others, in one of them: '. . . L. – demain, Cynthia – toujours là. . . .' This was written two months before he dropped me from his lists. Had I read those two ominous words at the time, I would probably have realized that the break I often dreaded was not far off.

But in December I met someone who swept all thoughts of suicide from my mind. Strangely enough, I discovered later that he was one of the many men who were hopelessly in love with one of the twins, his passion being for Mamaine. Though it did not last long, for the first time in more than three years I no longer dreamed of Arthur from dawn to dusk. All the same, when I went with another girl on a skiing holiday to Kitzbühel over Christmas I sent him a postcard which ended: 'I do hope all is going well and there'll be lots of the book for me to type.'

In February, Arthur gave a talk on the BBC about science fiction. In a letter to P. H. Newby, who was head of the Talks

Department, he had suggested as a title: 'The Boredom of Fantasy – A Talk about Martian Maidens, Space-Cadets, Carrotmen and Other Aspects of Science Fiction', and added, 'The idea is, roughly, that science fiction is good entertainment, but can never develop into good Art, for more or less the same reason that the historical novel got into a dead end.'

After recording the talk, he wrote in his notebook about 'the torture of my accent' of which he was becoming 'more and more painfully conscious as the desire for growing roots here gets stronger.' Spring had come – his first in the house which was 'all he hoped for' – and the almond trees were in blossom in Montpelier Square; yet, he added, 'I shall always remain the stranger on the Square.'

About the beginning of March, he recorded in the notebook that he had finished the part of the autobiography concerned with his journeys through Russia and Soviet Central Asia in 1932 – a hundred pages in all. When he reached Ashkhabad, the capital of Turkmenistan, he had met the American Negro poet, Langston Hughes, and they travelled together for a time. In Hughes's autobiography* there is a striking portrait of the young Koestler seen from a different and detached point of view. Had he changed, I wondered, when I read it? In 1932 so many chapters of his life lay ahead of him: imprisonment in Spain under the threat of being shot, leaving the Party, the concentration camp at Le Vernet, the war and the holocaust. Langston Hughes describes himself as a 'writer of sorts, but a writer who wrote mostly because when I felt bad, writing kept me from feeling worse; it put my inner emotions into an exterior form, and gave me an outlet for words that never came in conversation.'

Perhaps because of their contrasting characters, there was an affinity between the two men. Both were sad, wrote Hughes, but 'Koestler wore his sadness on his sleeve'; probably because of a love affair in Baku two weeks earlier to which he devoted a chapter, called 'Nadeshda', in *The Invisible Writing*.

Langston Hughes makes much of the squalor, filth and bad

* Volume II: *I Wonder as I Wander*, New York, 1956.

sanitation in Soviet Asia and of Arthur's squeamishness, and there are some amusing accounts of this. In the village of Permetyab they were informed by the doctor nurse, as they drank tea from 'grimy bowls', that 90 per cent of the population had syphilis ('Koestler almost keeled over'). There was the custom of drinking tea from a common tea bowl which was passed from hand to hand (' "Slobbering in each other's bowls," Koestler said, ". . . a filthy habit." ' Whenever possible 'Koestler got away from the main circle of tea bowl passing . . . to avoid drinking from bowls that dozens of strange moustaches had touched.' This aspect of his travels he hardly mentions in *The Invisible Writing,* although he describes 'counting the familiar stains on the wall which crushed bed-bugs left behind' and 'the latrine across the corridor, which was blocked and permanently overflowing.'

'By a strange hazard,' Arthur wrote, 'I stumbled on the first great show trial in Central Asia – a foretaste of things to come.' Langston Hughes too describes the trial of Attakurdov and a group of Turkmenians, who were accused of crimes against the state, in a chapter called 'Darkness Before Noon'. He himself had been bored by the trial and had sat 'in the public square where formerly no coloured folks were allowed' during the long hours Arthur spent in court. To Hughes the chief defendant, Attakurdov, 'looked like a portly bull-necked Chicago ward boss connected with the numbers racket.' But Arthur, he wrote, had been very much upset and later went to the Party offices to obtain further details of the charges.

I said, 'Atta Kurdov [*sic*] looks guilty to me, of what I don't know, but he just *looks* like a rogue.' But Koestler did not think much of my reasoning and said so quite seriously. I knew mine was not proper reasoning either and had nothing to do with due process of law. But when I saw that it upset him, I repeated that night just for fun, 'Well, anyhow Atta Kurdov does look like a rascal.' Koestler went to his room and I didn't see him any more until the next day, although I thought he might come back to listen to some jazz or to share a hunk of camel sausages with me around midnight. But he didn't come back. The trial disturbed him.

A few weeks later, in Tashkent, Arthur was still disturbed

about the trial and he evidently felt that Attakurdov was innocent, as Langston Hughes relates:

Suddenly Koestler looked up and stared at me intently. 'Here in
Tashkent the jails are full of people, the Atta Kurdovs of Asia.'
 'Don't you think that some of them belong in jail?'
 'Not so many,' said Koestler. 'Not all – maybe none.'

Langston Hughes also tells a story which reveals Arthur's
rather unnerving way of pouncing on seemingly ordinary,
decent sentiments and exposing their hypocrisy.

In Bokhara they visited the old Jewish quarter of the town
and met a young, native-born Jewish journalist who was
working on the daily paper, and the story concerned Langston
Hughes's 'last American pencil'. Good lead pencils were hard
to find and Soviet pencils wore down quickly and had to
be frequently resharpened. One afternoon the young Jewish
newspaperman paid Hughes a visit in his room and in the
course of conversation asked if he could have Hughes's pencil
as a souvenir of America.

'Oh, why, of course,' I said, not thinking at the moment how
valuable that pencil was to me. 'Please accept it.'
 'I will give you my pencil,' said the young man, 'and I will keep
yours forever as a souvenir from your country. Thank you very
much.'
 . . . Later when I started to write with his Soviet pencil, after a
few words the lead wore down so quickly that I really became upset.
Here I was without a single decent pencil in the middle of Asia
where there were only Russian pencils like the one I had in my hand.
 'Gee, Koestler,' I said, 'I wish I hadn't given that fellow my last
good pencil.'
 'Your last pencil!' Koestler exclaimed. 'Why did you give it to
him?'
 'Because he wanted a souvenir from America,' I said. 'But I'd
much rather have given him a shirt.'
 'Nothing's more valuable to a writer than the tools of his trade,'
said Koestler. 'That fellow's a newspaperman. Souvenir from
America – so much camouflage! He knows Soviet pencils are no
good. He tricked you. That Jew!' Koestler said, 'I'm ashamed!
Ashamed! Langston, I'll get your pencil back for you.'

'Oh, no man,' I said. 'Let him have it for a keepsake.'

'Keepsake, bah!' cried Koestler in a rage. 'Can you write with the pencil he left you? No! He didn't want a souvenir, I tell you – he wanted your pencil!' With that Koestler grabbed his coat – he never went out improperly garbed – and stormed off to retrieve my pencil.

I was embarrassed. I had not intended to make an issue of it – a mere pencil. In high school with hundreds of Jewish youngsters I had learned how sensitive some Jewish people can be when another does something considered shameful – just as many Negroes feel keenly any sort of behaviour which they think 'disgraces the race'. But I had not thought of Jewishness at all when I mentioned wishing I had my pencil back. Yet, as soon as I saw Koestler's face, and heard him explode, 'That Jew!' I felt that he thought one of his own had misbehaved, so he set out to do something about it. It took Koestler two or three hours to find the young reporter. But when he returned he had my pencil.

During the spring of 1953, Arthur corresponded intermittently with the Society for Psychical Research. One of his interests concerned research into ESP between identical twins; he hoped to involve Mamaine and Celia in this but without success.

He tried to relive certain episodes of his life which he wanted to write about in *The Invisible Writing* and consulted a psychiatrist. In his notebook he reported: 'Experimented with psychiatrist under pentothal, but total flop.'

Meanwhile, I continued to lead my own life and, as I only saw Arthur during working hours, I never discussed it with him as I had done in the past. One morning I came in to find myself caught in a tempest; it concerned some filing work, and I was the culprit. Hopefully he would soon forget it, I thought, since he never remembered anything irrelevant. Sometimes as I left his study I glanced back at him reading at his desk, an air of solitude about him. I was too wrapped up in my own problems to wonder what he was feeling, but that image remained, perhaps because I was used to seeing him with Mamaine, with whom he shared everything.

Once he broke the unspoken rule and took me out. We spent the day at the zoo and talked. The llamas looked on,

foolishly surprised, and the lions glared, then – bored no doubt
– stretched and yawned. I had reached a turning point in my
life and, with his overwhelming urge to help his fellow-beings,
he opened my eyes before it was too late.

A couple of months later, a friend with whom I frequently
corresponded, returned to England on holiday. He worked
for a publishing company in America. We got married before
he returned to New York.

I stayed behind in order to get my American visa so that I
could join him at the beginning of August. In the meantime
I continued to work for Arthur.

4

It was about this time that Arthur was moved by a depressing
letter from Whittaker Chambers. He had suffered a heart
attack and had spent four months in bed. Arthur had come
out on his side at the height of the Hiss–Chambers trials in an
article called 'Chambers, The Villain'* which was published
in the *New York Times* in February 1950. This article, the
editor told him, had cost him half his American readers. Later
Arthur met Whittaker and far from finding him the monster
depicted in the press (particularly in photographs), he had been
impressed by his qualities and they became friends. On receipt
of Whittaker's letter, Arthur wrote to Malraux:

I have just had a letter from Whittaker Chambers. He had an attack
of heart thrombosis and it is doubtful how long he will live.

I don't know how much you know about Chambers' Odyssey
and personality. If you have any faith in my judgment – he is one
of the most outstanding, most maligned and most sincere characters
whom I have met, and his story is a bizarre and symbolic twentieth-
century martyrdom.

The purpose of my letter is to ask you to write him a spontaneous
and private line of 'amitiés'. He lives in terrible physical and spiritual
loneliness, and a line from you will mean very much to him. This
request will seem less far-fetched to you when you have read the
enclosed copy of Whittaker's last letter to me. . . .

* See *The Trail of the Dinosaur*.

At the same time, he wrote in a similar vein to the editor of the *Manchester Guardian,* A. P. Wadsworth, quoting from Whittaker's letter. The *Guardian* had recently printed an anti-Whittaker article, and Arthur felt this should be answered 'thoroughly, factually and dispassionately'. He suggested that Wadsworth should ask Professor Sidney Hook of New York University to do it. But the quote from Whittaker's letter, with which Arthur hoped to gain Wadsworth's sympathy, fell upon stony ground:

Chambers leaves me cold. I grant that he is an interesting character, stepping right out of Dostoevsky or Koestler. (You might have invented him.) But he is a rogue all the same. His letter to you strikes me as perfectly in keeping. . . . He has done immense harm to liberal values and deserves what he gets. . . . I am sorry to seem bitter but this is one of the few subjects that really rouses me. . . . Why is the American renegade Communist so different from the European type?

Arthur replied:

I am glad about the frankness of your letter and sad about its contents. . . . But allow me a remark on a side issue which you raised: the difference between American and European ex-Communists. If you mean by that that you prefer Koestler to Chambers, I must disappoint you. I was, as a Continental ex, in the fortunate position of not having any relevant information which would have forced me into the dreaded part of a renegade informer. Had I possessed such information about the secret life of Klaus Fuchs or Guy Burgess, I would have run post-haste to M.I.5. If, moreover, say Fuchs had been an intimate friend of mine as Hiss was to Chambers, the conflict would probably have produced the same hesitations and neurotic symptoms as Chambers has occasionally displayed.

There remains, of course, a difference in atmosphere between this country and America – but that applies not only to ex-Communists. . . .

There was an unexpected sequel to this correspondence. When Whittaker's book *Witness* was published in England three months later, Wadsworth invited Arthur to write a notice of it for the *Guardian.* 'I don't know that I should put my head in the lion's mouth like this,' he wrote. 'But still, what do you say?'

'This is indeed a fair and generous offer,' Arthur replied. He declined, having already refused to review the book for the *Observer* and the *Sunday Times* 'on the grounds that if one ex-Communist reviews another ex-Communist's book, there is an unavoidable sound of axe-grinding, which defeats the purpose.' However, 'in the unlikely case that you should be at a loss for a reviewer for this and similarly controversial books,' he recommended a young American who had just arrived in England. This was Irving Kristol who, with Stephen Spender, had founded a new monthly magazine, *Encounter*.

Arthur also had an exchange of letters with Frederic Warburg who, inspired by Arthur's talk on science fiction, sent him a book he was soon to bring out, and about which he was full of enthusiasm. Would Arthur read it and give his opinion? Arthur replied:

Nobody can resist the word 'implore', so I partly read and partly skipped through the book. It is a monstrously clever and hideously fascinating book, apparently conceived by an electronic brain with over-heated tubes. Seriously, it is about the cleverest science fiction book I have seen, but in spite of its literary pretension, I fear the artistic value is nearly zero.

Despite this sugar-coated pill, the incorrigible Warburg asked if he could use as a quote the passage in Arthur's letter from 'It is a monstrously' to 'cleverest science fiction book I have seen'.

Arthur wrote back:

What a Machiavellian trap! My letter meant to explain to you why I couldn't say anything quotable. If you think 'monstrously' and 'hideously' nevertheless quotable, it is all right with me, but please leave out the second phrase.

But Warburg was reluctant to give up that second phrase. As a compromise he suggested omitting the word 'seriously'. Arthur replied:

I am sorry to appear pedantic, but I do feel puritanical about quotes on jackets. . . . I understand that from a publisher's point of view you like the superlative 'cleverest', but that is just what I am opposed to. I used the superlative in a private letter on the spur of the moment, but I wouldn't use it in print. So, forgive me if I am stubborn in asking you to quote, if at all, only the first phrase.

Sometimes Arthur wrote in his notebook that the autobiography was making good progress; at other times that he was 'plodding on'. He also recorded an 'extraordinary euphoria': he had sat at his desk until four in the morning and written twelve pages of a chapter called 'The House on the Lake' – 'which is, I believe, a lifetime's record'. The euphoria lasted for several days; in its wake came the inevitable depression. According to his notebook, a similar euphoria had been preceded by what he called 'another smash-up': he had driven his car over a traffic island while drunk and had quarrelled with the police.

Often bored when he went out in the evenings, Arthur wrote in his notebook about the 'insoluble dilemma': while intellectuals were often 'unconvivial company', the circle of people with whom he enjoyed wining and dining provided an intellectual stimulus which was 'zero'. Even intellectuals, he lamented, 'after 3 meetings also become uninspiring.' Boredom also led, as he wrote elsewhere in the notebook, to 'me behaving impossibly'.

In May he mentioned an incident which resulted in my (briefly) getting the sack. I had absent-mindedly lost the bank paying-in book. When he found out, it proved to be the last straw and I was given notice to leave at the end of the week. As I was going to New York as soon as I got my American visa, I told myself that I did not care. 'Arthur's given me the sack,' I said to Mamaine in a joking way. We were walking down Montpelier Street together, having left Arthur's house at the same time. She did not answer me; perhaps because she did not believe me or because of her loyalty to Arthur.

On my last morning, I was not prepared for the depression which filled me. At some point we looked at each other; I suppose he read my thoughts, because he relented. I was only too happy to forget about it. Ever since I had first thought of suicide, I had been too demoralized to work properly.

Before I left England, Mamaine invited me to lunch at a Polish restaurant near the Brompton Oratory. She gave me a slightly searching look, as if expecting to find a change now that I was married – perhaps she thought I might have grown up a bit. As we walked out into the sunny street after lunch, she looked for a moment tired and depressed. Nearly two years had passed since her fateful decision at Verte Rive. It was no good my wishing she had not made it; it could not be reversed.

In the week before I left, Arthur finished a vital chapter, 'The Hours by the Window', which I typed in those last days. 'Very exhausted,' he wrote in his notebook. During that week he had met at a dinner party a distinguished Catholic priest who 'shocked me by saying that mystic experience doesn't mean a thing. . . . They regard mysticism with as much distrust as the Comintern leadership regards genuine communists.'

His chronicle for that week ended with the remark: 'But my harem is wearing me out.'

He was also revising the German translation of *Arrow in the Blue* – 'the most gruelling job'. In a letter to his German publisher he wrote:

[The translator] is no doubt conscientious and has tried to do his best. Unfortunately, his knowledge of colloquial English is limited.

An autobiography is a self-portrait, and therefore a delicate matter, entirely dependent on nuances. I have treated my youthful self and also my family background with a kind of benevolent irony. By leaving the irony out, a quite different, pompous and boastful picture emerges.

On my farewell evening Arthur took Mamaine and me to see *Guys and Dolls*. I had never liked musicals and would have preferred the ballet or a concert. Arthur sat between us in the stalls and, though biased, I enjoyed it tremendously. Arthur had given me as a wedding present a red leather dressing case from Fortnum's; inside it were elegant little jars and boxes with brass tops and outside were my initials in gold lettering. Mamaine gave me a gift token to spend at a posh department store in New York.

After the show we had supper at the Ivy. It was the last time I was ever to see Mamaine. Arthur liked to do things in style and preferred being the host to being a guest. He looked at Mamaine and urged her to eat more. He did his best to tempt her with her favourite food and encouraged her with remarks like '*en mangeant vient l'appétit*'. But she had been through this determined cajoling too many times in the past and was sick of it. She would have preferred a conversation on more highbrow topics than food and pouted her disapproval. As he was getting nowhere, he turned to me. I could not eat another thing, but I was bullied into have a mousse *au chocolat* and plied with wine. He offered me half his dessert and then plonked nearly all of it on my plate with a dollop of crème Chantilly. My protests were ignored. 'Oh, come on, don't fuss,' he said, a frown beginning to cloud his face. I knew I would be terribly sick afterwards, but did not care. It was not so much that I was eager to please (though I cannot deny that) but that I found his passion for sharing irresistible. However, he was still not satisfied: 'Now you must have a sorbet,' he declared. My head was swimming with the wine. To 'complete the architecture of the meal' we had coffee and brandy.

The following morning was my last at Montpelier Square. Arthur gave me a huge bunch of flowers and drove me home, though I lived just round the corner. I was always rather proud of the way I could keep my feelings under control. During my schooldays we had been taken to see a film called *Mrs Miniver* and while the whole school sobbed during the performance, I had not shed a tear. But now the iron grip I had on my self-control was woefully lacking. As the car turned into the Brompton Road, my view of Burkett's the fishmongers, was blurred and I saw the assistants in their jolly straw boaters as if in a distorting mirror. All the will in the world only made things worse. I fled into the house.

Arthur wrote in his Hermès diary: 'Very sad adieux from Cynthia.'

A month after my departure Arthur wrote in the notebook:

Painfully plodding towards the end of Vol. II. Cynthia left on July 30 – got unexpectedly terribly depressed at losing her. Partly because really exceptionally sweet, cheerful, naive, pretty, devoted; and also because it is a breaking off of another bit of my life. Had very pleasant adieux.

I was to find out, when I reached New York, how infantile my illusions about married life had been. They had no place in the bright light of everyday life; before long we parted, and the marriage was dissolved.

10

Working for Ely Culbertson

When he finished the first draft of *The Invisible Writing* at the beginning of October, Arthur sent me a cable: 'Book finished 6.45 p.m. Love and thanks.'

I frequently sent him reports of how I was getting on. They began with a note from the boat train to Southampton. Later in New York I sent him a long letter about the failure of my marriage.

In September I started to look for a job in New York. Arthur wrote to Al Hart, his editor at Macmillans, and it was through Al that I was offered a job of secretary to the head of their editorial department. But I really wanted to work for a writer again and reluctantly refused their offer.

At last I saw in the *New York Times* an advertisement which sounded promising: a writer was looking for a secretary, and I applied. The writer turned out to be Ely Culbertson, the bridge expert. Though not a bridge player, I knew the name well.

Unfortunately two interviews for jobs were crammed into one morning. At eleven I was seeing Andrew Salter* and at one o'clock Ely Culbertson. Mr Salter gave me an IQ test. It must have been an easy one for me to have passed it; but it

---

* Arthur had read a book of his called *What Is Hypnosis?* in 1949 and had at that time written to ask him if he knew of a hypnotist in France. Apparently he was even then anxious to uncover memories submerged in the subconscious. Andrew Salter was unable to help.

gave me self-confidence and I got the job. Feeling in a euphoric mood, I betook myself to a public telephone box to ring Ely Culbertson's secretary and cancel my appointment with him. To my embarrassment the telephone was answered by Mr Culbertson himself. 'Where are you? You're late – I'm waiting for you,' he said. He had an extraordinary accent, predominantly Russian, but also very American. I could only stammer that I was on my way. I had no idea what I was going to do and felt like an impostor.

His flat was on West 57th Street opposite Carnegie Hall and the Russian Tea Room. He sat at his desk in the sitting room eating lunch from a tray. There was a small kitchenette in the room, barely two feet from his desk, with its doors folded back, and his Scandinavian maid Christine was discreetly making tea. He was not bothered by my being late and offered me some lunch. As I discovered later, he had no sense of time.

Ely Culbertson was tall, with a fair complexion and blue eyes. He had beautiful hands, the fingers long and slightly tapering; they always held a cigarette. He wore a shirt of heavy silk in a pastel colour and the tie of an aesthete. As he questioned me, I found myself telling him far more than I intended to. In the background there was a faint clatter of cutlery. He caught my expression: 'Oh, Christine knows everything,' he said, giving her a charming smile. 'There are no secrets from Christine.' She smiled back gravely.

During the interview I discovered that bridge was not his real vocation but merely, as he put it, his bread and butter. His passion in life was his peace plan. He had formed the World Federation Inc., and later the Citizens' Committee for United Nations Reform to organize a UN police force. He had lectured all over the country to promote his ideas. Time was running out, he said, and we were drifting towards another war. His goal was to achieve a lasting peace before it was too late. He had written two books on his system of collective defence: *Summary of the World Federation Plan* and *Total Peace*. He had also written his autobiography, which had an intriguing title: *Strange Lives of One Man*.

The door of the sitting room opened and his wife came in. Ely Culbertson was sixty-two and ill health made him look even older; Dorothy, his second wife, was thirty-three years younger. She was blonde and her face glowed with health and vitality. Dorothy shook hands with me unsmilingly; her eyes slightly narrowed as she studied me.

A few days later, when I learned that I had got the job, I had to pluck up my courage and explain that I had already accepted another job. When he heard this, Ely Culbertson asked me to come and see him. He was drinking a glass of tea and smoking when I came in. What was this job I had taken, he wanted to know. On hearing the details he looked at me a little quizzically. Did I think it was the right job for someone like me, he asked, somewhat sceptically. But I couldn't possibly change my mind now, I protested, I had given my word. He was a diabolical arguer and I had to admire him for it. There were two kinds of people in the world, he explained: those with two-dimensional minds (he waved them aside) and a few who had three-dimensional minds. I probably had a two-and-a-half-dimensional mind, he said kindly. But if I worked for him for two years I would have a three-dimensional mind. I was filled with wonder at the thought of this different me which would emerge in so short a time. Carried away, I said I would work for him. He made me telephone Mr Salter from the next room.

However, I found out after a while that another applicant had got the Culbertson job before me. It had not worked out and I was his second choice.

I frequently wrote to Arthur, telling him all my news, and in October I wrote:

Through an ad in the *N.Y. Times* I got a job as secretary to Ely Culbertson whom I believe you met. I long to know what you think. Actually, it seems to me that you have a lot in common politically. He has a small apartment in New York and a house in Vermont as well as one in Mexico. I have already spent some time in Vermont which was heaven. He may go to Mexico for 2 months this winter and I may go too, which would also be heaven. Naturally I got the job purely because I was your secretary for 4 years (not 6 years as you always tell people!). His wife is my age and very beautiful. She has read practically all your books – more than he. . . .

Dorothy had been married to Ely Culbertson for seven years. She had met him soon after graduating from Vassar. She had a vibrant curiosity about all aspects of life. I was overwhelmed with questions about myself, Arthur, Mamaine, my mother, my sister and my childhood. And she had a quite uninhibited way of confiding her own feelings and experiences.

Ely had told me that Dorothy was his Galatea* and he was proud that she had successfully passed the first half of her PhD. She was an only child. Her parents came from Prussia and soon after their marriage they emigrated to America, where Dorothy was born. She was brought up in Connecticut. Sometimes Ely said she looked like Hitler's dream girl. Her blonde hair, when let down, reached her waist, her eyes were a pale blue and her skin pale gold. She loved to have her back and neck stroked and would call upon one of the children, her mother, me, anyone to do this, giving sighs of happiness from the sofa.

She also loved having children. But the Culbertson family was all too often touched by tragedy. Of the four children she bore, only the youngest survived – Alexander, aged one, or Sasha, as his father called him. The other children in the house were Victoria, a little Mexican girl, whom Ely was turning into another Galatea, and Stevie, his only grandson. Ely's children by his first wife and bridge partner, Josephine, were grown up, and Stevie was the son of his beloved daughter, Nadia.

As Ely's secretary, I became part of the household and a member of the family. No wonder Dorothy had looked at me so critically when we first met. I kept the office going in New York and spent part of the time in Vermont. Twice a month Ely spent a few days in New York.

He had been born in the Caucasus, where his American father developed the oil fields of Grozny, three hundred miles north of Baku. As a young mining engineer, his father had carried off the daughter of a Cossack general and married her. Ely spent his youth in the Caucasus. In 1908 he was thrown

* The statue brought to life by Pygmalion – Editor.

into a tsarist jail in Sochi with six other social revolutionists who were awaiting execution. He was released because he was a minor and technically an American.

He wrote:

In those days I was desperately in love with the most beautiful abstractions: Humanity, Justice, People, Liberty, Peace. I hated the tyrants and despised the war-makers. I lived in the shadow of the great gatherers of noble truths, and I sought to follow the precepts of humanity's emancipators. These ideals were my science and my commandments.

Though his ideals remained the same, his way of fighting for them changed. His passion for knowledge led him to study at six universities in Europe. When the family fortune was expropriated after the Revolution, he left Russia. After a period in Paris, where he spent his nights gambling and his days sleeping, he arrived penniless in New York in the early twenties. He stood in breadlines, picked fruit and planted corn.

'I had always been fascinated by the bizarre world of cards,' he wrote. In order to earn a living and pursue his studies, he became a scientific gambler and built up the system of bridge which made him a millionaire. He spent his millions on his peace project and there was not much left by the time I knew him in 1953. He was always working out complicated ways of borrowing money. By then, too, he was suffering from a lung disease.

He was writing an abstract of his UN police plan as well as another volume of autobiography. Sometimes he would attack the fan mail, starting with the letters at the bottom of a file; these were two, even three, years old. After a while, he would heave a sigh and say despairingly: 'Oh, Cyntushka, would you bring me some more tea?' When I returned with the Russian tea glass and plenty of lemon, he had abandoned letter-writing and was working on his peace plan again.

Though his accent was frightful, his English was colourful and correct, except for the Russian difficulty with the definite and indefinite articles. It had never occurred to me that they might be unnecessary in a language. He often left them out, or substituted one for the other. Soon I was thoroughly muddled myself, and for years afterwards I had to think which was the right one to use.

On his visits to New York he took me out to dinner. He was always delighted with the proverbial rudeness of the New York taxi drivers; the ruder they were the better pleased he was, as it proved beyond doubt that in America all men were free and all men were equal. But he loved both his countries – America and Russia – and they had been the inspiration of his life's work.

2

Like some women who are awkwardly pregnant during the summer, Arthur was unable to take a holiday until he had finished the first draft of *The Invisible Writing*. On 19 September he left for Ischia to spend three weeks with L. who, to his delight, had bought a yacht. Whilst there, he bought a house 'on the spur of the moment'. He wrote in his notebook: 'Having abandoned France, adopted Italy as Mediterranean pied à terre.'

He finished the second draft of the book by the end of 1953 and noted: 'No depression as yet. But again unsettled life, with L. coming and going, and the rest of the harem unstable and boring.'

It was around this time that he began a soul-destroying affair with a woman whose face is reminiscent of one of Botticelli's angels. In the old files there are drafts of his letters to her. One, a page of single-space typing, was finally distilled into four lines; but even those four lines were never sent – they are still in their envelope marked 'By Hand'. Somewhere in the middle of the draft and crossed out, was this passage:

As I am emotionally more solvent in my continental ways than the average native of this country, who counts every penny of passion thrice before he spends it, I have probably paid more heavily in the currency of the heart. But in that particular currency one likes to be a sucker.

He was working on a new book, a volume of essays. This was *The Trail of the Dinosaur,* in the preface of which he made a vow to give up writing about politics.

Nicko and Mary Henderson* invited him to stay at the British Embassy in Vienna. 'My hesitation,' he replied, 'is due to the fear that the Vienna of my youth, which I haven't seen for almost exactly twenty years, would be rather a heartbreak and make me depressed to the extent of even losing at chess against Nicko.'

However, in March he went to Vienna after all, accompanied by Botticelli. The result of that visit was an idea for a novel with a background of postwar Vienna. 'I think I have found the background for the novel I was looking for,' he wrote to Nicko Henderson. 'I have started writing it and shall probably have to return to Vienna – probably end of July or beginning of August – for some additional atmosphere. Don't get frightened. I shall come alone and stay at Sacher's. . . .'

In April he let the house in Montpelier Square for the summer and began to pack for his sojourn in Ischia with L. in the newly acquired house. She was preparing the house and sending him affectionate cables. But before leaving, his obsession with Botticelli reached its peak. 'Unable to do burningly urgent page-proofs,' he wrote.

This part of the notebook he called 'Chronology of an Obsession'. He lunched with a friend – 'God knows how' – and visited other friends – 'only ½ alive'. He asked Botticelli to spend two days in France with him. She replied, 'Can't.' In despair he sent her by hand a seven-page letter at ten in the morning, having presumably worked on it till the early hours. He 'told her if she doesn't ring by 12, shall know it's all over.' The saga continues:

Ten to 12. A double Scotch. With wonderful effect. The glass of rum of the man going to be hanged.

Incantation to a telephone: Ring, black, cradled brute. . . .

* Sir Nicholas Henderson was British Ambassador in Vienna, 1953-56. The Hendersons were old friends of Koestler – Editor.

4 to 12. Until now have sense of humour. Now panic: realise finality.

12.5. Panic over, depression & resentment, hatred starts.

12.10. The world has turned grey. Hitting rock bottom. . . .

Many who crossed Botticelli's path became victims of her power to turn her lovers casually into empty shells. He might have derived a little comfort from his own verse, written four years previously in *The Age of Longing*:

> Thine absence is a void
> Which thy presence cannot fill.
> Thine absence is a wound
> Which thy presence cannot heal.*

He called this obsession with Botticelli a 'shattering change-of-age crisis'.

All that pent-up ardour had to find some release. On the car journey to Ischia he got involved in an adventure which was of a nature that was dear to his heart – the chase after forbidden fruit. It happened high up in the mountains to the north of Chamonix. Whilst sitting at a table in a crowded bar he saw an Italian girl with her fiancé sitting at the far side of the room, and was unable to take his eyes off her. He carried her off for the night and was thrilled by this feat. Paola came from the southern part of Italy and was fair. Later she escaped to spend a night with him in Milan.

'Very sad adieux,' he wrote in his diary.

The house in Ischia was still full of builders, so Arthur and L. had to live in a cottage belonging to an artist. 'Shirocco,' Arthur wrote in his Hermès. 'Impatient and irritable: still no home to work.' He began to have 'another builder obsession' and was 'depressed and furious at prospect house won't be ready for 3-4 weeks.'

He was to do little writing in Ischia. He got rid of the letters waiting to be answered and cleared the decks to establish peace of mind. But every day he went sailing and when the weather

---

* In fact these lines allude to the lost faith of the Catholic Hydie.

was bad he was too depressed to work: 'Read all day Evelyn Waugh.' Auden was living in Ischia at the time and they often dined together. Robin Maugham was also there and Arthur took him sailing in his Canadian canoe of Verte Rive days.

The time was drawing near to an event which was to shake him profoundly and change the course of his life. This event had a Koestlerian quality about it – like all the dramatic moments of his life – almost as if it had been devised solely for him, to torment his guilt-racked soul. It seems symbolic that Arthur – in his 'change-of-age crisis', as he put it – should have chosen to live so close to the ancient town of Capua. He had explored Capua in his writings and knew both her charms and her darker side. In *The Age of Longing,* the Soviet diplomat in Paris, Fedya, reflects on her enticing ways:

In Capua, Hannibal's army had gone soft by abandoning itself to the temptations of an older, refined and decadent civilisation. . . .Fedya knew that it would not happen to him. He was no puritan, and took whatever pleasure Capua had to offer, but never forgetting that it was Capua who offered it. The correct approach to the devil was to sup with him and let him pay the bill.

But her amphitheatre bears witness to her darker side, and it was from Capua that Spartacus and his fellow gladiators escaped. Arthur had been immersed in that moment of history when he wrote about the revolt of Spartacus in *The Gladiators.* In the prologue to the novel, there is a description of Lentulus, seen through the eyes of the scribe Apronius:

He came to Capua only two years ago, and founded his gladiator school which already enjoys an excellent reputation. . . . He has succeeded in impressing on his men as an iron rule that, once beaten, they should never ask to be spared, should cut a good figure whilst being finished off and not disgust the audience with any sort of fuss.

'Anyone can live – but dying is an art and takes some learning,' he kept on admonishing his gladiators. . . .

Arthur's first day on the island of Ischia (26 April) had been portentous. He received a cable informing him of the death of a close friend, Jack Newsom.★ Arthur had been greatly looking forward to the arrival in Naples of Jack Newsom and his wife, Chris; their boat, the S S *Roma,* had left New York and was due to dock in Naples in ten days' time. Jack had died of a heart attack on board ship. Arthur wrote to Mamaine about it, commenting: 'Somehow one can never escape *la vie tragique.*'

When the S S *Roma* reached Naples, Arthur was waiting to meet Jack's widow. The next day he wrote in the Hermès diary: 'Naples: coping with corpse.' It was Jack's wish to be cremated, which caused problems in a Catholic country. Eventually, with the help of the American Consulate in Rome, the cremation took place, according to Jack's will, and Arthur returned to Ischia. On 16 May, he went with friends to a fair and felt 'depressed; walked home alone; strong suic. temptation'.

He did not know it, but Mamaine was again desperately ill in hospital. She had been in hospital in late April, but had written to Arthur to say she was well enough to leave. On 19 May, he received a letter from her which began: 'As you see I'm back inside.' She had been found by her twin in an acute state of asthma and been rushed to hospital. This was the last letter she ever wrote to Arthur; he wrote back at once. On 2 June she died.

Arthur, bronzed from sailing in the Gulf of Naples, flew to London and went to the funeral, which was held in a country churchyard on a hot summer's day. Death, for some perverse reason, prefers sunlit places.

How could the doctors have allowed this to happen? Needless to say, Arthur made investigations and gave his verdict in the Hermès: 'Ought to have been permanently on ACTH; 4th ventricle failure; guilty.'

I heard the news while travelling in a train to Vermont with Ely Culbertson. He handed me, without comment, the

---

★ An author's note at the beginning of *Arrow in the Blue* states: 'My warm and sincere thanks are due to Jack and Chris Newsom, of Point Pleasant, Pennsylvania, for working over the manuscript, for their friendship, criticism and encouragement.'

afternoon paper, with a sympathetic look. I read the paragraph in the middle of the front page. It's a mistake, I thought. Surely they mean Arthur's mother (then in her eighties). Later in the month I had a letter from Arthur blaming himself for what had happened and for making her life with him intolerable. I felt he was magnifying their quarrels, though, as I wrote in a lengthy letter, 'I do not deny the fact that you nagged her a lot.' Feeling inadequate, I ended: 'Don't torture yourself.'

3

Back in Ischia on 8 June, four days after Mamaine's funeral, Arthur moved into the new house with L. The first day was spent 'joylessly arranging house; constant rows'. On the following day he wrote, 'ditto'.

L. may have been quite glad to go away to Paris for two weeks. Arthur wrote in his notebook: 'Saw a lot of Auden. More sex-obsessed than anybody I know. Said: you ought to write autobiography – not novels.' Could this 'depressing advice', given at such an unhappy time, have made a deep impression? In the notebook he wrote: 'One should only write novels which, if unwritten, would leave a hole.'

Unable to work, he spent his days sailing or going to the beach. The novel set in postwar Vienna must have been abandoned: in his last letter to Mamaine, dated 19 May, he had written: 'I made two or three false starts with the new novel, and still don't know whether I am on the right track.'

He tried to write an essay on snobbery which had been at the back of his mind for at least three years, but was unable to spend more than a day on it. Next day he sailed the canoe near the island's shores; a fierce wind drove him out into rough seas and he finally managed to land on the small neighbouring island of Procida. Sailing a flimsy craft like the Canadian canoe needs a light touch, for it is all too ready to capsize. Perhaps in those turbulent waters he did not much care what the outcome would be; but having brought it off successfully he felt 'happily exhausted'.

L. returned, bringing with her Leo Valiani, who stayed

over the weekend. Arthur and Leo had been together in the concentration camp of Le Vernet near the Pyrenees. Soon after the outbreak of war, the French authorities had started to round up aliens with a political record or a suspected political record. Arthur and Leo had been arrested and it was at Le Vernet that their lives converged. Leo is Mario in *Scum of the Earth,* and one of Arthur's closest friends.

'The life we led,' Arthur wrote of his experiences in Le Vernet, 'was a proof of man's capacity for adaptation. I think that even the condemned souls in purgatory after a time develop a sort of homely routine.'

Leo had spent nearly the whole decade of the thirties in prison as a member of the anti-Fascist underground and been tortured by electric shocks. When first arrested he was a mere teenager. Soon after Arthur was released from Le Vernet, Leo managed to escape and in 1943 he got back to Italy to join the Resistance. He is the author of a number of books, including his memoirs of the Resistance and a history of the Socialist movement.

After the recent interlude with Paola in the mountains near Chamonix, Arthur had visited Leo in Milan and written in the Hermès: 'Milano with Leo and Paola.'

After the weekend on Ischia with Arthur and L., Leo left and friends arrived from England. Arthur had little time for reflection – he was back in *la vie triviale*. They sailed and swam and cruised in L.'s yacht, dropping anchor in Sorrento, Positano, Salerno ('the Milan of the South, the Arabs having never got there'), and farther south at Paestum. They visited Pompeii and Ravello. In Ravello there was 'tension' – the poor guests were 'exhausted by mad-hatter's pace'. The skipper of this thirty-three-foot yacht was Arthur. Having taught himself, with a book in one hand, to sail his Canadian canoe on the Seine around Verte Rive, he proceeded to apply his experience to sailing a yacht in Mediterranean waters, single-handed.

On their return, Arthur began packing. He was leaving Ischia and going to the mountains to be alone and to write. With the shock of Mamaine's death had come a presentiment that he had for some time been 'drifting in a magnetic storm'.

As he wrote in *Arrow in the Blue:* 'Cosmic disturbances some-times cause a magnetic storm on earth. Man has no organ to detect it, and seafarers often do not realise that their compass has gone haywire.'

To recover his lost bearings he wanted to go away by himself. At the end of July, he and L. left Ischia together and she accompanied him on the journey as far as Verona. In Verona they 'parted, happily after 2 bottles of wine'. L. cannot have been really happy about this parting of the ways, though she found a way of softening the blow, as will be seen. Her name appears constantly throughout the notebook and diaries from the summer of 1951 to 1954. At one time, though, she went too far in her efforts to please him. One evening, when she had caviar and food sent round from Pruniers to Mont-pelier Square he flung the caviar out of the kitchen window. He wasn't going to become a gigolo.

Arthur was going to stay in Canazei in the Dolomites, where a friend – a former political prisoner whom, like Leo Valiani, he had got to know at Le Vernet – ran a hotel.

As a youth Arthur had been a keen mountaineer. He could scarcely have chosen a more savage landscape than the moun-tains of the Dolomites in which to attain the inner peace he longed for and a lifting of his depression. They send a chill down one's spine. One peak resembles the fang of a wild beast. A few kilometres from Canazei, the Marmolada, with its sheer walls of granite, soars to the skies.

Exhilarated by the long drive through the mountains and by the *Höhenluft,* Arthur arrived at Canazei, to be greeted by his concentration-camp companion and wife, and got 'very drunk' with them and 'some dumb blonde'.

He lost no time in exploring the mountains around him: to the north, the Sella massif, and to the south, the Marmolada: 'Absolutely wonderful ascent in Sessellift to Marmolada; glac-iers and rugged majesty; Sella looks like forbidding Olympus.'

At the top, he picked up a young Italian post-graduate student and drove her home over the Passo di San Pellegrino, returning to Canazei over a different pass. 'Went to Lake Carezza – what a name!' he exclaimed, though adding that it was originally called Karersee. His first attempt at climbing had been pitiful; he had to turn back halfway up ('1st time in life'), unable to stand the exertion. The life of Capua had been too soft for him.

Despite a depression which 'goes on and on, now seems chronic', he began to write a novel about Ischia. In the evening after work, his imagination was set on fire with 'every bottle of wine'. Nevertheless he remained 'doubtful' about it and soon wrote: 'Saw that story won't work. Started again (5th or 6th time) thru girl's eyes.' From his notebook it appears that the character of the girl was based on me.

Someone close can seem to come dramatically alive for a while after dying, almost as if tugging at one's sleeve. The 'wound broke open again,' Arthur wrote in the Hermès. Fragments of memory surfaced, such as climbing with Mamaine in Snowdonia, and he heard her voice with the clearness of an 'acoustic halucination'. A letter arrived informing him that the sale of the island in the Delaware river had been completed. At first he got 'v. excited', and then he fell into a daydream in which he spent the profit on a Vuillard for Mamaine. The painting was to be a surprise on her birthday. He imagined it filling her with the same delight that he had felt when he got his first food parcel in prison in Seville.

He was unable to continue with the novel: he wrote a page or two more and typed out the MS, but it had turned to ashes. Nevertheless those 'depressing weeks of loneliness' had borne fruit for it was now that he resolved to devote time to work in parapsychology. After a month in the Dolomites he went to Lago Maggiore where Manes Sperber, his wife Zenka and family were spending the summer holidays. 'Talked all morning and lunched with Munio who tried to lift my morale,' he wrote in the Hermès. Erich Maria Remarque and his wife Paulette Goddard were also in the Ticino. After their first dinner, Arthur 'smashed up car'. Remarque, he wrote, was 'just pulling out of dypsomaniac bout', but nevertheless they went on after dinner to an Ascona nightclub where they stayed till daylight.

When the car was repaired Arthur drove north, stopping in Paris, and arrived back at Montpelier Square at the beginning of September.

I I

The Anti-Hanging Campaign

I

'I wish I knew what you were writing about,' I wrote to Arthur in the autumn of 1954, 'but perhaps I will find out from Al Hart.' The lack of news in his brief letters hardly nourished my starved imagination.

According to his diary, he was revising the French translation of *The Invisible Writing* and correcting the pageproofs of the German edition. Unhappy about parts of the French translation, he wrote to his publisher, Robert Calmann-Lévy: 'I am really very worried about this book. Will you, for my reassurance, have proofs sent to me *together with the typescript* so that I can follow [my] corrections (made in red)?' And to Manes Sperber, who was associated with the French publishers, he wrote:

You know that for nearly six months I have been unable to work and on the brink of going off my rocker. Now at last, touch wood, I've got going, still in a precarious way, and I do not want to interrupt the new book I am working on by the full-time revision of the French translation. I can only do a few pages a day in my spare time. . . . If that means postponing publication, it just can't be helped.

In the same letter he told Sperber about the book which was so precariously coming into being:

The book I am working on is a collection of essays, covering the last twelve years, with three original essays added: 'The Anatomy of Snobbery', 'The Conversion of Jewry',* and 'The General Absence of Values, or the Approaching End of the World'. This last one will be very cheerful as I am waiting for that end with growing impatience and glee.

In fact it was to become the title essay of *The Trail of the Dinosaur* (which, he told Sperber, would make those who read it 'rush to commit suicide'). As for the 'Anatomy of Snobbery', he had worked on it in Ischia for one day before abandoning it.

In another letter to Sperber he asked him to send a copy of Simone de Beauvoir's new novel, *Les Mandarins*: 'People say there is a venomous portrait of me in it and vulgar curiosity prompts me to look it up.'

That autumn, his correspondence contained the usual batch of letters from readers, one of whom he thanked for giving him encouragement 'in a period of gloom and depression'. Another compared him with Orwell. 'Perhaps what I find in you and not in Orwell is your almost overpowering humanity,' he wrote and he complained of Orwell's 'repressed Utopianism' and 'lack of tolerance'. Defending his old friend, Arthur replied:

I think you are too hard on Orwell. In 'The Lion and the Unicorn' for instance, he gives a reasoned and constructive and not at all Utopian programme for a non-existent, specifically English Socialist movement. His chronic illness made him irritable and short-tempered with fools but he had an enormous store of kindness and even tenderness in him, which I admired and sometimes envied.

His reply to a fan letter about *The Age of Longing* had an ironical sting in the tail:

I agree with you that it is easier to be 'a fallen angel' among Catholics than among Communists. But this has not always been the case, and one wonders if it would be to the same extent the case if the Church wielded the same secular power as the Kremlin does. And when all is said, thirty years in an Arctic labour camp is still preferable to eternal damnation.

* Later changed to 'Judah at the Crossroads'.

In September he had written to me asking when my planned visit to London was supposed to take place, but I had already answered the question in a letter which crossed with his: 'Don't forget that I am coming to Europe next year. My ports of call will be: Gibraltar, Naples, Cannes, Paris, England, so I ought to come within a reasonable distance of where you will be staying then.'

He mentioned in another letter that he had at last got 'a nice secretary. She can't spell and her shorthand is awful but otherwise she is very pleasant.' I replied that I was delighted, though 'on reading the news your poor old ex-slave could not help feeling a few twinges of jealousy.'

He began 1955 in conventional fashion with a 'gigantic hangover', in the throes of which he spent New Year's Day answering correspondence, presumably to keep at bay the feelings of guilt and self-doubt clamouring to take their revenge.

On 10 February he finished *The Trail of the Dinosaur* and in the preface he made his farewell to politics: 'Now the errors are atoned for, the bitter passion has burnt itself out; Cassandra has gone hoarse, and is due for a vocational change.'

On 4 February he had written to Rebecca West, 'I am now turning with immense relief to a fat and scholarly tome in the seventeenth century – a kind of five year plan.'

He elaborated a little in a letter to Manes Sperber, to whom he said that he was now 'going to write my chef d'oeuvre, a biography of Johannes Kepler, which I have been planning to do for some twenty years and hope to finish before senility finally sets in.'

His diary entry for 21 February reads: 'Most of the day at London Lib[rary],' and on 1 March, 'At last some real reading re Kepler.' He wrote to Veronica Wedgwood:

Incidentally, I have embarked on a triangular biography of Kepler, Galileo and Bruno. If you have half an hour to spare in the near future, I would love to pick your brain, over a drink, not about the people in question but about background reading.

In fact Giordano Bruno (whom, in *The Trail of the Dinosaur,* he called an *enfant terrible,* 'the Bertrand Russell of his age') was dropped as one of the main characters of the new book. They became Copernicus, Kepler and Galileo and the book, of course, was *The Sleepwalkers.*

To me he wrote: 'I am starting on a new book – set in the 17th century and very exciting; but it will take at least a couple of years to write. In the meantime I need somebody to support me; don't you know of any elderly Brazilian widow?'

I replied two and a half months later, saying that I hoped 'the novel' was going well (thinking, as I did then, that only novels could be 'very exciting'). At the end of my letter I entreated him not to look for an elderly Brazilian widow. Of all his girlfriends I liked Sarah the most and hoped he would marry her.

In fact, at this turning point in his life, he was indeed contemplating getting married again and had even proposed, though his mood seemed at odds with his aspirations. He had his first row with his betrothed four days later 'for not making quadrilat[eral] conversation'.* He was seldom less than 'very irritated', though on one terrible day he complained: 'irritation at peak'.

There was 'more irritation' on 2 March. He spent the evening with friends ('dinner bumpy') and the diary note ends: 'But discovered K = K!'

What was it that had excited him? The mystery of this magic formula is revealed next day: 'Happy reading about K.' Kepler had been one of his heroes since the time of his youth, but it was only now – as he began this long-postponed biography – that he discovered in him a kindred spirit. Indeed, at the time of his magic formula, he must have been reading the horoscope that Kepler cast for himself and which Arthur called 'a remarkable document, a self-analysis more unsparing than Rousseau's'.

* * *

---

* i.e. for turning to a guest at the dinner table and carrying on a little private conversation, instead of taking part in the seminar into which he liked to turn his dinner parties in order to extract the maximum out of all his guests.

When Mamaine died, Arthur had become devoted to her twin. Celia had remarried shortly before Mamaine's death. Her husband, Arthur Goodman – a Roman Catholic with an eclectic mind – had formerly been a diplomat and now worked in the City. Arthur often spent weekends with them at their house in Hampshire. He worried incessantly about Celia, for like her twin she had asthma and was sometimes gravely ill. 'Rang Dr. M re Celia,' he wrote in his diary. And again: 'Celia *much* better.'

In February when he went to stay with them he learned that she was pregnant. Fond as he was of Celia's Arthur, he feared that this precious twin's life might be endangered by having a baby. 'A was out shooting when we arrived; Celia in bed. She loves pineapple; & pregnant to boot; why doesn't he *buy* her some!' he exclaimed indignantly in his diary.

He bought a canoe which he called *Blue Arrow*. Nearly eighteen feet long, it could be dismantled and put on the car's luggage rack. With his temporary fiancée he spent weekends on the river Wey, and on Frensham Pond near the Goodmans, or on the Thames. 'Wonderful canoeing in Shepperton,' he wrote.

In early April he spent a 'sombre dimanche' with the fiancée: 'Drinks, sleep, quarrel, maudlin psychoanalysing.' On Monday he felt depressed. The unhappy end was in sight – it was only a matter of time. Wednesday, 13 April, 'started actually writing "Watershed" '.* By Thursday he was 'working furiously'. Friday, too, was a 'good working day'. The trouble was that the weekend loomed before him, and he was only too willing to be lured away from his desk. He spent the weekend with friends in Chiswick 'canoeing with heaps of children'.

'In this man,' writes Kepler, 'there are two opposite tendencies: always to regret any wasted time, and always to waste it willingly. For Mercury makes one inclined to amusements, games, and other light pleasures. . . .'†

---

* 'The Watershed' was the original title of *The Sleepwalkers;* it later became the title of Part Four of the book.

† In his horoscope, Kepler mostly referred to himself in the third person.

Next, 'furniture shifting' took precedence over the book and went on for several days. Pictures had to be hung – an entertaining occupation which required yardstick and pencil to get the correct height. But it was time-consuming, for if he considered the picture had been hung a fraction too high or too low, it must be taken down and the whole operation of measuring and hammering in another picture hook began again and was sometimes repeated. This eventually led to his inventing an adjustable picture hook, for which he actually acquired a patent and he was very proud of becoming a member of the Institute of Patentees and Inventors.★ Alas, he was never able to sell his invention. To his surprise there was not sufficient demand.

On 28 April he wrote: 'Got working well – just before leaving for Berlin', where he was to give a lecture on 'The Ambiguity of Tolerance'. But the real reason for his trip to Germany was to visit Weil-der-Stadt, the birthplace of Kepler. There is a colourful description of his impressions in *The Sleepwalkers*. At the library in Stuttgart he met Dr Franz Hammer, the devoted editor of Kepler's *Collected Works*. Franz and his wife Esther were to become lifelong friends and spend many hours discussing Kepler as if he were a wayward mutual friend whom they often saw.

In the month of June, he was again considering getting married, and this time more seriously. The candidate had brown hair, a pale, arresting face and excellent bone structure. Perhaps her depressive nature also appealed to him as well as the slight resemblance she bore to Mamaine.

He summed up the first tentative stages in his diary: 'Inconclusive'. Later he thought he should have psychiatric 'treatment in order to be able to marry'. But she said he 'ought not to change. Little does she know.' In a depressed mood she sent him a letter. 'She retires,' he wrote in his diary at the end of the month.

He had written on 'the crisis re women' in a notebook

★ He was an enthusiastic, if unsuccessful, inventor. He once demonstrated to my wife a device he had invented to stop spoons and forks slipping into dishes and salad bowls – Editor.

during the month of soul-searching in the Dolomites the summer before: 'I can neither live alone, nor with somebody. It is true, I always picked one type: beautiful Cinderellas, infantile & inhibited, prone to be subdued by bullying. But this realisation doesn't solve the problem.' A little later he was lamenting: 'Women like a man to be sure of himself – even for the wrong reasons and in the wrong way; that's the trouble.' And on another occasion: 'I am so easy to please – & so easy to displease.'

2

In that summer of 1955 the Italian boat *Saturnia* set sail from New York for the Mediterranean. During the voyage I fell for the charms of a journalist from Genoa, but he only noticed me two days before I left the boat at Cannes. (I must have given him Arthur's telephone number, because more than twenty years later, when he visited London, he rang me from Heathrow Airport – a touching reminder of a shipboard romance.)

My mother, dressed in shades of hyacinth and lavender, was waiting to meet me at Cannes. After kissing me, she glanced quickly at my clothes and gasped with horror at my brown face. One should always protect one's face from the sun, she told me.

I had never been to the Mediterranean before and was disappointed by the beach at Cannes with its rows and rows of sunburned, well-oiled bodies. Yet I went there every day for fear of losing my tan.

On Bastille night, kept awake by distant cries of late-night revellers and the spluttering of fireworks, I thought of the first chapter in *The Age of Longing* and wondered how Arthur would have spent the Quatorze Juillet if he had been in Cannes – certainly not alone in a stuffy hotel room. On that same Quatorze Juillet he sent me a postcard: 'Welcome to Europe! Am still in London – working on two books at once; won't be able to get away until later in August. Enjoy yourself and let me know when you arrive. Love – ex-boss.'

How could he be working on two books at once? On the

day he sent me the postcard he rang Victor Gollancz and noted in his diary: '*Cap. punishment crusade started.*'

As John Grigg was to write twenty-five years later in *Astride the Two Cultures:**

It seemed to Arthur that the time was ripe for a full-scale assault on the institution of capital punishment in Britain. In the summer of 1955 he approached Victor Gollancz with the suggestion that they should together organise a national campaign. Gollancz had never been an intimate friend but he had published Arthur's first book in English, *Spanish Testament,* and they had worked together as Zionists. Arthur admired Gollancz's enthusiasm and his prowess as an impresario of good causes. Their joint efforts for abolition were to prove fruitful but stormy.

On 25 July, Arthur noted in his diary: 'Work on "Reflections" only; Kepler shelved. Cynthia arrives.'

I telephoned Arthur at once and he invited me to Montpelier Square the following evening at seven. I wished tomorrow would come quickly. I couldn't sleep and whiled away the hours trying to imagine what the evening would be like. After two whole years he must have changed a lot, I thought.

At last I was standing outside his house. I pressed the bell and waited, gazing hypnotized at the front door.

'Hello,' said a nonchalant voice above my head. Astonished, I looked up. Arthur was standing on the first-floor balcony above my head. He didn't give me much of a smile but he seemed in a good mood and not in any way different.

A jolly atmosphere prevailed within the walls of Bachelor's Fortress. His tenant in the basement flat, Anne Keay, was having drinks with him. They called each other Landlord and Lodger. A few minutes later his pretty, young secretary came in with a letter to be signed. She laughed delightedly at one of his jokes, and looked to see if I was joining in the fun.

The sitting room had lost its French-salon look. The parquet floor was covered with a fitted carpet and L.'s feminine, yellow curtains had been replaced by muted striped ones.

---

* A festschrift by various hands in honour of Koestler's seventieth birthday – Editor.

Later he took me out to dinner. We had no sooner got into the street than he gave me his frank opinion of my American accent. For one who sang out of tune unless accompanied, he suddenly mimicked me with an uncanny ear. 'Largical,' he said mockingly. I certainly overdid the use of the work 'logical'. Feeling somewhat unnerved, I tried to keep in step with him as he walked, but after a few long strides I had to do a hop and a skip to catch up with him. Although he said nothing, it seemed to bother him if I walked out of step.

In a Spanish restaurant facing the back of Harrods he told me about the capital punishment campaign and *Reflections on Hanging*. I remembered a grey morning early in 1953 when Bentley was hanged at nine o'clock and I remembered the grey despair in Arthur's face.

He wanted to know now what I thought about the abolition of capital punishment. Of course I was in favour of it, I told him, but shouldn't some calculating, cold-blooded murderers be hanged? Such cases were extremely rare, he explained patiently. As for murderers like Christie and Heath, they were mentally sick. Hanging was an archaic institution and should be abolished. I needed little convincing.

He was 'burning to write' his book, he said, but he could only dictate it to me. He thought he could finish it by the time I was due to return to New York in early September. But I had promised to spend August with my family in Portland, I reminded him. The whole month? He seemed surprised at such 'lunacy' – a week would be long enough. 'Oh, but I can't put them off,' I said anxiously. I lacked Arthur's alarming flexibility which allowed him to change course in midstream. 'You'll only quarrel,' he told me. I soon gave in – how could I not? – and my holiday in Portland was drastically reduced to five days or, rather, four and a half.

After dinner he told me the latest news about L. Soon after their affair ended she had written to tell him that she was pregnant. She had a daughter. The thought of Arthur being a father caused me some amusement – especially being the father of a daughter.

When we got back to Montpelier Square it was like returning to a past which had remained unchanged. I knew that

Arthur did not want me to become too attached to him for my own sake and I had done my best to become independent. I had an exciting job with Ely Culbertson, a flat I loved overlooking Sutton Gardens in New York, and even an American boyfriend. Nevertheless while I was away I had longed for a glimpse into his life. I had tried to see it in my imagination but it eluded me, just as his face did when I tried to conjure it up – one of the mind's perverse tricks.

That first evening with him during my visit to London was full of surprises and indeed I could hardly have expected it to be otherwise. I was caught up again in a hurricane. Its ways were .unpredictable and to spend the next few weeks in its turmoil was all I could possibly wish for.

When I turned up for work one Sunday morning, Arthur told me that L. was in London. She had flown over from Paris to see him – they had not met since the child was born. He had shown me some snapshots of the baby. He kept them in the bottom drawer of his desk. I saw a lively, fat, contented infant of three months whose smile was not unfamiliar. L.'s husband had readily recognized the child as his own.

L. was trying to inveigle Arthur into a clandestine meeting in the park in Paris where the nanny took the baby for a daily walk. The mere idea of Arthur bending over the pram in the park was enough to reduce me to giggles. Since he would have no hand in the child's education, he did not think it right for him to see her and had told L. so. She was coming for lunch today, he said, and he didn't want to be left alone with her. 'Made her stay in Dorchester,' he wrote in his diary.

The three of us sat in the sun on the roof garden which was on the first floor. She looked unhappy and bewildered. I caught a glance of hers at me which seemed to say, 'How can he have sunk to *that!*' And I was wondering what Arthur saw in her, particularly because of Mamaine. Her clothes were intended to look subdued, but somehow looked flashy in a subdued sort of way. I felt again the furious stirrings of jealousy. After that uneasy meeting she returned to Paris.

In his notebook Arthur gave a different view of L.'s visit. He had been 'very shaken' by it. 'She looked so lovely & sad,' he wrote, filled with pity. 'Unable to understand why I insisted on her staying at the Dorch[ester]. [The child] looks really a darling. Am I missing my last chance?'

3

While Arthur dictated *Reflections on Hanging* I sat in his study, curled up in the armchair beside the fireplace. Every available bit of space was covered with books, lying open or piled up, bristling with bookmarks in the form of brightly coloured tapers, which he bought at Woolworths for lighting the fire. He was constantly referring to them – quite a juggling act with so many books – while he dictated chapter I, 'The Heritage of the Past'. We were living in a world of gallows and gibbets, which were common objects in the early nineteenth-century countryside, 'creaking and groaning with the bodies of criminals'. He had warned me that parts of the book would be stomach-turning. Sometimes he turned pale when dealing with the physiological facts about hanging and looked to see whether I could bear it. Surely he's used to it, I thought. At lunch and dinner I tried not to think of rotting corpses.

Though people in England were shocked by the hanging of Ruth Ellis – the last woman in England to be hanged – who shot her lover in a fit of jealousy, most of the national press stood firmly on the side of capital punishment. The *Observer,* the *Manchester Guardian* and the *Yorkshire Post* were among the few exceptions. I trembled as I read the comments in *The Times* – how could the climate of opinion possibly be changed? But I relished Arthur's attacks on the bastions of the Establishment and in particular on the hanging judges. His *bête noire* was the Lord Chief Justice himself. He wrote:

I have no personal animosity against Lord Chief Justice Rayner Goddard; but as the highest judge in the realm, he is the symbol of authority, and his opinions, which I shall have frequent occasion to quote, carry immense weight in the debate about hanging.

He intended to write the book in a 'cool and detached manner', but it was not turning out that way. Surely he should be more dispassionate, I sometimes thought. All that highly charged, restrained emotion was like a fist in my solar plexus. He got some of it out of his system in the first draft and toned it down, but as he wrote in the preface:

In 1937, during the Civil War in Spain, I spent three months under sentence of death as a suspected spy, witnessing the executions of my fellow-prisoners and awaiting my own. These three months left me with a vested interest in capital punishment. . . . I shall never achieve real peace of mind until hanging is abolished. I have stated my bias. It colours the arguments in the book; it does not affect the facts in it, and most of its content is factual.

'Work, work, work,' he wrote in his diary. The book was beginning to grow into an obsession.

When he finished the chapter on 'Free Will and Determinism or the Philosophy of Hanging' – he called it the most difficult one – he was more than halfway through the book. He was like somebody possessed and the subject was never far from his mind. If we went to a pub for a-drink, he would start up a discussion with the publican – perhaps one of his ways of feeling the pulse of the nation. All publicans were pro-hanging, which, of course, was just what Arthur was hoping for, and he would present a diabolically reasoned and objective case for abolition. Although he never managed to convert a single die-hard publican, he never gave up hope. Even at the end of a working day, the obsession would continue to pursue him and the evenings were spent dictating notes to me for the following morning's work. In that heightened state of sensibility all his ideas seemed to fall on fertile ground and blossom. One night he decided to invent a fictional dialogue between a young abolitionist and a wise old hanging judge. In the cold light of day this idea was rejected and the pages he had dictated to me were torn up.

In his diary he wrote: 'Mania at peak.' He could not stop talking or reading about capital punishment when he was not writing about it. At night he continued to dictate the book to me in his sleep. I tried hard to memorize his words as they poured out – punctuated every now and then by 'full stop', 'semi-colon', or 'new para'. When I repeated my recollections to him in the morning, they turned out to be gibberish, but in the middle of the night they had seemed vital.

Arthur called this shared obsession a *folie à deux*. It was the beginning of my becoming, in his words, a 'junior partner', though I did not realize it then.

A heat wave was on. From the study window, which overlooks the tops of plane trees, there was a small rectangle of sky far too blue to be English. It was hot under the roof and the walls with their pine panelling raised the temperature even more. Occasionally the rural sound of a pigeon cooing would come down the chimney straight into the room. Infuriated, Arthur would spring to his feet and give the chimney breast a bang with a fire iron. The silence that followed was often only temporary. The pigeons seemed to like roosting on his chimney, and if there was one thing he couldn't stand it was their gentle cooing.

During the heat wave, he began Part Three of the book: 'The End of the Nightmare'. This part was unsparing in its glimpses of the struggles of prisoners on their way to the gallows, some 'carried tied to a chair' or dragged with 'arms pinioned to the back, like animals'. I could not help thinking of a passage in his autobiography, which he had also dictated to me and which was about one of his earliest and most traumatic memories. At the age of five he had had his tonsils removed, without anaesthetic, in a doctor's surgery in Budapest. This image of the young Koestler, his arms and legs secured to a chair by leather straps, rendered helpless, choking and coughing up blood – this image was my silent companion during the writing of *Reflections on Hanging*.

In the middle of August Arthur began to worry about Celia who was expecting her baby at any minute. He feared she might have an asthma attack and would not survive the birth. He infected me with his fears. Reliving the tragedy of Mamaine, he seemed sure that the same fate would befall her twin. In his diary he wrote of his 'anguish' about Celia. But on 14 August she had a daughter. 'Birth of Ariane,' he wrote in his diary with relief and had a brandy to recover.

One day he told me that an Italian ex-girlfriend had come on a short visit to London. 'I shall have to dine with her alone,' he said; 'poor thing, she has had a miserable time and has been sick, too.' Could I get her a room for the night in the place where I was staying? he wondered. He couldn't resist mentioning that he had first seen her with her fiancé in a restaurant in the Haute-Savoie and had stolen her for a night.*

I imagined him, rather sunburned, sitting by himself – his left hand propped up against the side of his face, as he appears in some photographs – looking at her with a certain expression he reserved for women. 'How did you get her away from her fiancé?' I asked, thrilled by the exploit. I could hardly catch his reply. He muttered something in an embarrassed way about the fiancé leaving her for a moment, then he brushed the whole thing aside.

The beautiful Paola did not put on airs and I liked her forthright manner as she gave my hand a hearty shake. She spoke excellent English.

I had supper that evening in a restaurant in Knightsbridge which served pseudo-Italian food. Arthur would never set foot in such a place, I thought, and he certainly would not have touched the soggy ravioli I was eating. But soggy ravioli was a relief after the quantities of raw garlic, green peppers and paprika which Arthur sprinkled liberally on anything he thought insipid.

My room was in a nearby late-Victorian building whose stairs and long corridors consisted of bare boards which echoed with every step. When I turned out my light that night I lay wide awake, listening for the returning footsteps of Paola. However, there was nothing but an unbearable silence. I imagined the candles glowing in the bedroom and the nude lady painted by Civet which hung over the mantelpiece, bathed in an esoteric light. . . . The next morning I felt a fool about that sudden jealousy. I had fallen asleep in the end and had not heard Paola come in. I was glad that I had no idea what had happened.

★　　★　　★

* See page 179.

The sprint to finish the first draft of *Reflections on Hanging* continued until 30 August. In his diary he simply scrawled 'work' or 'ditto' except for the mention of a cocktail party to which he 'forgot to go'. Whilst dictating the book, he walked diagonally up and down the room, from the study door to the mantelpiece. Sometimes he stopped and stared, unseeing, out of the window or he hunted in the stacks of books for a reference. When not converting his words into shorthand, I looked at a strand of carpet or the inlay on a piece of furniture or at the lady over the mantelpiece who shared his study. She seemed contented.

As soon as the first draft was finished Arthur began correcting it. But at the weekend he took a break – the first in twelve days – to go canoeing. We drove out of London in the open car, passing other cars often to the accompaniment of indignant hooting. I was unnerved by Arthur's bold leapfrogging to the top of a queue and by the noisy reaction of other motorists. But he couldn't bear the snail's pace of the average English motorist in those days. Why don't they all buy donkeys, he demanded, nearly driven mad.

When we reached the river there was peace. *Blue Arrow* was unpacked from her bags and reassembled on the shore. Soon she began to look like her name.

Monday, 5 September, was Arthur's fiftieth birthday. I was surprised that he remembered it. In his diary he wrote: 'Alas, only once.' In a state of gloom he opened the telegrams but felt cheered by the prospect of playing truant from work and going out for lunch. Just before we set forth he came downstairs from his study looking rather sick. He mentioned in passing that he had burned all the telegrams.

We had lunch on the first floor of Overton's, a fish restaurant in Victoria. Towards the end, as I was wishing it would go on for ever, I looked out of the window. It was raining and people were hurrying about on the grey streets which looked greyer than ever against the tropical red of the buses. I hoped Arthur would not be depressed as he surveyed the scene. He made no comment but in his diary he wrote: 'Very depressed, despite spectacular lunch at Overtons.'

The date for my return to New York was fixed for early

September, but as Arthur was still hard at work on the final draft, I postponed it by ten days. I was filled with euphoria: I had another ten, whole, magical days before me. Needless to say, the days dwindled fast. If only I could have just one more week; it was a futile thought – no amount of time would ever be long enough.

On my last Sunday we went to Guildford to fetch the canoe which was moored on the river Wey and had dinner with Celia and her husband in their house near Farnham. Arthur held the tiny baby, Ariane, to whom he explained in a matter-of-fact way that he was her Uncle Arthur. Would she be like Mamaine and Celia when she grew up? I wondered. Would I ever know?

It was during this summer that I discovered that Arthur sometimes got drunk. In all the years I had known him I had never been aware of this. Perhaps my uncritical view of him had blinded me. I had only noticed that the more he drank, the more lucid he became – something I had not come across in anybody else. But the evening we spent with Celia and Arthur Goodman ended unexpectedly.

After dinner we left to drive back to London. We got no farther than a pub at the end of the village called the Cricketer, where we stopped for a quick drink. A few locals were having beer with the publican. Naturally Arthur turned the topic of conversation to hanging. He could hardly have chosen a subject which provoked more interest – apart from sex (indeed hanging often aroused the same kind of lurid curiosity). In that stronghold of 'hang-hards', he entered the fray with hopeful enthusiasm. It soon became clear that he was getting nowhere, but this only added fuel to his infinite desire to share his feelings. Many rounds later, we made our way to the car. The hour was midnight – long past closing time.

That whisky was hooch, said Arthur, trying to shake it out of his head. We never got back to London that night, but spent it en route in a slummy little hotel. Arthur was beset with nightmares. He gasped and shuddered, suddenly giving a violent shout, then mumbling. The sounds would die away, come back as if all the furies were pursuing him, and die away again. After that night on a bare mountain we drove silently in the open car through the dreary sunlit suburbs back to Montpelier Square.

Two days before leaving, I went with Arthur to the Old Bailey where a murder trial was being held. The defendant, Donald Brown, aged nineteen, had killed an elderly tobacconist in his little shop and robbed the till. The court was nearly empty since the case had nothing sensational about it. Nevertheless it did seem strange that the trial was conducted to the sound of snoring – macabre, Arthur called it. The elderly official who was responsible for it sat near the judge and had once been shaken gently by the shoulder, but soon succumbed again and this time he was left in peace.

When the jury returned a verdict of guilty, the official whose snoring had been so persistent suddenly came to life and now played his appointed role in the act. He handed the black cap to the judge, who set it on his wig and passed the death sentence. The defendant was told that he would be hanged by the neck until dead and his body removed for burial in the prison grounds. The youth, standing in the dock with his jailers seated behind him, looked down at the floor, dazed and a little defiant. 'Terrible,' wrote Arthur in his diary. Later he told me with relief that Donald Brown had been reprieved.

We worked on the book up to the last moment. It was not yet finished – two chapters had still to be corrected and the preface written. The day before I left Arthur wrote in his diary: 'Departure depression crescendo.' If he had told me, I would not have believed him.

The next day we worked until noon and had a farewell lunch in the kitchen – lobster from Burkett's, the fishmongers round the corner who wore straw boaters, and white wine. Later Arthur took me back to my hotel 'loaden with flowers' as he put it rather comically in his diary. I felt strangely elated as we said goodbye on the hotel doorstep; some inner strength seemed to flow through my veins, which was quite electrifying. I saw the same face that had looked at me from the balcony in Montpelier Square seven and a half weeks ago. Those two moments were photographed in my memory. I jumped up the hotel stairs two at a time. The rest of the day my heart kept turning over in pain and delight. I must stop it, I thought, or it will give out.

On board the *Nieuw Amsterdam* I spent the voyage on my bunk reading. Sometimes I went to the dining room, but was unable to eat, and it was not the rough seas that bothered me. One dreary day I went out on deck and got picked up by the kind of young man who wore a bow tie and read the *New Yorker* every week. It was all a matter of indifference to me.

'Let's play telepathy,' he said. Knowing what Arthur thought about the subject, I felt a spark of interest. We sat at a table on the desolate, windswept deck. 'I'll draw something,' he said, 'and you must guess what it is.' He shielded a piece of paper with one hand as he drew, then put it into his pocket and looked at me challengingly. 'It's a horse,' I said. Triumphantly he flourished the drawing. It was the head of a horse – in actual fact, a knight in chess.

Excited by this instant success, he suggested we have another go. But it never worked again. When he drew telegraph lines I thought of rabbits hopping about in a field. I drifted back to my bunk.

The book I was reading, acquired at a bookstand in Southampton, was called *A Book of Trials – Personal Recollections of an Eminent Judge of the High Court*. I was hoping to find something of interest in it for Arthur. I had a daydream of returning to London to work for him again. But I knew he wanted me to be sensible and lead my own life.

'It was a *wonderful* summer and terribly hard to recover from,' I wrote to him. My good intentions were hopeless – in that letter I mentioned a mere four times my daydream of coming back in the near future. Nevertheless I was determined to pull myself together. At least I could imagine for a while the life he was leading: he was finishing *Reflections on Hanging*; and he would continue to see his friends, go out to dinner, buy a picture or an *objet d'art,* and spend his Sundays lazing with someone (though I preferred not to think of that).

When the boat arrived at New York harbour my boyfriend, looking rather simpatico, was there to meet me. But I didn't like the present of a glamorous American nightdress which he brought me.

After I left, Arthur suffered from a pain in the thorax 'like a fist turning, churning'. He went to the house of friends, the diary goes on, and had a ghastly dinner of an 'alive-burnt artichoke' – a rather Koestlerian description. For the rest of the week he worked, despite a mysterious attack of gastric flu which he attributed to 'that artichoke'.

I had sometimes heard Arthur bewail the fact that his friends only knew Koestler B – they knew nothing of Koestler A. His diary that autumn chronicles the lives of both of them, not to mention a depression which reached 'rock bottom'.

Koestler B was no contemplative. He liked good food and wine, conviviality and wit – in both senses of the word. 'My evenings are wasted' is the complaint in a notebook of 1954, 'yet I need these alcoholic evening-inspirations, even though most of them are worthless.' Alcohol, the balm of the writer, might lead him to a fertile oasis – or to a mirage.

Koestler A was no hedonist. He lived a spartan existence in his study on the top floor, amongst his books, ruled manuscript paper on his desk. In the mornings, as soon as he was awake he got up. I was amazed that there had ever been a time – described in *Arrow in the Blue* – when as a student he had rotted 'in a crumpled bed until afternoon . . . sinking into an abyss of depravity.' He went down to the kitchen for breakfast and barely had time for some bitter, black coffee and a dry crust of bread sprinkled with salt. He went upstairs again, impatient to suffer the delights of a cold shower. Before nine he was at his desk – his hair plastered down and still sopping wet – to attack the mail. Long letters were put in a file to be read later and the bench behind his desk was stacked with periodicals, offprints on divers subjects and other people's manuscripts – to be read over the weekend. Having cleared his desk he waited hopefully for that inner peace which made his writing possible.

As evening approached, his mood changed too. The room grew dark, except for the illuminated lady over the mantelpiece and the circle of light on his desk, where he sat writing. Alone in that blessed cocoon of darkness and silence, all the

conflicting elements of his nature fell into harmony and for a
while he became himself – the writer's happy or unhappy fate.

The Trail of the Dinosaur had just come out in England.
Stephen Spender gave it what the diary called a 'beastly first
review' in one of the Sunday papers.

On 3 October Arthur finished *Reflections on Hanging* and sent
the typescript off to Gollancz. This coincided with another
mysterious attack of gastric flu which persisted for a week
('damn it,' he wrote). Perhaps it is a psychosomatic disease of
the writer? Notwithstanding, he managed within two days to
answer three months of neglected correspondence, and
worked on the footnotes and appendices for *Reflections on
Hanging*. At last he returned to the fifteenth century: '*Back to
Copernic*,' he wrote with relief, but it was short-lived.

'Lovely Sunday morning with Mozart and white wine,' he
wrote of a weekend with one of his shadowy companions. In
the afternoon they went to Oxford and visited a 'suicidal
electro-shocked don, collector of hideous rugs and books'. By
evening Arthur was himself depressed, and feeling disenchan-
ted with his companion.

His obsessive nature next fastened itself on a girl he had
met at the dinner of 'burnt-alive artichoke'. She had been
away since that occasion and during her absence his obsession
grew. 'Waiting for Kikuyu to ring,' he wrote in the diary.
Though she had a not unusual English name, he called her
Kikuyu as she came from Kenya, home of the Kikuyu tribe.
Meant only as a joke, the nickname hinted in an uncanny way
at the torture in store for him. 'Bursting with adrenalin, yet at
the same time grinning at myself,' he scribbled. In the section
on humour in *The Act of Creation* there is a fitting description
of his predicament: 'The puppet on strings is a timeless
symbol, either comic or tragic, of man as a plaything of
destiny – whether he is jerked about by the gods or suspended
on his own chromosomes and glands.'

At last the 'blessed' telephone rang.

Next day he visited Celia, who was in a London clinic after
an asthma attack – the second in three months – and then he
lunched with Arthur Goodman, who was 'in a desperate state'
about her precarious health. He dined that night with Griselda

and Louis Kentner – the Hungarian pianist – Robin Maugham, Sir Richard Rees, and the Kikuyu. That evening in Montpelier Square was catastrophic. Robin Maugham was conversing with Kikuyu. With his dark and dashing looks he was being too charming by half. Enraged by this unexpected trespassing, Arthur 'threw Robin out into the street'. His guilt for this 'impardonable and cowardly act' turned into horror when he later learned that the victim of his temper had a war injury which still caused him to suffer from headaches. He wrote an agonized letter of apology.

Over the weekend, Kikuyu stood him up at the last minute. By now he was off his head about her. In despair he rang the girl with whom he had gone to Oxford the week before. They drove to Oxford again, dined with six undergraduates and stayed overnight at a hotel. When his companion vanished to somebody else's hotel room, his self-control abandoned him for the second time in four days. In his diary he wrote of becoming 'half-crazed' and 'beating her up terribly' and '1/2 murdering' her. In the morning he drove back to London to find that his tenant's basement flat in Montpelier Square had been burgled.

During this 'breakdown week' he made no progress with his work on Copernicus. Indeed, he had no sooner started it than he was interrupted. Gerald Gardiner QC had read *Reflections on Hanging* for Arthur's publisher, Gollancz, and considered quite a few passages libellous.

Gerald Gardiner, who later became Lord Chancellor, was one of the leading lights of the capital punishment campaign. His own book on the subject was also being published by Gollancz. 'In their different ways,' to quote John Grigg, 'these two books provided an overwhelming statement of the case for abolition.'* Though Gardiner was passionately against capital punishment, his style was cool and detached, and no doubt *Reflections on Hanging* challenged the cautious attitude of a legal mind. 'Nearly finished last Gardiner-caused corrections,' Arthur wrote with resignation in his diary. He had spent two weeks on a job he considered a waste of time.

* *Astride the Two Cultures*, p. 126.

On 27 October he sent off the final typescript of *Reflections on Hanging* to Gollancz and on the same day went to the British Museum Library to take up the thread at last of his work on Copernicus and Kepler. In his diary he wrote: 'Beginning, I hope, to convalesce after break-down week.' He was longing to get back to writing, but soon he developed a 'stinking cold', and was plagued with one of his psychosomatic ailments – this time 'nausea'.

'Cold even worse,' he noted, and spent most of the day in bed reading some biographies of Casanova, for he was toying with the idea of writing an essay on Casanova and Don Juan. Still in bed with a temperature on 5 November, he listened to *Fidelio* on the radio from Vienna, and later got up to see some friends.

'Then blank – then cable to Cynthia.'

12

Back to the Square

I

In the cable Arthur mentioned 'new developments' and asked me to come back to London and work for him for six months. Thrilled by this sudden bombshell, I tried to fathom the meaning of the 'new developments', but as usual my feeble imagination gave out.*

A week after the cable came a letter. It began:

There is really no mystery. The fat book about Copernicus, Kepler, Galileo, etc., has turned out to be a book of the kind that ought to be dictated, so as to force myself to get on with it, otherwise it would take five years. . . . And since you kept saying that if there was a job for you, you would come back; and since it looks as if you wouldn't be missing much in New York just now, I took one

---

* There is no record of Arthur's cable. But her cabled reply, sent late on 6 November 1955, said simply: 'YES WRITING LOVE CYNTHIA'. An ecstatic letter followed on 7 November: 'Dearest Arthur, I am so overwhelmed! What can this all be about? It sounds so exciting I can't wait to hear. And I suppose I shan't get a letter from you until about November 9, for you won't write until you have my cable saying yes (which I sent off last night in case you want confirmation.) WHAT CAN IT BE? I have spent a night in the clouds – I didn't even need sleep! I will be able to arrange my life so as to be in London by November 20th. . . .'

This letter goes on to discuss some details of financial arrangements which she had to make in New York and concludes: 'Really, life is full of thunderbolts and whirlpools. Now I must stop and try to organise myself in the exhausting whirlpool of the next two weeks. How wonderful! How exciting! I long to know about your plan. THANK YOU A MILLION. Much love from your slavey (formerly ex-ex), Cynthia.' Arthur's reply to this letter is in the text – Editor.

208

of those quick decisions in suggesting that we do this book together. It will be less exciting (and less stomach-turning) than the hanging book. . . . The people in it, at any rate, are very fascinating looney geniuses; one gets burned alive, and the other's mother is indicted as a witch. . . .

I have to go for a week to Paris next Saturday, the 12th. I shall be back in London on Saturday, 19th. If you can alter your booking to a flight to Paris, we could drive back to London together one day later, on Sunday (I am taking the car), which would be fun. Do let me know what arrangements you make. . . .

Celia had a bad bout of asthma and had to go to a clinic for a fortnight, but is now better. Her baby is flourishing.

Dorothy Culbertson was sharing my flat, using it as a *pied-à-terre* whenever she came to New York. The marriage between Ely and herself had broken down some time before. Dorothy had the craving of an only child to confide, transforming a confidante into the imagined sibling, perhaps once longed for, of early childhood. I had no similar urges, preferring to keep my secrets to myself. Such a friend as Dorothy is rare. She had a critical mind and she could analyse in a reasoned way the most unreasonable of emotions.

She was with me when Arthur's letter arrived, and was mystified by the hurry I was in to pack up, find a new secretary for Ely, leave my boyfriend and apartment, and fly back to London to be at Arthur's beck and call. I tried in an embarrassed way to express my feelings.

'But,' she said scornfully, 'how can anyone – *for years* – live on unrequited love?'

That awful word shook me. It was not 'unrequited' I quickly said, then mumbled something about being lovers – a dark secret for the first time seeing the light of day.

Dorothy looked sceptical. What does the letter say, she wanted to know. I gave it to her reluctantly and she stood reading it intently, the light shining on her straight blonde hair. The reason I had been reluctant for her to see it was that it began 'Dear Old Cynthia' – the words made my heart sink like lead.

'Panic re C.,' Arthur wrote in his diary on the day after he sent that urgent cable. It was a Sunday and he spent it nursing his cold: 'Except for short visit to pub, in bed all day.' It was not the first time that he had acted in a similar vein and in the aftermath suffered from cold feet. When twenty, a lightning decision – made after a long and impassioned argument about free will and determinism – changed the course of his life. He called that chapter in *Arrow in the Blue* 'The Blessings of Unreason'. The book itself ends with another abrupt change of course.*

He received my reply on the Monday, and comforted himself by invoking 'Socrates and his daemon'. 'Feel better about it,' the diary adds. There is no further mention of the cold.

During the week he went to one of Lady Rothermere's literary luncheons and dined with Rebecca West and her husband. 'Rebecca incredibly spiteful about everybody,' he commented, '& when I talked about "rich and poor" [she] thought am rejoining CP.' But she 'joined' him in his feelings about the death penalty.

On 10 November in a crowded London hall the first meeting of the National Campaign for the Abolition of Capital Punishment was held. 'V.G. pays tribute to me as initiator; felt very proud,' he wrote in the diary. He had gone to the meeting with Arthur Goodman, David and Bridget Astor and others, and afterwards had supper with the Astors, Gerald Gardiner and J. B. Priestley and his wife, Jaquetta Hawkes.

'Due to start Pariswards tomorrow, but kidney symptoms,' he noted on 11 November. The symptoms evidently did not develop. He was away for eight nights and seems to have wasted not a moment of that precious time.

On the ferryboat he met a friend and took a fancy to the girl who was with him. She was allowed to keep him company

---

* The two incidents referred to are the burning of his matriculation papers which meant he could not complete his course at Vienna University; and joining the Communist Party – Editor.

on part of the drive to Paris – 'kidnap-ride to Abbéville,' he wrote in the diary. Less than twenty-four hours later he was having a 'siesta' with her, after a rendezvous at Weber's close to the Madeleine, where 'the sun shone down pleasantly, warming the wicker-chairs on the terrace with all those pretty women wondering with whom they should go to bed next' (so thought Fedya in *The Age of Longing*).

'Beastly lunch à trois,' he wrote crossly of one of the two days on which he failed to have a siesta. He had taken the new girlfriend to have lunch with an old girlfriend – Sarah, the one I had liked so much in 1953 and hoped he might marry.

He went shopping, viewed an exhibition of Etruscan art and had a 'long lunch' with Manes Sperber. One evening he went out to see Anna and Maxim and Sabby and took them to dinner in Fontainebleau. He had drinks at the Pont Royal bar and another favourite haunt, Fouquet's. He drove his new girlfriend to Melun where his canoe of Verte Rive days was stored, had lunch in Fontainebleau and a siesta there, too. The nights were spent with Paola in her flat. One evening he dined with the Raymond Arons, and on another with the Rothschilds, revisiting two other favourite haunts: the lesbian *boîte de nuit*, Monocle, and Les Halles for a *soupe à l'oignon*. Two days running he lunched with a dazzling French girl. A row with Paola was made up on their farewell night: 'En te disant adieu, je dis adieu à ma jeunesse.'

He departed as he had arrived – with the girl he had bagged on the ferry. At Boulogne there was the 'usual farewell row with waiter'. They returned together to Montpelier Square. 'Delighted to be back,' the diary says at the end of his sentimental journey.

I only managed to get to London two days later, having had to cancel my flight to Paris where we had intended to meet. This was fortunate perhaps for I should undoubtedly have been *de trop*. I turned up on the doorstep of Montpelier Square on a wintry morning and was let in by Arthur's cross-looking char. Leaving my luggage in the hall, I walked up the three flights of stairs as slowly as I was able and found Arthur at his desk, looking quite cheerful, if a little pale. He told me rather mournfully that after I left for New York he had had six new girlfriends and that was quite enough. He wasn't going to be a sugar daddy, he muttered frowning. The mere thought of Arthur as a sugar daddy gave me the giggles, but he was not amused.

A month later, Ely Culbertson died. I had known him for two years and his influence on me cannot be forgotten. (I was to feel even more intensely the death of Dorothy – always so radiantly alive – who was but a year older than I. She remarried and three years later died in childbirth. How could the birds still sing, I thought, as I awoke to the dawn chorus the next day?)

3

Within two days Arthur was at work again on his 'fat book about Copernicus, Kepler, Galileo, etc.'. He was also passionately involved in the capital punishment campaign, attending an executive committee on the day of my return. Towards the end of November, Edward Hulton, proprietor of *Picture Post,* and Gerald Gardiner came 'solemnly for drinks' at Montpelier Square. 'H. says converted,' Arthur noted. The campaign had few allies among the press – from *The Times* down they were all out for retention, and only a tiny minority were for abolition.

He dictated to me what he had written about Copernicus, but a week later discovered to his frustration that he would have to delve even farther back into the history of science – to Pythagoras. He was longing to get to the book's central character – the complicated and contradictory Johannes Kepler, whose portrait in a small frame was propped up on his desk.

I found myself a room on the top floor of a vast and depressing late-Victorian house in Hans Place, a stone's throw from Montpelier Square. With records and books borrowed from Arthur, I was far from depressed when spending an evening alone. One afternoon, while we were playing truant from work, he told me in a joky way that I was the favourite. I felt awestruck and for days tried not to behave self-consciously, afraid of spoiling things. My predecessor was a novelist. She had actually lived in the house and she sounded the ideal woman for Arthur. They must have had a fearful row. I wondered what it could have been about.

One Sunday morning a doctor friend dropped in for a drink. After a while Arthur left the room briefly. The doctor sat on the sofa beside me and I felt as usual tongue-tied. He asked a question and I looked up into blue eyes that widened in a most lively expression of curiosity and warmth. I learned later that he was a Jungian analyst whom Arthur had seen in the hopes of curing depressions and writing blocks.

The capital punishment campaign was getting into full swing and during that winter I worked part time at the campaign's headquarters in the publishing house of Gollancz in Henrietta Street, Covent Garden. A cubicle had been partitioned off from the packing department on the ground floor and served as an office for Peggy Duff, the secretary and treasurer, and her handful of voluntary workers. Peggy had campaigned before for Gollancz on Save Europe Now. Nervous at first of her blunt manner and daunting ability to cope with the daily crises, I soon became as devoted to Peggy as all her workers were.

Occasionally Victor Gollancz breezed in – a genial patriarch whose features resembled those of a hawk. Despite his whims which Arthur was fighting against during those turbulent months, I had a paradoxical liking for him. Even at the first meeting of the executive committee during the summer, Gollancz and Arthur had clashed. Arthur wrote in his diary that V.G. 'embarrassed everyone' by wanting his wife Ruth on the committee: 'Only I stuck my neck out & opposed. Rather depressing, but since I can't help it, don't mind.' It meant of course that V.G. had two votes instead of one.

Gollancz had apparently hoped that *Reflections on Hanging* would stress the religious aspects of capital punishment, upon which he himself drew heavily in the campaign pamphlet he wrote, 'Capital Punishment: The Heart of the Matter', which Arthur privately dismissed as beating about the bush. The other campaign pamphlet, written by Gerald Gardiner and Arthur, was called 'Capital Punishment: The Facts'. V.G.'s religious feelings, together with a desire to hold the centre of the stage, caused endless delays in the publishing of *Reflections on Hanging*. It took two months to write, but seven to publish.

Arthur felt that his foreign accent would damage the cause and refused to lecture on capital punishment, except once – to Cambridge undergraduates. Gerald Gardiner, he said, was a brilliant speaker, whose restraint made him all the more convincing – acting had been a pastime in his student days. Though sharing Arthur's passion for abolition, he was not always an ally at executive committee meetings. Perhaps the more cautious, legal mind of the future Lord Chancellor made him sit on the fence, but Arthur said it was because he was terrorized by V.G.

Arthur spent Christmas 1955 with the Goodmans and was 'very worried' about Celia ('only 6 stone'). A few days later he saw a new play, *Waiting for Godot,* which he found 'a remarkable mixture of allegory, poetry and nonsense'.

On New Year's Eve, he wrote to David Astor, editor of the *Observer,* which was going to serialize *Reflections on Hanging* in early February:

For a happy start of the New Year three people are scheduled to be hanged on January 3rd and 6th respectively. All three are obviously psychiatric cases. . . . I would like to write a few lines (anonymous) for 'Table Talk' or any other appropriate column. This raises the more general issue of a systematic coverage of these semi-anonymous cases who are dispatched in our name without fanfares. . . .

Thus began 'Vigil', a pseudonym under which Arthur wrote in the *Observer* and which, he felt, gave him the freedom to fight more effectively for the cause rather than under his own name which was that of a notorious pro-abolitionist. Also, he wanted Vigil to be a collective pseudonym for a team, but David Astor was against this. Arthur had a 'hard fight' (as he wrote in the diary) before David Astor reluctantly agreed 'to make Vigil a team'.

Clarence William Ward, a labourer of below average intelligence, was due to be executed on 26 January. The *Observer* printed Vigil's first piece, attacking the Appeal Court judge –

none other than Lord Chief Justice Goddard. David Astor sent Arthur a copy of the newspaper, hot from the press, on the Saturday night, 21 January, with a handwritten note:

> My dear Vigil I,
> Here it is.
> En avant!
> Yours
> David

'Ward reprieved,' wrote Arthur in the diary three days later. 'Editorial in M[*anchester*] G[*uardian*] attributing it to Vigil.'

Occasionally I caught glimpses of David Astor when he came to Montpelier Square. During those tempestuous months he was an unfailing ally of Arthur's and stood by him with a courage that was awe-inspiring.

Two obsessions beset Arthur that winter – the abolition crusade and the new book. '1/2 despaired re Plato. Black fog.' I remember one bleak winter's night when his obsession with Plato and Aristotle, 'the twin stars' as he called them, became unbearable. He had to talk to somebody about it. Henry Green lived round the corner and had studied classics, so we went to see him. Arthur, alas, got little out of the visit, apart from letting off steam. Henry had nothing to say about Plato and Aristotle, but he looked on and listened, obviously bemused by the sight of a man with a burning obsession. His son plied Arthur with vodkas, but even they did not help. When at last we left he was as tormented as ever and somewhat the worse for wear. Staggering slightly, he wondered if his mind would give him any peace to sleep.

'Am dead beat,' he wrote in the diary and, 'On the brink of exhaustion.' Switching from one obsession to the other, he commented: 'This split existence creates experimental neurosis as with Pavlov dog.'

In January the first campaign *Bulletin,* of which he was the author, appeared – a monthly production circularized to the sixty-five members of the campaign's Committee of Honour, the press and other contacts. A feature of the *Bulletin* was the 'Newgate Calendar 1956', which gave brief case histories of defendants in murder trials. The first issue reported the cases of four men who had been reprieved, after a sojourn in the condemned cell. Arthur wrote to David Astor:

> . . . I do not share the general optimism regarding the capital punishment issue. Wait for two or three particularly nasty murders in London – they always come in series as recently in Glasgow – and there will be a great comeback of the retentionists, blaming it all on too many recent reprieves.
>
> When I started 'Vigil', I meant it to be a collective pseudonym for a team. . . . I feel that since we were lucky with the first Vigil piece, people will watch out for the next and that once started we should let this Frankenstein march on.

A debate in the House of Commons on capital punishment, with a free vote, was imminent. In early February, Gerald Gardiner and Peggy Duff came to Montpelier Square one evening. Over drinks Peggy said that V.G. had 'completely lost interest' in the campaign. On 14 February – the eve of the Commons debate – Arthur feared the 'shock of morrow's defeat'. But his pessimism was unfounded.

There was an excellent view from the Visitors' Gallery. On the Front Bench the members of the Cabinet – Churchill among them – reclined, their legs comfortably outstretched. Sydney Silverman gave one of the main speeches in favour of abolition. As he returned to his seat, walking past the Front Bench, Churchill glanced at him briefly with faint contempt.

'*Unforgettable*. . . . Incredible surprise vote,' Arthur wrote in the diary. Afterwards a group of abolitionists gathered at the entrance of the Commons in a buoyant mood. A woman in a well-worn winter coat – the organizer of one of the campaign's provincial offices – rushed up to Victor Gollancz to ask if they should cancel their forthcoming meeting. To Arthur's horror Gollancz said yes.★ 'Anti-climax,' he wrote in the diary. 'Row with V.G. in front of Commons not to pack up.' Perhaps others who witnessed the scene also longed, like me, to sink beneath the floor. The general mood of

---

★ The reason for his 'horror' was of course that the House of Lords might throw out the Bill, as indeed happened. It was not until 1965 that the death penalty was suspended and it was 1970 before it was finally abolished – Editor.

rejoicing dissolved into uneasy confusion. Gollancz reluctantly agreed to a meeting of the executive committee.

As a result of Gollancz's loss of interest and the overoptimistic feelings of many abolitionists, the campaign lost some of its initial vitality, but it remained in being as a valuable watchdog for many years – thanks to the funds raised by an auction sale. To quote John Grigg:

The Campaign's finances were at a desperately low ebb, and to rectify this state of affairs Arthur took an initiative which led to the raising of a large fund. He suggested to his friend June Osborn that she should organise an auction sale of literary manuscripts and works of art, the proceeds to go towards abolition and penal reform. June, recently widowed, threw herself into the work with her own peculiarly infectious gusto and ruthless powers of persuasion. With the help of a few friends she assembled a remarkable collection of objects, including the works of many famous contemporary artists, presented by themselves. These were sold in London on 30 May at an auction conducted by her cousin, Peter Wilson of Sotheby's. The sum raised was about £4400. . . .*

In March Arthur had barely got back into the lives of medieval astronomers when he was again plunged in at the deep end of a controversy on capital punishment. Lord Waverley, who, as Sir John Anderson, had been Home Secretary and was an ardent retentionist, raised a question in the House of Lords:

To ask Her Majesty's Government whether their attention has been drawn to an article by Arthur Koestler in *The Observer* of March 4th entitled 'Behind the Bulletins' which purports to quote a confidential Home Office instruction to Prison Governors and refers to incidents alleged to have occurred at the execution of Edith Thompson; and whether they have any statement to make.

Lord Hailsham, another retentionist, supported him.

The article in question came from *Reflections on Hanging* – still not published by Gollancz – which was being serialized

---

* *Astride the Two Cultures*, p. 129.

by the *Observer*. The extract from a confidential Home Office instruction to prison governors, dated 10 January 1925, ran as follows:

Any reference to the manner in which an execution has been carried out should be confined to as few words as possible, e.g., 'it was carried out expeditiously and without a hitch'. No record should be taken as to the number of seconds and, if pressed for details of this kind, the Governor should say he cannot give them, and he did not time the proceedings, but 'a very short interval elapsed', or some general expression of opinion to the same effect.

Fourteen years later, in 1970, Arthur described the incident in a footnote to the Danube Edition of *Reflections on Hanging*:

This extract came to light during the trial of Major Blake, former Governor of Pentonville, for publishing official secrets in December 1926. For thirty years it had been quoted in the literature on the subject, and its authenticity was never challenged. But when, in March 1956, I quoted that infamous Instruction in an article in *The Observer*, Lord Mancroft, Under-Secretary, Home Office, accused me, in the House of Lords debate of March 8, of having omitted two vital phrases: 'After the words "without a hitch", the following sentence should be inserted: "If there has been any hitch or unusual event the fact must, of course, be stated and a full explanation given".' Subsequently the Home Office admitted that these two oddly worded phrases had never been published until Lord Mancroft produced them. They had evidently been added to the Instructions at a date which the Home Office refused to disclose. On March 15, in the House of Lords, Lord Mancroft apologised to the Editor of *The Observer* and myself.

It was only now that the connection occurred to Arthur between his vehement feelings on hanging and the tonsilectomy he had undergone as a child without anaesthesia. Yet this was an association with which I had lived during the writing of *Reflections on Hanging*. It seems obvious, but, as he wrote in *The Act of Creation,* such discoveries often become apparent only afterwards.

★   ★   ★

On 16 March there is an entry in the diary: 'Cynthia has food poisoning.' This was a kind of code. In fact, I had got up early and before 9 a.m. was ringing the doorbell of a strange house north of Hyde Park. On the first floor an operating table had been set up, upon which I lay, embarrassed by the false bonhomie of the Mayfair doctor and nurse. They disappeared briefly and came back transformed in sinister black gowns of rubber which made a rustling sound. Held down by the nurse, I tried not to struggle as the doctor wielded his scalpel.

Thus ended a nightmare in slow motion which many couples have experienced – from the first dawning suspicions to the clandestine visit to the abortionist weeks later. I was soon in a taxi bound for Montpelier Square, melodramatically haunted by the scene in *Arrow in the Blue* of that childhood tonsilectomy and also by the hangman in a black gown. The nightmare happened again in later years, though the squalid trip north of the park was replaced by two days in a clinic with an anaesthetic, as the climate of opinion had begun to change.

I wished Arthur were not so infectious. He also infected me with his moods – his depressions and melancholias.

Sometimes when one wakes up after a bad dream, one loses consciousness again, only to be catapulted into a new horror. So it was with us the following week. We spent the time at the Press Association going through old files in search of material for a piece Arthur was writing called 'Patterns of Murder'.

In the Parliamentary debate on the second reading of the Abolition Bill, the Home Secretary, Mr Gwilym Lloyd George, had declared that 'of the murderers executed between 1949 and 1953, something like 60 would have had to be detained for periods of up to 20 years and some 25 for longer, some of them for the whole course of their natural lives. . . .' And he added, 'I have looked into this possibility with great care.'

Arthur had the idea, which was perhaps decisive for the fate of the campaign, of going through the press reports of the eighty-five men and women who had been hanged in the five-year period which the Home Secretary said he had 'looked into'. Who were the men and women hanged between 1949 and 1953? In our hearts we knew that the picture painted by the Home Secretary was different from that which would emerge from the Press Association's archives.

Every day for a week we sat in an empty room upstairs in the Press Association building, next to a window which overlooked Fleet Street. A kindly attendant brought us the battered files, marked 'Murder', and we read through the case histories of those anonymous 'wretches' – as they are called in *Reflections on Hanging* – who had been through 'the pain and terror' of meeting their end on the gallows. One had merely to summarize in a few lines the relevant features of each case to be confronted with the awful truth. The following two samples serve as an illustration; almost all the other cases were in a similar vein, reflecting the infinite variety of human misery:

Benjamin Roberts, a miner, twenty-three, found his girl-friend in the arms of another man. Shot her, then shot himself in the head with a double-barrelled sporting gun. Was nursed back to life and hanged on December 14, 1949, in defiance of a Jury recommendation to mercy.

Thomas Eames, thirty-one, a labourer, killed his mistress, Muriel Bent, after she told him that she intended to marry another man. Then gave himself up. Jury recommendation to mercy. Hanged on July 15, 1952.

At lunch time we emerged into Fleet Street in a semi-daze and feeling physically sick. Overhead a March sun lit the narrow sky. Arthur needed a stiff drink and so did I. The evidence was more shocking than we had dreamed: the disregard of the jury's recommendation to mercy (in 10 per cent of the cases) and the prevalence of mental disorder and crime passionel.

To sit in the condemned cell awaiting one's end is an archetypal horror to be experienced only in one's imagination; but Arthur had actually been through it – for 102 days. Trying to revive my memory of our research at the Press Association, I asked him recently what his memories of that week were. He remembered the attendant who befriended us; that we worked in an empty room; and that only drink could help obliterate the ghostly parade of hanged men and women to which we had become spectators. Oddly enough he thought we had worked in a cellar.

'Patterns of Murder' appeared in the *Observer* on 14 April – Arthur's last piece under the pseudonym of Vigil. It was also printed in pamphlet form and sent to all MPs, upon whom its effect was not inconsiderable.

4

'Drinks with Henry (who "can't stand any more" of hanging talk),' the diary said on 20 March.

On Sunday mornings we were in the habit of wandering across the square to the George IV pub where Henry Green was to be found, together with a rather eccentric rear-admiral; other friends dropped in too.

One could see that Henry had been handsome in his youth – from the painting by Matthew Smith hanging in his house. Matthew Smith painted Henry against a backdrop of iridescent greens – perhaps an artistic pun, for Henry Green was the nom de plume of Henry Yorke. I can only think of him against a grey background. He no longer wrote and it was said his depressions were only made bearable by gin. The dark eyes with winged eyebrows which seemed to dance according to his feelings – one or the other was often raised – were set in a face whose pallor rarely saw the light of day. His sense of humour was of the black variety. He was rather deaf and what maddened Arthur was his refusal to wear a hearing aid – somehow symbolizing his desire to opt out. In fact, Henry used his deafness adroitly, watching people's faces, catching a phrase or two of an amusing story, but avoiding boring stretches of dialogue. Arthur had other methods of countering this boredom. As an only child he had been starved of the company of children, and describes in *Arrow in the Blue* how he coped on the rare occasions when he was allowed to meet them:

As soon as the adults had settled down at the *jour* table and we children were left alone in the nursery, my timidity wore off and I changed into a frenzied little maniac. The ingenious games I had devised in my daydreams all had to be tried out during those infinitely precious moments, after the manner of lovers who, meeting between periods of long separation, put into hurried practice their erotic reveries. The other child, whether younger or older, would usually be swept off its feet by this torrent of new games and ideas, and within a quarter of an hour I would become transformed from a tongue-tied puppet into a fierce bully who had to have it all his own way. . . .

The child became a part of the man and the fear of that early deprivation is a leitmotif of his life. At dinner parties in Montpelier Square he was inclined to turn the conversation into a seminar in order to extract the maximum out of all his guests. As I have recorded, the guest who liked to carry on a private little conversation with a neighbour, instead of taking part in 'quadrilateral conversation', was indeed in his bad books.

The best Sundays were when Arthur invited friends to Bachelor's Fortress for Mozart and Moselle before lunch – M and M for short. Many of the women were ex-girlfriends – mostly feminine and sylph-like, some with a masculine trait, bossy and clever. All had one thing in common: at some point in their lives they had been scarred by sorrow, and it showed.

Arthur's favourite Mozart consisted of the Horn Concerti played by Dennis Brain. When Dennis Brain was tragically killed in a car crash, it became too precious to play often, and those Sunday mornings were like the music – light-hearted, but occasionally shadowed by a reminiscent dark chord.

The guests would leave and after lunch Arthur fell happily asleep. When he awoke his mood was changed: *sombre Dimanche* had closed in on him. Dostoyevsky had once written that, even in solitary confinement and ignorant of the calendar, he would still sense when it was Sunday. Arthur's picture of gloomy Sunday is different: a provincial town in France, the family sleeping off a gargantuan lunch, whilst the teenage daughter of the house painfully practises her scales on the piano and outside the rain drives down on the empty cobbled streets. On Sunday evenings Arthur craved company and if by chance we were alone, he turned the force of his despair on me.

He decided to move to the country, and in April recorded in his diary: 'House hunting in Sussex. Sudden depression: seeing myself in [house we viewed] on evenings, with C., rather pointlessly.' It was a massive eighteenth-century house, imbued with the Victorian virtues of past inhabitants; locked in the straitjacket of their era, one could almost hear them breathing. Arthur would have looked singularly out of place.

The depression was only dispelled when he got back to Copernicus. He was working feverishly to finish that part of the book before our holiday, to which, as he wrote in the diary, he was 'madly looking forward'. We were about to spend the first three weeks of May in France, canoeing down the Dordogne. The Sunday morning before leaving was devoted to working out our route with Michelin maps and a *carte nautique* of the Dordogne – a task he found 'particularly pleasant'. Three days before leaving, he wrote impatiently: 'Counting the hours till departure.'

To appease his wayward guilt feelings, he proposed to write about the expedition and keep a log on the journey. When we made our second expedition a year later, he described canoeing (in the *Observer*) as 'the ideal cure for people who, like myself, suffer from holiday neurosis – a common affliction not mentioned in psychiatric textbooks; the people for whom lazing on a beach is hell, and pre-planned pleasure a guarantee of disappointment.'

5

I had never travelled with Arthur before and was wildly excited at the prospect of being with him day and night for three weeks – though also daunted. The thought of having to speak French in front of him was agony; perhaps I could get away with a few monosyllables.

A radiant sun was in the sky when I came to Montpelier Square to find Arthur loading the car which was parked beside Bachelor's Fortress. He frowned when he saw my luggage – a bulging suitcase and two shopping bags containing the overflow – and muttered darkly something about travelling in a gypsy caravan. None the less, driving fast in the open car soon put him in a good mood. We flew through Kentish orchards – which spring, reversing the order of time, had restored to youth. It seemed that we were beginning to emerge from the long black tunnel of winter with its obsessions and fears – a winter which had extracted its due. One morning I had noticed, while standing beside Arthur's desk as he signed the letters, a few grey hairs growing from the geometrically straight line of his parting.

On board the ferry Arthur did not cast a glance at the receding English coast. He ordered a demi champagne. It was only ten o'clock, too early to drink, I thought. It seemed sinful to be drinking champagne at that hour and perhaps that was why it tasted so delicious. Soon we floated on wings. The sea was a luminous blue and on the horizon one could distinguish the shores of France, like a distant mirage. As the land grew nearer Arthur got up and gazed out of the saloon, as might a lover who waits impatiently a reunion long dreamed of, a smile upon his lips. Many times in the past I had made the dull cross-Channel trip to France; it had never been like this. How thrilling to travel with Arthur, I thought. This aspect of Koestler B was unknown to me.

The first meal in France was memorable. The customs man in Boulogne waved us on and the car plunged into the fast-moving traffic as if it had never known the left-hand side of the road. Arthur's method of finding a restaurant was to follow his nose, and we proceeded along a boulevard until the car came to a sudden halt in front of a tall, narrow-chested restaurant with a gabled roof. Arthur was certain his nose had led him to the right place. Soon we were sitting upstairs in a room crowded with locals, tucking in to *hors d'oeuvres variés*. Why does French food taste as the Lord meant food to taste, Arthur kept wondering throughout the meal. With the coffee came brandy balloons for the *petit verre* – a line encircling them to indicate the exact measure. '*Laissez la main trembler un peu,*' Arthur encouraged the waiter as his glass was being filled.

The sun burned and the wind blew away the last of the wine as we raced across the countryside in the open car, passing deserted villages with peeling shutters. Beyond the wide views of fields and coppices the sea could occasionally be glimpsed. How unlike the English miniature landscape, said Arthur; the sky was much bigger than the English sky.

In a small town with a merry-go-round in its square we stopped for a *café arrosé au rhum.* Arthur studied the faces of the people, which he managed to do without staring, and stood for ages reading the small print on some old political poster and other notices.

In Paris, in the middle of the night, I woke up to find Arthur wandering around lost in the hotel room, calling the name of an old girlfriend. I led him back to bed, where he muttered to himself in French for a while. I had often wondered whether he knew who was beside him at night, for sometimes an arm reached over to feel or he turned his head in the semi-darkness, as if he wasn't sure. I vaguely pondered the mystery. Perhaps I should have felt jealous, but I only felt lucky to be sharing his life.

We had an early-morning drink before leaving Paris the next day at a little bar near our Left Bank hotel. Arthur's face lit up when he saw the zinc bar and a few elderly habitués drinking a *coup de rouge* in the shabby surroundings. His love of the French petite bourgeoisie, of which he saw so much at the age of twenty-four when he first lived in Paris, struck me as rather strange for he described them in astringent terms in *Arrow in the Blue.* On our journey he engaged in hopeful dialogue with waiters, barmaids, concierges, and old men with a glass of cloudy Pernod before them.

Soon we were on the road we knew so well from Verte Rive days, passing through the green tunnel of trees. Brie-Comte-Robert with the leafy terrace outside its little restaurant, the bridge at Melun over the majestic Seine and the signposts saying 'Corbeil', 'Chartrettes', 'Bois-le-Roi' and 'Fontaine-le-Port'. I was glad when we left the Forest of Fontainebleau behind and Arthur no longer looked tormented.

Although it was only the beginning of May, the heatwave made it feel like summer the farther south we travelled. In the open car Arthur's face gradually turned a golden brown and mine, to my chagrin, bright scarlet.

As we were lunching in a bistro Arthur suddenly said: 'They're quarrelling.' I heard a muffled sound of shouts coming from the direction of the kitchen. It seemed to me to be only the waiters, raising their voices above the general clatter to make their orders heard, but Arthur took no notice of my reasonable hypothesis. Variations on this trivial scene have taken place over the years. Sometimes Arthur would notice two people in a restaurant, eating their food in silence, their movements jerky; or a couple sitting on a sunlit café terrace, their eyes fixed on the ground. 'They're quarrelling,' would be his frequent refrain. His antennae seemed too well attuned to dark undercurrents in the most unlikely places.

We arrived at our starting point – Beaulieu-sur-Dordogne – three days after leaving London, and the next morning *Blue Arrow,* the red ensign flying from her stern, was launched on what Arthur called an African Queenie expedition. The river followed her own wayward course, reflecting the light from the blue Dordogne sky or the deep shadow where overhanging trees merged with the water. Cocooned in the intimate world of the river, which was not very wide, gave one a feeling of peace. But we were barely acquainted with the Dordogne's character and her changing moods, and it was not long before our peace was disrupted.

Something frothy and white appeared on the water in the distance which Arthur regarded with suspicion, and without further ado he turned the canoe towards the shore. We would have to reconnoitre, he said. We heaved ourselves out on to a steep, prickly slope and scrambled up the bank. Under the boiling sun we walked to the spot where the river danced in a merry whirl of little waves. The word *maigres* (shallows) was to become all too familiar as the days passed. Arthur found a narrow channel just deep enough for *Blue Arrow* to pass through. We could make it, he explained, provided we paddled at top speed. We returned to the boat and gained headway, making straight for the *maigres*. The sound of rushing water grew louder and we raced through the narrow channel at breakneck speed.

I did not relish these hair-raising dashes between the *maigres* as much as Arthur seemed to, but kept my cowardly thought to myself. It was often touch and go whether we would find the eye of the needle in time. Due to the heatwave, the water level was unusually low and the *maigres* were a frequent sight. *Blue Arrow* did not always get through unscathed and on the second day her punctures had to be patched up on a pebbly beach near the bridge of Meyronne.

It was on the second day that the Dordogne showed her capricious nature. We had run aground in shallow water and had to get out and push *Blue Arrow* along the sandy river bed. Absorbed in our efforts, we were taken by surprise when the canoe suddenly surged forward. As we grabbed hold of her, we were submerged in deep water up to our necks, hanging on to *Blue Arrow* for dear life as she careered down the river. The current was swift and carried us along in the sunlight, Arthur at the bow, whilst I clung to the stern. I pictured the end of our expedition: *Blue Arrow* breaking free and, out of control, heading downstream alone, with all our precious possessions. At that moment I felt the boat being tugged towards the shore; Arthur had grasped a tow rope and was swimming to the steep green river bank, pulling *Blue Arrow* and me, feeling like a sack of potatoes, to safety. After we had secured the boat and climbed the bank, Arthur lay on his back under the hard blue sky for a while, quite out of breath. Then he smoked a cigarette. We had been plummeted into hidden depths and they had a sobering effect.

Besides 'playing second paddle', one of the duties of Crew (as I was named by Arthur) was to follow our course on the Michelin map with its intriguing little symbols for a chateau or ruins or a fortress. From the river, we often had no view of the surrounding countryside because of the high banks; it was a bit like being in a Kentish smugglers' lane, hidden between the hedges. Often a hamlet which, according to the map, lay almost beside the river was invisible.

The compass which Arthur kept propped up in front of him never ceased to fascinate him. I failed to see what was so magical about a compass – the idea that it should be of any use on the Dordogne seemed to me ridiculous. As usual, I was soon proved wrong for it became invaluable. As the winding river carried us in a southerly direction, then north, then west, in an unending series of bends, the Capitaine was able to work out exactly where we were and to avoid over-shooting a village where we planned to spend the night.

Describing 'canoeing without tears' in his *Observer* piece in 1957, Arthur wrote:

Last year . . . I became addicted to a new hobby; at a loss for an adequate English expression, I shall call it *le canotage gastronomique*. The idea is to travel, in a canoe, down one of the great rivers of France – the Dordogne or the Loire; to spend one's days on the water and one's nights at a comfortable hotel; to combine the virtuous satisfaction of a sporting achievement with a guilt-free guzzle in the evening.

On 9 May we ate some lunch on a sandy beach and swam. On the opposite shore a wall of white rock rose out of the Dordogne – the first intimations of the limestone caves at Lascaux a hundred kilometres away. It was my twenty-ninth birthday; despite this advanced age, I still suffered from a paralysing lack of self-assurance, and it was doubly annoying not to look my age. I could not wait to be thirty-five.

We were paddling through the heartland of the Perigord Noir on our way to Souillac, whose Grand Hôtel had a gastronomic star in the Michelin guide. We walked through the town carrying our blue canvas overnight bags and the paddles, having got into decent dress in the canoe. Carrying the paddles with us every evening when entering a hotel was a tactic of Arthur's to allay any suspicions the locals might harbour for such strange tourists. The result was that we were regarded as '*des sportifs*' instead of tramps, materializing out of the blue without a car and proper luggage.

The rich treasures of Perigord went into the dinner that night and we drank the exotic, if rough, local wine. No longer did we rave about the food as during our first meal in Boulogne, but ate rather critically. Like Fedya in *The Age of*

Longing, Arthur had merely to raise his hand a fraction for waiters to come hurrying over. However, when this instant mesmerizing failed to work he looked depressed, a shadow crossing his face. We had two bottles of wine. Not wanting to be a spoilsport, I drank a huge amount. Besides, it was the only way of stopping Arthur from drinking too much. At the end of dinner he ordered coffee and a *digestif* of the region. The hotel had none of the local *prune* and brought out instead a marc de Bourgogne in a bottle which Arthur called *'chichiteux'* and regarded with misgiving. Whilst drinking the coffee and marc we gauged the distance between our table and the door, and the obstacles of other tables we would have to encounter en route. We then rose and managed to walk unhurriedly out of the room, collect our key at the desk and walk upstairs with perfect decorum. 'Ah,' he sighed, looking at me, bemused by some revelation, 'I'm enjoying myself.' He was sparing in his compliments.

In the morning he was awake by 7.30 and it was my task to pick up the telephone and order breakfast. I hoped that he had gone back to sleep and would not hear my French. All I could see of him was his head with the dead straight parting in the mousy brown hair as I said uncertainly: *'Je voudrais commander le petit dejeuner.'*

We sat on a terrace in the early-morning sun, catching up with the log. Once completed, Arthur was impatient to get back to the river.

We were travelling through Fénélon country. Castle after castle, rising from the limestone rock, surveyed us as we slowly paddled past each apparition, viewing it from all angles and then turning our heads for a last look before it vanished from sight. This sightseeing from the river gave one a different perspective; one no longer felt a tourist, but a part of the landscape. We passed the castle in which Fénélon was born, high above the valley overlooking a vast expanse of river.

After the comfort and one-star meal in Souillac our next landfall was a slummy one. A rather small double bed filled the room. There were no pillows and Arthur had to descend the wooden staircase to ask for them. He had had a wonderful time that night, drinking the local *prune* and 'fraternizing' with the yokels, their smiling faces betraying a deep curiosity. A warmth of feeling made up for the tepid soup, and the *prune* was delicious. In the morning we were awakened by an insistent cockerel. The air was chilly and the smell of cows and manure wafted through the tiny bedroom window. The plumbing, as Arthur warned me, was primitive. Before leaving, we had a glass of white wine on the cold terrace overlooking the Dordogne.

Towards evening we reached Beynac-et-Cazenac, an ancient village growing out of the Dordogne rock, where Richard the Lionheart's men had engaged in bloody skirmishes with the French during the Hundred Years' War. The castle, which dominated the village, had been rebuilt after the Albigensian Crusade.

On landing we sat in the canoe, putting clothes on over our bathing suits and then walked to the hotel in anticipation of the one-star dinner promised by the Michelin guide. Though respectably dressed, we must have seemed a funny pair, as Arthur handed over his British passport to the receptionist for filling in the usual form required by the French police. Dressed like an Englishman in grey flannels and a tweed sports jacket, his eyes startlingly blue in a sunburned face, he could hardly have looked less English with his high cheekbones emphasizing his Eastern European origin. In my pale blue summer dress with white polka dots, I looked too young to be his wife, and my cramped manner and self-conscious movements doubtless led people to wonder why he had chosen such an odd mistress.

The dining-room windows gave on to the Dordogne; as dusk fell she disappeared in a melancholy mist. We were eating the trout fished from her waters.

Epilogue

BY HAROLD HARRIS

So ends the fragment of Cynthia's contribution to this joint autobiography. It is rather difficult to see how Arthur could have continued to insert alternate chapters beyond chapter 6 without a great deal of repetition, especially as Cynthia's account of her own life is kept to a minimum when they are apart and almost non-existent when they are together. A synopsis – typewritten except for a few handwritten insertions by Arthur – only goes as far as the first three chapters of Part Two, and although the second of these is initialled A.K., there is no indication of its proposed contents.

It may well be that Cynthia continued working on her contribution up to the last few days. 'I should have liked to finish my account of working for Arthur,' she wrote in the brief note quoted in the Introduction. The holiday in the Dordogne which concludes this book took place in 1956. From 1961 to 1974 she kept a diary in which she faithfully recorded their joint life. A considerable amount of editing and annotation will be required if it is to be made suitable for publication. Perhaps she intended to conclude the present book in 1961 when the diaries begin.

I hope that material has not been left in which, on reflection, she might have preferred to delete on revision. I do not think so, although it is possible that she would have occasionally commented on some of the more surprising pieces of information. For instance, she might have wished to insert her reasons for having two abortions. 'I only felt lucky to be sharing his life,' she had written à propos her lack of jealousy, and she would have known from the start that sharing his life precluded any prospect of motherhood. Though I knew nothing of the abortions myself until I read of them in these pages, Arthur had once told me that he had decided at an early age not to risk bringing up any children. He and Cynthia knew that he would have made an intolerable father. Indeed, her reaction on learning of his illegitimate daughter had been one of amusement.

Of course, there is an element of sadness in all this, just as there is in the way that she surrendered her life to his on an all-inclusive scale. But sadness was not the impression she gave to friends and acquaintances. She was happy in her total devotion as wife–secretary–cook–housekeeper–companion, and happy, above all, in Arthur's total reliance upon her.

The fact that, as revealed in these pages, she had contemplated suicide in 1952, if not perhaps very seriously, when Arthur's feelings towards her appeared to cool, may have had some significance in the final decision she came to thirty-one years later at the prospect of living without him. It is also relevant to mention that her father, whom she loved deeply, had committed suicide by cutting his wrists when she was ten years old. She was not told of his death for three days and did not learn that he had ended his own life until 1969. However, reading between the lines of a detailed account which she wrote of the entire circumstances in 1970, one suspects that she might have been subconsciously aware of his suicide all her life.

Whether or not these two episodes had any bearing on her final decision, readers of the joint account of the first seven years of this unique association will agree that its ending, twenty-seven years later, seems logical and almost inevitable. In those final hours in the house in Montpelier Square Arthur might indeed have felt some remorse or even guilt because of Cynthia's decision, but that was an emotion with which he had been familiar all his life. I am convinced that, for her part, Cynthia would have looked back upon the thirty-three years of their joint life with feelings only of gratitude and fulfilment.

Appendix
by A.K.

It would appear that Arthur Koestler intended this brief chapter to follow chapter 6, and for it to be followed by the present chapter 7 by Cynthia. As the events related in this chapter are dealt with more fully by Cynthia, and this is largely repetition, it has been omitted from the body of the book. It does, however, contain some fresh material, and as it may have been the last thing that Arthur Koestler wrote it is included here – Editor.

I

In July 1951, we were back in Verte Rive. In August, Mamaine left me and our marriage came to an abrupt end. She had been spending, as was her habit, some weeks with twin Celia in London; on the day of her return to Verte Rive she informed me that after endless soul-searching and discussions with Celia she had come to the conclusion that it was best for both of us to go our separate ways and 'remain pals'. I seem to remember that it was at the word 'pals' that she broke down in tears.

It was, as I said, an abrupt end to an affair* which had lasted seven years – including two when we were legally married – but the signs had been visible for a long time – cracks in the walls of an edifice in the process of disintegration. The reason Mamaine gave for her decision was the urge to lead her own

---

* There is an indication that Arthur intended to change the word 'affair' when revising – Editor.

life – painting, playing the piano, cultivating her own friends (most of whom I disapproved of, as they disapproved of me) – all of which, she felt, was impossible in a household ruled by a capricious tyrant. I saw her point only too clearly, pleaded for some compromise solution and promised to try to mend my ways – to no avail. I had no illusions about my character (unless this statement is in itself based on an illusion); nevertheless I felt that a compromise would still have been possible but for a reason which I could not openly discuss with her: Mamaine's state of health. Her chronic asthma made her unfit to lead the hectic kind of life to which I was accustomed at the time. Only now, in old age, afflicted by several chronic diseases, do I realize what it means to move constantly along the verge of exhaustion; to feel irritable because of sheer physical fatigue; to resent the vitality of others as an insult to me.

2

The year after Mamaine left me was another period of restlessness and indecision. We had planned to transplant the whole household – including Cynthia, Maxim and Anna – to the island; but without Mamaine the project became unmanageable, and in the late autumn of 1951 I returned to the Delaware once more alone. I spent the winter revising *Arrow in the Blue,* writing some essays, and wasting my time preparing endless memoranda for the lawsuit against Sidney Kingsley to regain some control over European translations of the stage version of *Darkness at Noon.* The play contained several scenes that gave a naively distorted view of life in the Communist movement which could pass before an American audience ignorant of that atmosphere – but not in France or Italy where the C P was represented by mass movements and where some of these scenes would have brought the house down with laughter. As it happened, no European producer would touch the play and I could have saved myself the trouble of a lawsuit (which I lost anyway since the small print in the contract deprived me of any legal right to control the contents of the play). But at the time the matter acquired the intensity of an obsession, as lawsuits tend to do – even in the case of less obsession-prone people than I am.

However, there was also a grotesque side to this unhappy affair. Some day at Verte Rive, when I was hurriedly dictating to Cynthia, I stumbled over the name Sidney Kingsley and telescoped it into Kidney. She found that funny, and it became a kind of family joke. But it was less funny when, after some weeks on the island, I developed a kidney stone. It passed mercifully without an operation, and I am still half convinced that its origin was psychosomatic. Anybody can develop psychosomatic ulcers, but a psychosomatic kidney stone is something one is justified to boast about.

3

In the spring of 1952, *Arrow in the Blue* was at last delivered to the publishers, the lawsuit fought and lost, and once more the question arose where to live. To divide the year between Europe and the USA had sounded, theoretically, an admirable idea; but what was the point of sharing a huge house with Miss Nellie as the only other inhabitant, on a huge island which threatened to turn into a jungle, while a lovely villa stood abandoned on the Seine? Obviously the solution to the problem of the two houses was to sell them both and buy a third one – this time in London.

The decision was not quite as insane as it may seem. The overriding consideration was language. Up to the age of thirty-five I had been writing in German. (The last book written in German was *Darkness at Noon*; the first book written in English was *Scum of the Earth*.) Before the change I did some journalism in English, as a sideline; from 1941 onward English became 'my' language and I considered myself *ipso facto* an English writer.

But changing languages is an immensely complex process of metamorphosis, especially for a writer. It involves several successive phases which are difficult to describe, because most of the changes occur gradually below the level of consciousness. In the earliest phase you *translate* the message to be conveyed from the original into the adopted language; at a later stage you catch yourself *thinking* in it – occasionally at first, and at last permanently. The final stage of the transformation has been completed when you not only think, but *dream,* in the language you are now wedded to.

However, this metamorphosis could be realized only if I lived in an English-speaking environment. This was the blatantly simple conclusion at which I had at last arrived after the tortuous, erratic peregrinations of my *Wanderjahre;* and among English-speaking countries, I had grown much deeper roots in England than in America. Moreover, London was only at a stone's throw from the continent of Europe; and with my Austro-Hungarian, Franco-English background, I felt first and foremost a European.

4

So I rented Island Farm to an Italian builder with five children who adored Miss Nellie, and in the spring of 1952 was back in London – house-hunting.

Index

Index

Index

with AK ends, 184; child by AK, 194, 195
Labour Party, 49
Lasky, Melvin, J., 114, 156
League for the Rights of Man, 41–4, 46
Left Book Club, 26
Le Vernet d'Arriège, 22, 24, 25, 183, 184
Literaturny Sovremennik, 104
Llan Festiniog, 41
Lloyd George, Gwilym, 219
Loewengard, Jupp, 99, 100
Loewengard, Kathrin, 99, 100
Lousada, Anthony, 159

McCarthy, Mary, 120
Malraux, André, 22, 46, 67, 73, 89, 132, 165
Mancroft, Lord, 218
Maritain, Jacques, 96
Martin, Kingsley, 26, 89
Mary's Diner, 121
Maugham, Robin, 180, 206
Maxim, 78–9, 81, 108, 128, 133, 139, 141, 211
Merleau-Ponty, 66, 76
Milton, John, 25
Mimault, Professor, 82–3
Miss Nellie, 111–12, 113, 118, 121, 122, 123, 148, 149, 235, 236
Montpelier Square, 151–2, 154, 155, 158, 161, 178, 185
Montpelier Walk, 144, 151, 152
Moppes, Denise van, 157
Moscow, 73
Mozart, Wolfgang Amadeus, 60, 222
Muenzenberg, Willi, 157
Muggeridge, Malcolm, 90

National Campaign for the Abolition of Capital Punishment, 210
Neumann, Clara von, 122, 146, 147

Neumann, Johnnie von, 121–2, 146, 147
Newby, P. H., 160–1
Newsom, Chris, 181
Newsom, Jack, 181

Orwell, George, 41, 42, 45, 49, 90, 128, 187
Osborn, June, 217
Ould, Hermon, 95, 106

Paget, Celia, 43, 45, 68, 69, 108, 128, 137, 201; AK worries about, 190, 198, 214; asthma, 190, 205, 209; similarity to Mamaine, 33–4, 63, 164; Mamaine discusses leaving AK, 233
Paget, Mamaine, *see* Koestler, Mamaine
Palestine, 35–8
Palestine Kennel Club, 82
'Paola', 179, 183, 199, 211
Pavlov, Ivan, 52
Peel, Lord, 35
PEN Club, 95, 106
Pentonville Prison, 25, 26
Peters, A. D., 60, 94, 137, 140, 148, 149, 150
Picasso, Pablo, 22
Pioneer Corps, 27–9
Plato, 215
Plesch, Egon, 153
Port Meirion, 39–40
Prague Trials, 156
Press Association, 219–21
Priestley, J. B., 210

Quennell, Peter, 157, 158

Rajk, Laszlo, 31, 76
Read, Herbert, 147
Rees, Sir Richard, 206
Remarque, Erich Maria, 185
Reuter, 42, 43
Revisionist Party, 20, 36
Roberts, Benjamin, 220
Rothermere, Lady, 210

241